What Others Are Saying About Ant Dens

"With *Ant Dens*, Mary Coley has written a superb sequel to *Cobwebs*, presenting us with yet another engaging mystery that not only focuses on the case at hand, but also gives us an even deeper look into the complexities of the human spirit."

—Teresa Miller
Author of *Means of Transit,*
Host of OETA/PBS's *Writing Outloud*

Jamie Aldrich longs to move on with her life, but complications from her past threaten to take her down. *Ant Dens*, a beautifully written suspense novel by Mary Coley, sends readers on a white-knuckle adventure through historic Las Vegas, New Mexico. This college town, set on the old Santa Fe Trail, furnishes a fascinating local history that Coley weaves into her story. *Ant Dens* is sure to keep readers turning pages until the heart-stopping conclusion.

—Jackie King
Author of *The Inconvenient Corpse*
and *The Corpse Who Walked in the Door*

Ant Dens grabbed me from the start, providing a wild ride of twists and turns as the story flowed swiftly along to its surprising end. A compelling story, readers will appreciate Coley's many surprises as she lets this modern, suspense-filled drama unfold amidst the unassuming backdrop of Las Vegas, New Mexico. A wonderfully unexpected book . . . Coley's unique voice makes this surprise-filled drama an easy read."

—C̶

Author

What Readers Are Saying About Mary Coley's Cobwebs: A Suspense Novel

"*Cobwebs* made me delightfully uneasy and kept me in suspense. I thoroughly enjoyed the intenseness all the way through. It kept me turning the pages. I highly recommend it to suspense lovers. I usually figure out the "who done it" but I didn't with Cobwebs. I'm glad it wasn't windy, stormy weather when I read it!"

—Jackie D.

"*Cobwebs* is a beautiful suspense novel on so many levels. The actual book is gorgeous, with a fantastic interior design and a marvelous cover. But once I started reading the story I was captured in the lovely silken web of words that this writer weaves so well. She brings readers right into the setting, to feel we're following Jamie as she walks and rides through the pages, closer and closer to the middle of the web created through history, deceit, memories, and fears. This is a psychological thriller that took hold of me from the first page and kept me riveted until the end. "

—J. Rhine

"This is a WONDERFULLY EXCITING BOOK THAT I JUST COULDN'T PUT DOWN!! I loved it so much that I had to buy another copy just to share with my family book exchange because I didn't want to GIVE UP MINE!! Mary Coley is a wonderful writer and I look forward to reading so much more from her!"

—MandyS.

"My mother and I devour suspense novels - you win some, you lose some. *Cobwebs* is definitely a winner! The characters and plot are finely drawn, but what makes this book stand out from the crowd is all the little details - especially the history of the area - that the author painstakingly included to enhance this mystery."

—Yomissami

"This book was such a joy to read! It was suspenseful from beginning to end, and gave you that 'creepy feeling' at the end of each chapter. I especially enjoyed the Oklahoma history woven throughout the book. I didn't figure out how to solve the mystery until the very end! I would recommend this book to everyone who enjoys a good mystery!"

—Jeri H.

ANT DENS

ANT DENS

a suspense novel

MARY COLEY

Ant Dens: A Suspense Novel

Published by Wheatmark®
1760 East River Road, Suite 145, Tucson, Arizona 85718 USA
www.wheatmark.com

ISBN: 978-1-62787-196-9 (paperback)
ISBN: 978-1-62787-197-6 (ebook)
LCCN: 2014951571

I dedicate this book to my family and my friends.

I am so thankful to have your support. Pursuing my writing dream has resulted in many hours when I have not been present for you. Instead, I have been researching, writing, editing or marketing as I pursue my passion.

Thank you for your understanding and your love.

Acknowledgments

Slavery exists.

It is not something people like to talk about, but the truth of the matter is that every day people are kidnapped from their homes, towns and villages and thrown into slavery. Their hopes for a happy future are crushed under the weight of a life they did not choose for themselves. The present is misery and the future is a black hole of despair.

Ant Dens is a Family Secrets mystery, but my hope is that the reader's awareness of a horrible injustice in the world will be stirred through the reading of this book.

Thank you to those dedicated individuals who work diligently to stop this corrupted way of life by finding the victims of human trafficking and returning them to their families and friends.

The Ants Go Marching

The ants go marching one by one, hurrah, hurrah.
The ants go marching one by one, hurrah, hurrah.
The ants go marching one by one,
the little one stops to suck her thumb,
and they all go marching down to the ground,
to get out of the rain, BOOM! BOOM! BOOM!

The ants go marching two by two, hurrah, hurrah
The ants go marching two by two, hurrah, hurrah
The ants go marching two by two,
The little one stops to tie her shoe
And they all go marching down to the ground
To get out of the rain, BOOM! BOOM! BOOM!

Unforgettable

Unforgettable, that's what you are
Unforgettable though near or far
Like a song of love that clings to me
How the thought of you does things to me
Never before has someone been more

Unforgettable in every way
And forever more, that's how you'll stay
That's why, darling, it's incredible
That someone so unforgettable
Thinks that I am unforgettable too

Unforgettable in every way
And forever more, that's how you'll stay
That's why, darling, it's incredible
That someone so unforgettable
Thinks that I am unforgettable too

Songwriters:
PHIL RAMACON/CORAL GORDON (P/K/A CHYNA)

Published by
Lyrics © EMI Music Publishing,
Universal Music Publishing Group

PROLOGUE

Sunday, August 13, 2000

The man waited behind the thick plastic construction drape, letting the shadows hide him. Cool air flowed through the open fourth floor window and licked at the drape. The plastic rippled with circulating construction dust and paint fumes.

A young woman stepped toward him from the far end of the long hallway. Her steps tapped, then stopped, then tapped again as she passed each wooden doorframe.

A tingle of anticipation ran up the man's spine. *It will not be long now.*

"Hello?" Rebecca called.

He smiled, knowing the deepening shadows made him invisible to her. He would play with her a little bit first to see how much courage she had.

"Where are you?" Her footsteps, which had been clicking closer on the newly refinished walnut floor, stopped. "Okay. No more games. I'm going back downstairs. You're freaking me out."

His heartbeat quickened. *She's not going to be a pushover. She's never heard my voice before. She needs coaxing.*

A sound like low thunder rumbled along the hallway as the construction drapes caught the moving air.

"I'm out of here," she shouted. Her footsteps clomped away.

"Rebecca," he called. He tried to stifle the sneeze building up in his sinuses from construction dust. "Achoo!"

Her footfalls stopped.

"Rebecca!" He called louder this time. "Back here."

"Where are you? Let me see you." Her strong voice quivered.

"I'm here." He took a step out from behind the drape but still stood halfway in the shadows.

She squinted in his direction and walked closer.

CHAPTER 1

Monday, August 14, 2000

Ben's spirit swirled around me in the rain-fresh afternoon air, stinging my heart like cactus spines. Maybe I had been wrong, maybe I was not ready to come home to the place where I had lost my husband 18 months ago. My boots clunked as I walked and my long skirt blew around me in the pine-scented breeze.

"Mrs. Aldrich?" An all-too familiar voice called.

My heart plummeted into my stomach. The burly brown-skinned man charged across the parking lot like an angry bison. Sweat glistened on his forehead in spite of the cooling breeze sailing in from New Mexico's Sangre de Cristo Mountains.

Every muscle in my body tightened. I smoothed my long hair back into the ponytail and swiped my little finger under my eye to remove any trace of tears.

For more than a year after Ben's death, Sheriff Jonah Clay had hounded me with insinuations that I had helped my husband commit suicide. I felt sure Clay still believed I was guilty, although he had never actually filed charges. Now, here he was on my first day home after months with my great aunt in Pawhuska, Oklahoma.

My breath caught. I focused on the stonewalls of the Highlands University administration building. As the sheriff of New Mexico's San Miguel County, Clay had a lot more territory to cover than the historic railroad town of Las Vegas on the old Santa Fe Trail.

The sheriff cleared his throat and lifted one hand to groom his dark moustache. He pulled a photograph out of his starched gray uniform shirt pocket and thrust it at me. "You know this girl?"

The smiling young woman with smooth brown skin, gleaming obsidian hair, huge walnut-colored eyes and perfect white teeth looked out of her high school graduation picture.

Piñon-scented air rushed into my lungs. I studied the lovely face. "It's my stepdaughter, Rebecca."

"She's missing," the sheriff said. "Her mother said the girl might have been in touch with you."

Laughter pealed as students strolled around us to step up on the wide sidewalk. A solitary student trailed the group, his black hoodie pulled around his head as if the recent rain had not given way to sun. My stomach clenched. *I want to banish hoodies as an apparel item after this past April's adventure.*

I thought of the cream-colored note from Rebecca I had found last night in my stack of mail. The brief note told me she planned to attend Highlands University where her father had taught in the history department before his death. With classes starting next week, Becca had probably settled into her dorm room this past weekend. She had not asked me for help moving in. *No surprise.*

The sheriff's eyes narrowed.

I handed the photograph back. "I did receive a note from her about coming to school here. When did she disappear?"

"We got the call early this morning. I'm here to determine who saw her last. Female students do not always return home when they are supposed to. She's only the latest one." His sharp eyes flicked over the passing students, and then back to me.

"The latest one? Recently?" I did not like the sound of this. I didn't have a clue what had been going on out here since Ben's death. I had not even set foot on the campus.

"A couple of other young women went missing this summer." Clay tucked the photo back into his front pocket. "Do you and your stepdaughter email each other or keep up on Facebook?"

I shook my head. "I don't even know her email address."

"If you hear from her, let me know." With a curt nod, he stalked across the parking lot.

I let the breeze tickle my face and ruffle my hair. Back here in New Mexico where Ben and I had lived together for twelve years, I still expected to see my husband hurrying down the steps of one of the University's classroom buildings or walking with his long loping stride on the sidewalks lacing the wide campus lawns. He had taught at Highlands University for all of our married life until cancer consumed him. I still imagined him here and on the tree-covered historic plaza a few blocks away.

Rebecca and I had never developed much of a relationship although she visited Ben and me frequently on weekends and holidays. A couple of times as a teenager, Becca had run away from her home in Gallup, where she lived with her mother and stepfather. Each time, her mother Maria freaked and called Ben. He would drive to Gallup to look for her, even searching the villages tucked among the nearby mesas. Each time, Becca would show up after a few days and act as if she had never been gone. Ben would return home shaking his head.

The wind breathed deeper down through the conifers carrying the unmistakable pine and cedar scents of the New Mexico forests as it rustled the leaves of the giant elms and cottonwoods. A few leaves, brown from the late summer heat, floated erratically down onto the shaded lawns.

It felt good to be home, back in this sleepy little town. Once a bustling Old West settlement on the final stretch of New Mexico's Santa Fe Trail, Las Vegas became a major depot on the Atchison, Topeka and Santa Fe railroad, complete with a famous Harvey House, The Hotel Castaneda, next door to the depot. How many times had I had to explain to people I'd met during the last fifteen years that Las Vegas, New Mexico was not Las Vegas, Nevada. No casinos here. No big time entertainers. No wedding chapels and open-all-night businesses. Just lots of family-owned cafes featuring New Mexican-style tacos or enchiladas and businesses that closed their doors at nine p.m.

"Jamie?"

My best friend Kate rushed across the green lawn toward me. "Thanks for coming," I said as I stepped into her hug.

"Packing up Ben's office could have waited for another day," she scolded, straightening the red chiffon scarf draped around her neck. As usual, she was stylishly dressed in trendy pink crops and a polka-dot t-shirt. Silver bracelets clanked on her left wrist and big hoop earrings dangled beneath her short blonde hair.

I stepped off the sidewalk and onto the grass to let more students pass on their way toward the Felix Martinez Building and the admissions offices. "Fall term starts next week and the new professor needs the office. I've kept him waiting way too long."

Kate cocked her head. "And what else? You look worried. Aunt Elizabeth okay?"

She knew me too well for me to pretend nothing was wrong. "Yes, she's holding her own. But, I've just heard some troubling news about Rebecca, Ben's daughter." A chill crept up my vertebrae and headed for my neck.

"What's she done now?"

As we entered Douglas Hall, voices and aromatic scents swirled around us.

"She's decided to attend Highlands University this fall. But today, her mother reported her missing."

Inside the building, a smelly mix of floor cleaner, fresh paint and varnish swirled in the air. "I don't like hearing this. It's especially not good in light of what has been happening here." Kate frowned.

If anyone had a pulse on what was going on locally it was

my friend Kate. Her job as a journalist, including work as the Las Vegas 'stringer' for the Albuquerque Journal, made her the go-to source about criminal activities anywhere in the area.

"Sheriff Clay told me there had been other disappearances. What's been going on?"

"Counting Rebecca, three students have been reported missing here in the past month. An investigative report I've been working on could put these disappearances in a frightening light." She chewed at her lip. "But knowing Rebecca's history, she'll probably show up in a few days." Kate pushed her hair behind her ear as her voice trailed off.

I shot her a sideways glance as we neared the stairs. I could not prompt her for more information right now. I wanted to know more but the task ahead demanded my full attention and called for a check on my emotions. I had dreaded this office cleanout for more than a year and it was finally happening. Light glared from overhead fixtures and reflected from the refinished wooden floors as we climbed the stairs.

On the second floor, I focused on the patterned red, beige and brown tiled floor leading down the hall to Ben's former office. Voices murmured behind the open doors of offices we passed.

In a recent email, the dean had said Ben's office had sat 'shrine-like' for too long. He was right. Now a freshly painted name gleamed on the frosted glass of the office door.

"McDaniel," Kate read aloud. "The new professor." She tried the knob and then turned to me when the door did not budge.

I dug Ben's key ring from my pocket and selected a shiny silver key for the lock.

"Damn," I muttered, twisting the key and thinking ahead to what I might find in the unused office. "I didn't bring anything to dust with. Probably stringy spider webs throughout and dust an inch thick." The events of my summer in Oklahoma had done nothing to help me get past my aversion to spiders. If anything, my arachnophobia seemed to be worse.

The door swung open soundlessly.

Even after more than a year, the faint scent of Ben's cologne wafted up as the air stirred. Kate moved toward the bookshelves lining the far wall as I crossed the room to my late husband's desk.

"Dean Russell told me the new professor set up a temporary office in a corner of the former student lounge on the third floor. He'll be glad to finally get a real office," I glanced around the room at framed photographs: Ben and I in Santa Fe, Ben and I in Telluride, Ben and I in Key Largo, all uniformly framed in warm, smooth oak. A silver frame decorated with Celtic symbols held a photo of Ben and Rebecca arm in arm on the Rio Grande Gorge bridge west of Taos.

I skirted the desk and focused on another picture on the windowsill. Once again, Ben and Rebecca, the youngest of our blended family and Ben's only child, posed on the beach with the azure Jamaican Sea glowing behind them.

"Ben told Rebecca she needed to keep in touch with me after he was gone. The note I got from her last night was the first communication I've received since the funeral." I caught my lower lip between my upper and lower teeth and felt the pinch. "She blames me. Says he shouldn't have died. Says I should have realized he wasn't feeling well and made him go to the doctor long before the cancer got so advanced."

"Do you believe that?"

I pondered the question like I had each day for the past eighteen months. "Ben always had a reserve –things he didn't share with me. I never worried about his secrecy. I have things in my past, from my first marriage, which I didn't share with him." Memories of my husband's face, his demeanor and activities in those months before his diagnosis, rolled across my mind like an ocean wave. I searched my memory for any sign of illness I might have missed, just as I had a thousand times before.

I fingered the sleeve of a thick gray sweatshirt hanging from the coat tree in the corner. "He often kept to himself. Research-ing. Writing." My throat tightened.

"Okay, then. Let's get this show on the road." Kate grabbed an empty cardboard box from a stack of three piled in a corner. Framed photographs clinked like dishware as she piled them inside one box.

"Two girls have gone missing in the past month. Summer school students." Kate sighed. "And now Rebecca. The admin-istration and the faculty must be concerned."

"No doubt. Not very encouraging for the parents of female students." Encouraging? Try terrifying. The very thought that such a thing could have happened to my daughter Alison chilled my soul. Had something horrible happened to Rebecca?

"After my article appears in the paper next Sunday, everyone will be concerned about those disappearances." Kate pointed one red fingernail at the piles of books and manila file folders spilling out from the shelves and onto the floor. "We won't have near enough boxes, honey."

My breath whooshed out. "I want to know more about your article." I lowered myself into the upholstered desk chair and rubbed at my temples where a jackhammer headache now pounded. "What do you mean by a 'frightening new light?'" I had detected something different in my friend's face, a worried look on her forehead. I scooted one box closer to the desk with my foot. "I'll have to bring more boxes tomorrow. It won't matter to Dean Russell if I don't finish today. He doesn't know I'm back."

Someone rapped on the doorframe.

"Maybe Russell doesn't know you're here, but I do," the tall, athletic man's voice boomed. He propped himself against the wooden doorframe, gray eyes sparkling behind black-framed glasses. "Joshua McDaniel. You must be Mrs. Aldrich." His long legs carried him into the room. He extended his right hand, his long fingers splayed.

"Yes, and this is my friend, Kate Gerard."

Joshua McDaniel saluted in Kate's direction. He peered at me. "Can I help with anything?"

Mentally I measured his lanky frame and evaluated the bulges under his t-shirt. Ready evidence of workout hours in a gym. "We need more boxes. Know where we could find any empty ones?"

His mouth stretched wide across slightly crooked teeth as he grinned. "I'll be right back."

Kate scooted another empty box across the floor and over to the bookshelf.

I soaked up the mixed scents of Ben's office: cologne, books, paper and a slight smell of cedar from a half-burnt candle on the desk. As I gathered more photographs and piled them into a box, Ben's image floated above the desk chair. He looked up at me over his reading glasses. A sudden burst of loneliness skewered my heart. I moved away from the desk to the corner computer station where I picked up the old petrified bone paperweight Ben and I had found on a trek to a north-western Oklahoma creek bed near Black Mesa. I set it gently in the box beside framed photos.

I squatted to check the desk's kneehole and found the black laptop case still stowed there. One quick look confirmed the computer was inside.

Joshua reappeared in the doorway, each hand clutching two boxes. "Think this will be enough?"

"I hope so. Thanks." I glanced around the room at the remaining items. "The challenge will be to get these boxes down to the car after they are all stuffed with books and files."

"No problem." He reached out into the hallway and pulled a wheeled freight cart halfway into the room. "We ought to be able to take it all in one trip."

Joshua stationed himself by the door and began to stack our filled boxes onto the cart, whistling tunelessly through his front teeth as he worked.

Minutes later, the office was empty.

Downstairs, the three of us moved with the cart toward the

front doors. Someone had posted a sign on the frosted window of the door.

"CURFEW IN EFFECT: 10 p.m. – no exceptions!" the hand-printed neon-orange card read.

I held the building's outer door open as Joshua pushed the cart through.

"I've been staying as far away from the fiasco surrounding these missing girls as I can," he stated. "But having an office in the student lounge does mean I hear all the gossip."

"What do the students say about these disappearances?" Kate asked.

He shrugged. "People speculate. No real evidence the girls didn't run away."

Kate leaned close to my ear. "We'll talk more when we get to the car," she breathed.

Joshua's tuneless whistling grated on my nerves as we loaded the packed boxes into the trunk of my car.

CHAPTER 2

"So, what's your take on these disappearances?" I asked as we fastened our seat belts and drove out of the parking lot. The late afternoon sun kissed the tops of the Sangre de Cristo Mountains, adding a yellow glow to the puffy clouds floating across the brilliant blue sky.

"Slightly different than Mr. Neanderthal Professor, McDaniel," Kate griped. "He didn't sound very concerned about the missing women." She flipped down the sun visor and checked her eye makeup, then rubbed at a slight smudge under one eye.

"Is there evidence that foul play was involved?"

"None. Doesn't mean something bad didn't happen."

"I agree. But it is possible Joshua is right about the girls taking off for a few days, isn't it?"

"You're thinking about Rebecca. She's run away before, hasn't she?" Kate asked. "Kind of an overprotective mother-rebellious daughter thing?"

"Unfortunately." I sighed. "Sneaking out with boyfriends. Staying out all night without calling home. Teenage stuff." I thought about my own daughter. Alison and I had had our share of mother-daughter problems during her teenage years. Thank goodness she had never even stayed out all night without permission.

Kate shifted in her bucket seat to face me, resting her

elbow on the armrest between us. "But Maria called the sheriff this time. Something must not be typical."

"When Becca ran off before, Maria called Ben. Now that he's gone, she had no choice but to call the authorities." I wanted to shrug off Rebecca's disappearance. However, something in my brain – and my heart – nagged at me. Why now? Why when she was about to start her college career?

Kate unknotted her red neck scarf. "When they find her, I hope her mother jerks her out of here and takes her home. Otherwise, you had better get ready for an entire semester of this. Rebecca disappears, Maria calls the police, the police call you."

I crossed my fingers and waved them in Kate's direction. "I'm hoping that's not the way it goes. Maria told the sheriff I might know where Rebecca had gone. Seems odd. My role as stepmother was always more like 'father's friend.' According to Maria, Rebecca already had a mother." I steered the car onto University Avenue. "Why shouldn't the police connect Rebecca's disappearance to the other two?"

Kate shrugged. "You got me. After the second girl disappeared, the administration ramped up campus security. But they haven't come up with any suspects that I've heard about."

"Tell me all you know," I urged. I turned the corner onto National, and then onto my street. The small Victorian cottage Ben and I had spent three years renovating was a few blocks ahead. The air chilled as the sun dropped beneath the jagged peaks of the mountains. I sucked in the cool air, relishing it after the heat of August in Oklahoma. This felt like heaven.

I backed into my driveway, leaving room to raise the SUV's lift gate and remove the boxes. Kate and I began the unloading process.

Where were Joshua and his dolly now? The new professor was probably already decorating his new office.

Twenty minutes later, I braced my legs to pick up one more heavy box and hand it off to Kate. Sweat trickled down my sides. "This is the last box. Thank goodness."

Darkness clung around us like a dense fog and with it came the heavy aroma of a nearby piñon fire.

A tan car with a sputtering muffler crept past the house. I glanced over my shoulder and watched it pass as Kate stepped through the door in front of me. "So, what's your current investigation about? And do you think it's related to these disappearances?" I kicked the front door closed with my foot.

"Crazy stuff. Did you know Interstate 40, south of here, is a key route across the United States to transport victims of human trafficking?" Kate pushed her box into the line we had started along the wall, and then she backed into the living room and flopped down on the sofa.

"Trafficking?" I stacked my box on top of hers and leaned against the living room archway. I was unfamiliar with the term.

"Sex or labor slaves, sold into bondage after being kidnapped or after coming to the U.S. as an illegal. Some of them get hooked on drugs, they fall into the hands of ruthless men and women who promise to help but then put them to work for literally pennies a day or sell them as slaves."

An icy chill tingled through my body. "You don't think Rebecca -?"

"With her history, she's just doing her teenage thing again." Kate picked at the front of her shirt. "But the investigation has been eye-opening for me. You have to promise not to say anything to anyone until after the article comes out Sunday. It's disturbing."

"Of course I won't say anything." I dropped onto the edge of an upholstered chair cushion. "But is it possible the traffickers took her?"

"Anything's possible but what is the most logical? Consider her previous behavior."

"I'll try to." *I was not sure I could ignore this new information.* "So, tell me more about your investigation."

"The FBI is trying to get a handle on human trafficking. Not all victims are immigrants. In fact, over 80 percent of those in the sex-traffic trade in the U.S. are kidnapped Americans." Kate moved to the edge of her chair. "Do you know how many unidentified bodies are found in this country every year? It's unbelievable. The authorities think many of them are probably victims of traffickers, most of them trapped in the sex trade."

My breath caught. "Unidentified bodies? Can't they identify them with dental records?"

"That would be the best case scenario. If the person had previous dental work and if they've been reported missing. When police make arrests for prostitution, they are sometimes allowed to take photos of the individual's tattoos and identifying features. Those pictures, along with the dental records, can help with identification when a body turns up."

I imagined a photo database full of tattoos, moles and scars labeled with the names of people separated from both society and their own families. A shiver shook me. *Not Rebecca. It can't have happened to Rebecca.*

"Once these people are deep in that system, most aren't willing to accept help to get out. Many of them are addicts. Coke, heroin, meth—or whatever their pimps or 'managers' give them. Brain washed and in such a deep hole, they can't see any way out. They won't seek help to get out of servitude," Kate continued.

We sat in silence for a moment.

"Pizza and some beer?" Kate finally asked, flying up off the sofa. "Tell me about your summer in Pawhuska. How is your great aunt? And the lawyer, Sam?" Her eyes sparked.

Even though my mind was locked onto her revelation about human trafficking, my cheeks reddened. Memories of Sam's straight, confident stance, his long, shining black hair and the deep brown wells of his emotion-filled eyes filled my mind. He had touched my heart, and now he was six hundred miles away and seemed like an illicit fling.

Kate winked. "Let's go eat and get caught up."

"As long as you tell me about your latest love interest. Is there one?"

She shook her head. "No one special. And, haven't I told you I will never get married again? I mean it."

Two hours later, it was dusk when I stopped at the end of the driveway to grab the day's mail from the mailbox. I had decided not to tell anyone in my family about Rebecca for a few days. When she returned safely—as I thought she would by the end of the week—her brief disappearance would be one more negative my mother could use against her.

My thoughts flashed to Sam as I got out of the SUV. I had not been entirely truthful with Kate about how I felt about him. The Osage attorney had become very important to me. Hardly an hour passed that I did not remember something he'd said or done during the five months we'd known each other. I knew the love I felt for Sam did *not* mean I had not loved Ben. It *did* mean I was finally able to move past the overwhelming help-lessness and emptiness I had felt over his illness and death.

"I love you, Jamie," Sam had said as he kissed me goodbye yesterday morning. "Don't ever doubt my love is true." He had stroked my cheek with a fingertip and stepped back to look at me. "I've loved you for so long. My life is finally whole again, with you back in it."

The look in his eyes was enough. I still wondered how I could have forgotten him so completely after all the summer-time weeks we had spent together in Pawhuska in our preteen years. The events of that summer visit when I was twelve years old had blocked out the good memories as well as the horrible ones.

Beneath the mailbox, a long steady line of black ants

marched along the curb, in and out of an anthill they were reconstructing after the afternoon rain. Tiny circular bits of dirt spilled from the lawn down onto the curb. I made a mental note to check for ants around the foundation of the house and call an exterminator if one was needed. Ant dens with intersecting tunnels could extend for yards and yards underground with many entrances and exits. My skin crawled and I brushed at my legs, flicking off imaginary ants.

I grabbed the few letters and ad circulars from the mailbox and got back into my car to pull it around to the freestanding garage behind the house.

Inside, I ignored the row of boxes in the hallway. Packing those boxes had been a mindless task with Kate and Joshua to help. Unpacking them would be another thing. It could wait for tomorrow or the next day.

Right now, a stack of mail five inches tall leaned against the cubbies of my desk in the small office. I added the few pieces I had just collected to the pile. My neighbor, Mildred, had watched the house while I had been gone last spring and over the summer months. Each week, Mildred had placed the mail in my small office.

I pictured my neighbor running all ten fingers through her short white bob and adjusting her oversized glasses on her button nose. "I shredded the credit card offers and pitched the mail order catalogs," she had said last night on the phone. "And of course I mailed the bills to your sister, like you said. Otherwise the whole desk would be a heap of paper. Three months is a long time."

Mildred was efficient to the point of irritation, nosy and quick to offer opinions. Yet, in the months of Ben's declining health, I had to acknowledge Mildred had been a Godsend. The woman had brought over countless meals and spent many hours sitting with Ben through the long nights.

The blinking light on the telephone answering machine distracted me from the pile of mail. I pushed the "play" button.

"Jamie. I must talk to you. Please call me. It is urgent." I recognized Maria's careful English; I sank back into the desk chair. Maria wanted to talk about Rebecca. Surely, she would not be as rude and haughty to me now as she had been during Ben's lifetime.

As I replayed Maria's message, I picked up the cream envelope I had opened last night. Inside the bright pink note card, Rebecca had written, *"Jamie, I'll be at Highlands next week! You know how Dad always talked up the freshman programs. I'll call when I'm settled in the dorm. Rebecca."*

The second message on the machine played. Once again, Maria. Sobs broke her message into pieces. "It is Rebecca. Has she called you? I not know where she is. Call, Jamie. Please."

I flipped the envelope over and studied the postmark. Rebecca had sent the note last week.

The recording moved on to the third message. Silence, then the sound of someone hanging up the phone.

I punched the machine's pause button, pulled my address book from the drawer, found Maria's number, and then reached for the phone. It rang.

"Jamie? This is Maria. I come there. Rebecca—I not know where she is." Her voice disintegrated into a sob.

"Maria?" I spoke calmly. "Rebecca's done this kind of thing before. Could she have run away?"

"She and the boy broke off. She wants to go to school. She promises."

"Come to my house when you get here and we'll go to the police together."

"I come tomorrow, as soon as my boss lets me off."

I hung up. If Ben were still alive, he would be beside himself with worry. I should be, too. Rebecca was all that was left of Ben in this world.

I punched the message button for message four.

Somebody breathed into the phone. Then, a gruff voice said, "Your stepdaughter tells me she hasn't seen you since her daddy died. Too bad."

CHAPTER 3

Tuesday, August 15

Early the next morning, the staff parking lot at Robertson High School was already half-full of vehicles when I parked my SUV. I trudged to the side door and entered the building. The smells of floor polish and bathroom disinfectant tickled my nose. A floor polisher ground away near the front office as I climbed the stairs to the second floor.

My mind replayed the message from the anonymous caller. What did his message mean? *What had happened to Rebecca?*

As soon as I had awakened this morning, I called the Sheriff's Department number. The operator routed me to Clay's office phone and his answering machine. The message I had left for him had been short and to the point. "It's Jamie Aldrich. Someone contacted me about Rebecca. Please call as soon as you can." I recited my cell phone number.

The classrooms off the second floor hallway stood dark and empty, with only a few open doors. I unlocked the science lab.

"Mrs. Aldrich. You're back."

I knew that voice. I twisted the doorknob as I looked up at the young man. Trey Woodard grinned down from six-foot-two inches of brawn and guile, straight white teeth gleaming. I pulled myself to my full height but the kid was still eight inches taller. His blue eyes glared. "Trey. Have a good summer?"

He rubbed his muscled neck with thick fingers. "Summer

school doesn't make for a good summer. But, I *am* going to graduate in the spring. Nobody's gonna stop me." His eyes narrowed. He had ripped the sleeves out of his oversized t-shirt and the thick muscles of his arms bulged. Sweat on his brow suggested he had just finished football practice.

I stuffed a rubber wedge under the bottom of the door. "I hope you're right. Keep your grades up and finish your class work. It's up to you, Trey." He was repeating my Biology II class this fall, the one he had failed last spring.

Trey's palm slammed into the doorframe; the sound echoed like a shotgun blast up and down the hallway. "It's not up to me, it's up to you. And I want *you* to make it happen."

I met his stare.

Seconds ticked by.

A grin worked its way up onto his face. "Just so we're clear on it, Mrs. Aldrich. Have a good one."

Trey sauntered away.

I dumped my workbag onto the desk. *Damn that kid.* There seemed to be one like him in nearly every class group. Trey did not need Biology II to graduate and he had passing grades in other science classes. He was harassing me not only for failing him, but also for having him suspended for an incident during a basketball game. Later, he had been suspended a second time during a field trip to Highlands when he had made a pass at a female student on the sidewalk. The kid was nothing but trouble.

I glanced up at the wall clock. Surely, Sheriff Clay had been in his office for hours, yet he had not called me back. So much for making Rebecca's disappearance a priority. I punched redial on my phone and got his answering machine again. Not much I could do about it if he ignored me.

My thoughts turned to the list of things I needed to do to prepare for the start of class on Monday. I promised myself I would accomplish at least one item on that list before taking a break and calling Clay again. I dug the lab inventory sheets out of a file folder in the top drawer of the desk and then moved to the cabinets in the back of the room to complete my supply checklist.

"Jamie?"

Principal Al Winters stood in the hall doorway. As usual, his thinning black hair swept across the bald top of his head, but his face seemed thinner than I remembered from last spring. His suit jacket was actually buttoned, the material pulled snugly across his midriff. "Hi, Al."

"Did you have a good summer?" he asked as he marched into the room.

"Pretty good," I said. "I'm glad you stopped by. I wanted to talk to you about Trey Woodard. He's enrolled in my Biology II class again."

"I remember. He wants to get the grade on his transcript changed to an A."

"I don't think it is a good idea to let him repeat my class. Enroll him in something else that will work for his University entry credits. Get him in a class with one of the other science teachers, please." I glanced down at the inventory checklist and up at the contents of the glass-fronted storage cabinets.

"He and I have discussed this," Winters said. "He wants to go into pre-med. We need to let him take the class over again and erase the F."

I laid down the list and peered at Winters. "He threatened me."

"What?"

I explained what had happened a few minutes ago during my encounter with Trey.

Winters smiled. "He's bluffing. He wants to do well. Trey excelled during the summer session. He was a model student. I think you will see a change once class starts."

I stared at him. He met my stare and raised his eyebrows. He was the principal, I was just a science teacher. I turned back to the supply cabinet.

Winters lingered, tapping one finger on the back of a nearby chair as I reached up to pull items off the storage shelves. "Get me your supply list as soon as you can," he finally said before he crossed the room and stepped through the door.

Trey Woodard was a bully. I knew it and so did everyone else. The kid would never change. I had no doubt he would do all he could to make my life miserable this semester if I gave him anything less than a C on any exam or experiment. Winters had become the principal here three years ago; he'd already proven many times that he would not always side with the teachers when a student was concerned. Looked like I was going to experience that attitude myself this semester.

I turned back to the lengthy inventory sheet and began working my way through the cabinets.

Trey had managed to distract me from thoughts of Rebecca for a few seconds. Now my mind raced back to my missing stepdaughter and to Kate's investigation of human trafficking.

Kidnapping, sex slaves and human trafficking. Who would have thought those types of events would create headlines in a small town like Las Vegas, New Mexico?

CHAPTER 4

The midday sun burst through the canopy of a huge cotton-wood tree as I drove into the Highlands University general parking lot for the second time in two days.

Shielding my eyes, I pulled my SUV into a short-term visitor's space and then sat with my eyes closed as the beams of light played over my face. I intended to be here only long enough to find out if Dean Stuart Russell had any news about Rebecca. Better to deal with him than Sheriff Clay, I thought.

Deputy Sheriff Steve Ross had returned my early morning call to the sheriff. "I've made note of your report regarding the late night caller. Please let us know if you hear anything else."

So Clay intended to sideline me to an underling. It was just as well. Our encounter yesterday had brought all the painful memories of his accusations rushing back. The less contact I had with him the better.

I slid out of the car and stepped onto the sidewalk.

"Hey, you?" A muscular middle-aged man in a black golf shirt and khakis stepped off the sidewalk and over to me.

The last time I had seen Professor Paul Everson was at Ben's funeral, a memory still cloaked in the deep fog of my grief. "Paul. How are you?"

"I'm good." He slipped one arm around my shoulders and squeezed. "You look terrific. How was your summer?"

I stepped away from his embrace and the smell of his heavy aftershave. Sam Mazie's face swam into my mind. "Good.

Thanks for asking." Paul did not need to know anything about what had happened earlier this year in Oklahoma.

"I looked for you around town. As small as this place is, I thought we would surely run into one another. You are teaching at the high school again this year?"

A group of students moved around us on the sidewalk.

I looked up at him. Faint white streaks across his temples hinted of sunny New Mexico summer days and sunglasses. "I left my biology class a few minutes ago. I had to check the lab supplies and order fresh chemicals. Six more days till classes start."

"Same here, unless the administration delays the start of classes because of the missing students."

"Anything new on that front?" As a professor, Paul might know the latest news about what was happening.

He shrugged. "Number three disappeared over the weekend."

"I know," I said. "The latest missing student is Ben's daughter."

"God, I'm sorry." A muscle in his cheek twitched.

"Her mother's coming in later today."

Paul frowned. "Is that a good idea? Add a hysterical mother to the mix?"

"She might have some idea where Becca went or who she might have gone with." This mid-forties never-married bachelor knew nothing of a mother's despair when her child was missing. Hysterics was part of it.

"Ten to one she and her daughter were hardly on speaking terms," he muttered. "I mean, don't mothers and their teenage daughters have a love/hate relationship?"

Almost sounded like he knew Maria and Rebecca.

A voice spoke behind me. "Hello, again, Mrs. Aldrich." Joshua McDaniel pulled open the door into the Rodgers Administration building as Paul Everson and I neared the building's steps.

"Morning, Joshua. Did you get your things moved into your new office?" I asked.

"Just a few personal items left to find room for. Thanks for cleaning it out." His teeth peeked out between his lips when he smiled.

In his dark green t-shirt and jeans, Joshua looked like a student, not faculty.

"You've moved into Ben's office?" Paul asked Joshua. He scowled at the younger man.

"Yesterday." Joshua ignored Paul's expression and kept smiling as he held the door open for the two of us.

"You should have called me," Paul complained, turning toward me. "I'd have been happy to come and help. Ben had so many books and files. How did you manage?"

"My friend Kate helped. And Joshua." My voice sounded sharp.

"I had hoped to help you get that done," he stammered. "I know you were not looking forward to it."

I pulled the frown off my face and told myself not to over-analyze his words. We had hardly spoken at the funeral and not at all since. How could he know what I was or was not looking forward to doing?

I paused in front of the doorway to the Dean's office. "Here's my stop."

Joshua waved a hand in the air and strode down the hall.

Paul leaned close. "I really had counted on helping you with the clean out, Jamie. I can come by your house and help you put Ben's things away. It could be a tough thing to do alone."

I looked up into his blue eyes as I pulled my arm from his grip. "I'll be ready to tackle that in a day or two." His sudden interest in helping me set off alarm bells in my brain. *What did he want?* My suspicious nature surfaced. Ben had not liked Paul. It had been obvious in the set of my husband's jaw whenever we were at a faculty event with Paul or whenever someone said his name. How would he feel about Paul going through his work materials?

"Call me." He flashed a bright smile and then sauntered away, good-looking and in great shape, just as Ben had been before he was ravaged by cancer. The graying hair at Paul's temples added a touch of character that most women would find appealing.

Call him? Why was he suddenly so interested in me? He seemed to want to be friends. My experiences earlier this year in Pawhuska made me hesitant to trust him, and it was not just because Ben had not liked him. The man was still a stranger to me. Strangers could turn deadly.

I pushed my hair away from my face and stepped into the dean's office. The scent of lemon oil hung in the air. Natural light from the windows reflected from a crystal chandelier. Bright lacquered glazes shimmered on the oriental style vases posed on a long narrow wall table.

The dean's secretary was speaking into her head set as she jotted a message on a notepad. "I'll see that he gets the message, Sheriff." The woman drew three thick lines beneath whatever she had written on the pad. She looked up at me as she replaced the phone receiver. "Help you?"

"Would you tell Dean Russell that Jamie Aldrich is here to see him?" I glanced around the vacant reception area at semi-circles of antique chairs and racks of colorful brochures detailing fields of study and summer programs abroad.

"Your name again?"

I repeated my name.

The woman motioned toward the seating area as she punched her intercom button.

Several minutes later when the door opened, the Dean marched out of his office. Russell wiped the palms of his hands on his tweed jacket. "Nice to see you again, Mrs. Aldrich." His light brown eyes glanced at the empty chairs. He cleared his throat. "Something I can help you with?"

"I'm checking in for Rebecca Aldrich's mother, Maria Sanchez. She will be here later today. Is there any news about Rebecca?"

The dean looked down at his brown tie shoes and rocked on the balls of his feet.

"Unfortunately, no. Nothing about Rebecca." He looked around the room again and sighed. "I hope she turns up quickly. This publicity is not good for the University, and we don't want our students to feel there's danger on campus." He cleared his throat again. "If she comes to her senses soon, perhaps the damage can be negated."

He scanned the empty room again. I got the picture. Classes started in a few days. This room should be full of students waiting to talk to him. The Dean had reason to worry. However, he obviously did not believe my stepdaughter was truly in danger.

"Rebecca's mother and I don't believe her disappearance is a prank. We are very upset. Please let me know if you hear anything."

I hurried out of the office, my own worry growing. Why wasn't the dean more concerned? And, why hadn't the sheriff called me personally, instead of assigning that task to Deputy Ross?

Downstairs, I spotted the neon orange card on the entryway bulletin board. *Curfew.* It would not make much difference. For teenagers, curfews were something to ignore.

As I neared my SUV in the parking lot, I noticed a man leaning against the front hood, talking to a young woman. The woman raked her highlighted hair back from her face with two fingers as she talked, and clutched a stack of books against her chest with one arm.

When she noticed me approaching the car, she backed a few steps away; the man did not.

"Give me a time and place, Babe," he insisted as I neared

the driver's door of my car. Finally, he saw me and stepped away, a wide grin stretching across his face.

Greasy long hair framed a thin face with a day-old beard and moustache. *Craig* was embroidered in red over the left pocket of his gray shirt with the word *Maintenance* stenciled below it. The University logo decorated the shirt's left shoulder.

"Sorry," he said.

"No problem." I opened the door and settled in. As the couple crossed the parking lot, the man draped his arm across the girl's shoulders.

I knew that this university, like all others, had rules about any employee or staff member consorting with a student. 'Craig' was breaking the hell out of it.

CHAPTER 5

A hint of fall swooped into Las Vegas with the wind as I pulled into my driveway. I stood in the breezeway between the house and the garage for a moment, soaking in the afternoon glow and the smells of cottonwood and pine I loved so much. Next door, all was still at Mildred's house.

My nosy neighbor had not been over to see me since I arrived home Sunday night. It was not like her to go more than a day without stopping by for some reason. Should I go over there? The answer was *probably*, but I was not feeling especially social right now. I felt certain she would make contact soon enough.

Inside, I glanced only once at the row of boxes lining the hallway. Heaviness settled over me. Paul had seemed serious about helping me go through Ben's papers. Some of the material might be useful to a history professor like Paul, or Ben's replacement, Joshua. I needed to forget Ben's dislike of Paul. I had no inkling why he felt that way, and most likely, I never would. Going through the class materials could wait another day and Paul could help, whenever he showed up.

I searched the boxes for those containing the framed photographs Ben had kept displayed in his office at the university. Once I found them, I pulled the pictures out one by one and laid them on the floor. It did not take me long to decide which one I should place on the living room bookshelf. I chose another for the lamp table. Then I carried three of them upstairs and added one to the hall table and one to the tops of the dressers in two of the bedrooms. The last picture—one of the three of us—I gave a place of honor on the desk in the office.

Now what? The quiet house felt oppressive. I did not remember ever feeling that way here, not even shortly after Ben's death. Maybe it had something to do with all the activity I had lived with this summer. Between Elizabeth, Trudy and Ben, someone was always near me, engaging me in life. Even Queenie, the basset hound mix I had adopted, had kept me totally engaged if no humans were around. Now, I felt lonely. I missed my children and I missed the little Chihuahua who had been a member of our family. I missed Ben and I missed Sam. I needed to stay busy, doing something. Anything.

Maria would be here in a few hours, if she left Gallup after work. Although unpacking the boxes from Ben's office seemed daunting, I could tackle a smaller bite of the process.

Ben's briefcase and laptop computer leaned against the wall inside the living room where I had deposited them last night; I lugged them both to the kitchen.

After flipping on the radio and dialing to my favorite oldies station, I climbed onto a bar stool at the butcher-block island, and then unlatched the briefcase. On top of the pile of documents stuffed into the case were reports from the fall semester two years ago, as well as copies of the grades and class rosters Ben had submitted shortly before his death. The briefcase also included piles of stapled newspaper or magazine articles, clipped together by categories. I flipped through them. Many were obviously research; some were simply historical Americana.

However, one set of articles held together with a large red binder clip seemed an odd inclusion. The headlines packed a punch. *Missing Woman Reported in Los Alamos Area. Chama Woman Missing. Santa Rosa Woman Disappears,* and so on. The news articles were all about women who had gone missing. The dates of the articles spanned a twenty-year period.

Crazy coincidence. Ben had clipped and studied all of these

cases over the years, and now his own daughter was missing. Stranger still, Ben had never mentioned his interest in these cases to me. Had these missing women been the focus of some paper he was writing or was his interest more personal? I set the group of articles to one side.

The final item in the briefcase was a narrow white binder. Ben had printed "Fort Union" on the binder's spine with a black Sharpie.

The binder held drafts of research papers Ben had written and submitted over the years to Western history journals. In a separate section at the back of the binder, I recognized drafts of two manuscripts he had been writing before he became ill. If I remembered correctly, he had intended to submit the articles and then develop displays of the information for the Fort Union Visitor's Center northeast of town near the old Santa Fe Trail.

I scanned the two drafts. The facility might still want the information. Each article contained an extensive bibliography helpful to any researcher. Although I had not been as fascinated with either Fort Union or his research topics, I knew there was value to his discoveries. Maybe someone else had gone ahead and written about these things, and maybe displays explaining the facts already existed. I did not know; I had not driven to old Fort Union since the doctors had diagnosed Ben's cancer.

I glanced out the kitchen window at our backyard and the row of evergreens and pines which separating my yard from the neighbor's yard behind. Two birds flitted out from the green branches, chirping and chasing one another. A butterfly swooped past on the breeze, and then flapped its way to puddle in the birdbath. Another day, I might have set the binder aside and gone out to sit in the quiet, enjoying the privacy of my back yard and watching clouds puff and shape shift in the sky above. But not today.

Fort Union was only a thirty-minute drive. At the earliest, Maria might arrive from Gallup about nine. I could stay here, feeling lonely, with the boxes calling from the hallway, or I could find something else to do. Fresh air and a drive through the short grass prairie of north central New Mexico might help clear my head.

I stowed the laptop in the office closet beneath Ben's doctoral robe, took the two unfinished articles out of the binder and placed them in an empty file folder before I stepped out into the beautiful August afternoon.

As I drove through Las Vegas to Interstate 25, I gulped deep breaths of the fresh air and prepared myself. For more than a year, I had known this day would come: I had to go out to the Fort, just as I had had to go to the University. I could not live my life putting off visits to the places Ben had frequented. Fort Union held memories for me, too. Good memories. The Fort had been Ben's pet project.

Twenty minutes later, I exited the expressway and followed the meandering asphalt road across the prairie to the historic site. The grass-covered landscape rolled northwest for thirty miles or more until it reached the foothills of the Sangre de Cristo Mountains. It was a desolate place for a fort, but the surrounding mountains to the north and west and the grasslands to the east and south offered beautiful views. Eventually, my SUV rumbled across the final cattle guard and through the gate of the historic complex. The interpretive building's mostly empty parking area stretched ahead.

"Owen?" I called as I stepped inside the reception area of the visitor's center. "Owen Mabry?" The modern building, decorated in brown earth tones with southwestern accents of turquoise, red and yellow, felt strangely comforting. Ben had spent so many hours here. The facility had been his second home.

A chair screeched against the cement floor in the nearby office, and seconds later a man about my age stepped through the door. The park superintendent's ruddy cheeks plumped as he smiled. "Jamie Aldrich! How are you? I've missed seeing you."

He stretched over the counter and reached to shake my hand.

"Great to see you, Owen. How are things out here?"

"Busy. Big celebration mid-November." He shrugged. "Other than that, things are about the same. We sure miss Ben."

I nodded and swallowed a lump in my throat. *So did I.*

"Too much to do and not enough time," he added. "We've hired extra crews to get the restorations finished. Making sure all the event details are handled takes even more time. Not my forte. Sure could use another hand to plan the celebration." He leaned across the reception counter, staring at me with brown eyes shrunk by thick corrective lenses.

I handed him the file folder. "I brought you two articles Ben had drafted. The first one is about the laundresses at the Indian Wars fort and the other is about the Civil War earthwork fort."

Mabry grinned. "Thanks. I remember he was working on these. Ben thought we should have some displays on those topics for the anniversary." He flipped through the dozen pages of the two manuscripts. "Maybe we can incorporate this into what we're planning. Somebody would have to get cracking on it right away, though."

"Get cracking on what?" Paul Everson strode in through the door and leaned against the counter next to me.

"Hey there, Paul. Look who's here." Owen smiled at me. "Jamie brought two articles Ben had been writing for the anniversary. Interesting stuff," Owen said.

Paul took the pages. "Are you thinking we could use this for publicity, or maybe prepare a display for the celebration?" he asked Owen. Paul glanced at the drafts then laid them on the counter.

"Wish we could. Be a chance to give some credit to Ben

for all the hours he spent out here as a volunteer curator and board member." Owen flashed me another wide smile. "What do you think, Paul?"

"It's a great idea, but we're going to need some help to see it through. Know any good volunteers?" Paul peered at me.

I could see where this conversation would lead. "I don't think—"

"We could use your help, Jamie," the park superintendent said. "You and Paul could come up with some way to use the materials, and while you're at it, you could serve on his committee lining up the agenda. What do you think?" Owen asked. "Ben would sure have appreciated your help if he were still here."

Owen was right. Working out here at the old fort had been Ben's 'mission.' Volunteering for the anniversary was a short-term commitment of my time, and it would be good for me to be involved in something Ben had loved.

"Okay. Hope I'm not getting myself in over my head." In the face of their enthusiasm, it was hard not to agree to help.

"We'll work on it together, with the rest of the agenda committee," Paul assured me. "We can all get it done without burdening anyone."

I hoped so. Was I ready to handle this commitment? I felt Ben's absence. *Painfully.*

"Great to have you aboard." Owen extended his hand over the counter again. I shook it and then turned to go.

I would have to think long and hard about the commitment I had made, and get my heart ready for constant reminders of my husband's avocation. As I headed for the door, a display about the Indian Wars grabbed my attention.

What would Sam think about my involvement with Ben's pet project? Like most Native Americans, he was fully aware that history according to the native, indigenous residents of the area known as North America was mostly suppressed. Out here, the 'glory days' of Western Expansion were still celebrated. Tourism advertisements for small Western towns like

Las Vegas, New Mexico were all about recounting the challenges of Western white settlement. That history could not be ignored. Sam would argue that historians should find a way to celebrate the bravery of the white settlers while also compassionately explaining the despair of the native people whose culture was challenged and eventually extinguished. The battles of the Indian Wars were historical facts. Nothing anyone did now could change the injustices that occurred during western expansion over a century ago.

However, I also had to wonder if Sam would resent my new involvement in my husband's pet project. Sam had been grieving when we first met; his wife's death had occurred only a year or so before Ben had died. He knew grief. This past summer, the two of us had spent many hours talking about our spouses and the grief process. We had also been open about how we were beginning to feel about each other. Life had new hope.

I could not imagine Sam would take my new commitment at the Fort as a threat to our growing relationship.

"Got a minute to take a quick walk?" Paul asked as I neared the door to the visitor's center.

I glanced at my watch. Maria's arrival was still hours away.

Paul took a firm hold on my elbow and then steered me over the threshold and onto the pathway leading to the ruins behind the interpretive center. A pair of ravens squawked from the top of an evergreen bush, and then flapped away as we neared.

Despite an errant cool breeze, the midday sun had warmed the air into the upper eighties here on the prairie. I glanced toward the mountains and saw storm clouds building, quick-forming dark gray masses common during the monsoon season of the Southwest. We walked toward the ruins. Half-walled adobe buildings lined the gravel avenues of what had once been a depot on the Santa Fe Trail. The complex looked like bombed-out ruins but it was time that had done the damage here.

"You remember, don't you Jamie, that Fort Union includes three historic forts, a wooden frontier fort built in 1851, a star-shaped earth fort built during the Civil War and then, after the war, this adobe fort or depot. Once railroads were constructed across the continent, the Santa Fe Trail was no longer used by settlers and the depot was abandoned."

My head filled with Ben's voice, telling stories, reminiscing about those days on the Santa Fe Trail, the last days of the West he loved to study. A heavy weight filled my chest. *He should be here.*

Paul turned onto an adjacent path leading from the adobe ruins to the old Civil War earthworks farther east. Thunder rumbled.

I resisted Paul's gentle pressure on my elbow and stopped. "Not now, Paul. Another time, maybe." My mouth trembled.

Paul released my elbow. "Are you all right?"

"It's a little too much. This is my first time out here since Ben died."

He stuck his hands into his pockets. "I thought maybe after your summer away . . . I get it."

I was not sure he really did. What did he know about losing someone who had been your other half? I still remembered Ben's scent, still smelled him in our house, still saw him in his office. I turned back to the visitor's center.

"Before you go," he called after me, "let's make a date to unpack those boxes. Tomorrow?"

"Okay." I said before I hurried away. Holding back a sob and blinking back tears, I rushed over the graveled path, stepping around a giant red ant mound on my way to the parking lot. Seconds later, I was driving over the cattle guard and through the gate. I had to pull over; tears overflowed and poured down my cheeks. Raindrops splashed my windshield.

For the moment, my love for Sam was washed away. I grieved for Ben again.

CHAPTER 6

First, I noticed the battered blue Chevy parked against the curb in front of my house. Then, I saw the woman on the top porch step, head down, arms wrapped around her knees. I swiped at the tight skin under my eyes to remove any traces of mascara left by my tears.

The woman on the porch stood. *Maria.*

Ben had loved this woman once, I told myself, in spite of how it had all turned out. They had a daughter together and now that daughter had disappeared. I owed it to Ben to help in any way I could. And, I owed it to Rebecca as her stepmother.

"Maria! Como esta?" I called as I scurried up to the porch. The late afternoon rain had not made it here yet, but the breeze carried the ozone-scented air ahead of the storm.

The black-haired woman hunched her shoulders and swayed. Deep clefts bracketed her mouth and her eyes drooped. This woman bore little resemblance to the fiery Latina who had once been Ben's wife.

"What do you hear? Is there any news about my Becca?" Maria extended her hands palms up as I climbed the front steps. She grasped my shoulders and sobbed when I reached her.

"Madre de Dios. Donde esta mi bebe?" She keened, sinking to her knees. She swayed.

As I knelt beside her, I caught sight of movement next door. Mildred stood on the property line between our yards, the upper half of her body leaning our way, head cocked.

Maria dissolved into hysterical tears.

Maybe Paul had been right and Maria's presence in Las Vegas was a bad idea.

"Let's get inside, Maria. Come with me. Please." I helped her to her feet and then unlocked the door, guiding her through it before returning to the porch to grab the luggage she had left near the steps. A glance at the side yard showed Mildred still watching. Within an hour, I expected her to ring my doorbell on the pretense of wanting to help when all she really wanted was to know what was going on.

I helped Maria into the living room where she collapsed on the sofa, hunched over the cushion's edge, arms once again clasped around her knees, rocking her body.

"Where is she?" Maria repeated, staring out the front window.

This was not the Maria I knew. That woman had been haughty and often hostile, berating Ben in Spanish even when I was present. Her adult daughter had been out of touch for only two days. Apparently, she believed the worst had happened.

Eventually, with the help of some hot herbal tea as well as cheese and crackers, Maria regained her self-control. She had spent all her tears and repeated her prayer phrases countless times. She closed her eyes and sat still.

What had I always thought so beautiful about this woman? Her narrow nose was slightly hooked. Red rimmed her huge, soulful black eyes. Today, Maria's usually wavy shoulder-length hair jutted out from her head at odd angles as if she had not brushed it in days. Smears of black eye liner and mascara were all that remained of any makeup she had applied earlier.

She was the image of a mother in distress.

"Maria? What can you tell me that might help the police?"

Maria started in Spanish, speaking so quickly she lost me almost immediately. I held up my hands. "Whoa. I do not understand. No hablo. Speak English please, Maria." I leaned towards her.

"Si. I mean, yes. English. Oh, Jamie. We must find her." Maria's lower lip quivered.

I could not help Maria or Rebecca if the woman did nothing but cry. "Let's start at the beginning, when Rebecca left home to come to school here at the University. What kind of mood was she in? Had you been arguing?"

"The police asked that, too. It was a little argument, nothing to cause this. Nothing to make her run away. She wasn't seeing that boy anymore. He was out of her life. She told me so for many days. She came here for school. To study. Said she would feel close to her father here, and I believed her. She misses him so." Maria choked back another sob.

"Is there a chance she was lying about having broken off that relationship? Maybe her coming here was a cover for running off with her boyfriend."

Maria stiffened and shook her head frantically. "No. She meant it to be over. Something bad happened to her. I know it. Please, Jamie. Help me find her. The police, they no believe anything bad happen. But, a mother knows in her heart." Maria sucked in several quick breaths and then blew out a long whooshing sigh.

"Rebecca sent me a note while I was out of state. She seemed excited to be coming here to school."

Maria grasped the thought. "Oh, yes. She was excited. She knows what she wants and where she should be."

I glimpsed the other Maria for an instant, forehead smooth, eyes alight but then her expression crumbled.

"Why did this happen?" she moaned.

"You said you argued. Maybe she was more upset than you thought."

Maria shook her head again. "We argue about Eduardo. My husband. Rebecca and he . . . they not get along. The two of them argue all the time."

Ben had told me about Eduardo and about how Rebecca

felt about him. He had wondered if Rebecca's frequent weekend visits to us in Las Vegas were as much an escape from Eduardo as a way to spend time with Ben.

Maria stared into my eyes and repeated. "Eddie did not do this. If police only look at him, we never know what happened. Please, Jamie, help me find her."

Sometime later, when my cell phone rang, I was glad to take a break from Maria's sobbing rants. Nothing I said calmed her, and I had learned nothing to help locate Rebecca. I dashed down the hall and grabbed my cell from my purse.

"Hello," I said, drawing in a breath.

"Hello, yourself."

I heard the smile in Sam's voice, and weight lifted from my shoulders as lightness filled my chest. "Oh, Sam. I'm so glad you called." I glanced up at the small metal-framed mirror I had hung on the kitchen wall. My cheeks glowed, and so did my green eyes. There was no denying that this Oklahoma man brought out the best in me.

"You're welcome, sweetheart. I miss you."

"And I miss you." My love for Sam tingled through my body. This afternoon I had wondered if my feelings for him were true. How could I still feel such strong grief for my husband if I had fallen in love with someone else? I had no answers, but I knew the reality of the love I felt for Sam, who was now six hundred miles away in northern Oklahoma.

"I want to be there with you," Sam said.

My insides melted; I sank down onto a barstool. "Me, too, honey."

"I'm glad that's settled. Now, what's wrong? I hear something in your voice."

I longed to spill it all out to him. Maria huddled in the living room within earshot, crying. I lowered my voice. "Something's happened. Ben's daughter Rebecca enrolled in the University for the semester. Last weekend she disappeared. Her mother is here with me now."

"That's disturbing. Any clue where she might have gone?"

"Maria is sure Rebecca didn't run away, but the girl ran off a few times before, during high school. The police don't seem to be concerned."

As Sam and I talked, I heard Maria moving about in the house. I stepped out onto the back deck for some privacy. "How's Trudy, Sam? Have you seen her this week?"

"Yes," he said his voice strong and confident. "I stopped by the house on my way home from the office today. She was making cookies while humming 'Do You Know the Muffin Man.'"

A shiver tingled across my neck and goose bumps rose on my arms. "Good thing I wasn't there. That nursery rhyme gives me the creeps, now. I am glad it still has good memories for Trudy, though." I stepped back inside the house and listened for Maria. "I know I did the right thing by coming home, but it was difficult to leave."

The sound of sobbing floated down the hall and into the kitchen. I peered toward the front of the house. Maria stood outlined in the open front door, her shoulders heaving with sobs.

"I've got to go, Sam. Maria is hysterical again. Can I call you back?"

"Is there anything I can do? I'll drive right out if you need me."

"I'm afraid there's not a lot to do right now but let the sheriff investigate. Maria and I need to figure out if there is anything *we* can do. I'll call you back."

"You better, honey. Love you."

"Me, too."

I clicked off my cell and hurried to the front of the house. Maria paced back and forth on the front porch.

My neighbor, Mildred, stood on the walk, halfway up to the porch. She keyed in on me with a sharp look as she marched forward. "Jamie! Everything all right?" Her look jerked from me to Maria and back again.

"Not really," I replied.

Maria sobbed and muttered to herself in Spanish.

Mildred stared at Maria's back. "What's wrong with her?" Her chin pointed toward Maria.

What was the use in keeping this a secret? The police would broadcast Rebecca's name soon, if they had not done so already. Mildred would make the connection to me. "Ben's daughter Rebecca is missing. This is her mother, Maria. She drove in from Gallup to help the police, and to wait for Rebecca to come back."

"Ah." Mildred straightened her shoulders. She rose up slightly on her toes. "Missing. As in, 'run away to the big city,' or as in 'who knows?'"

"Maria doesn't think she ran away."

"No, no, no, no, no," Maria moaned. "She did not run away. She gave up those stage life dreams. She did not run away."

Stage life dreams? This was something new, and I did not like the sound of it. *The girl probably had run away.*

Maria took one look at my face and burst into another round of crying.

Mildred's eyes widened and she darted across the front yard and back into her house.

What was wrong with Mildred? She was not acting at all like herself.

CHAPTER 7

An hour later, I stood in Sheriff Jonah Clay's office, clenching my fists.

"Yes, she had recently talked about a career in modeling or acting, but her mother is convinced she didn't run away. She intended to get her BA degree from the University," I said.

The man's steely look cut right through me. Good thing Maria had waited outside the police station in the car. The woman did not have the stamina right now to face this man's disbelief.

"The husband—Eduardo Sanchez? She's sure he had nothing to do with the girl's disappearance?" He turned to Deputy Ross, who leaned against another desk. "We'll check him out anyway. Run his sheet," he instructed. The sheriff swiveled his wooden desk chair around to face me. "What about the daughter's boyfriend? I need a name and a number."

Maria had insisted the young man was not relevant, but how could she know? The man could have been stalking Rebecca, followed her here and then kidnapped her. On the other hand, maybe the pair had kissed and made up and left together. "I'll go out and get it from her."

"There is no evidence of foul play," the sheriff reminded me. "The girl is over 18. There has been no ransom note or contact from her." Clay stood. "I have a news conference in ten minutes. I need to update the public on the other two students, the ones who had no prior history of running away."

"What about the phone call, and the message that was left for me? Even though the caller did not threaten Rebecca, and made no demands, he knew something," I insisted. "Rebecca left all of her things in the dorm room. If she left town, she would have taken some clothes or essentials."

"Not necessarily."

I did not want him to be right. If not for Maria's insistence and the brief phone message on the answering machine, I would probably also believe Rebecca had left willingly.

The sun had dropped behind the mountains and darkness hovered outside as I slipped into the front seat of my car and pulled the door shut a few minutes later.

"What did he say?" Fresh tears wet Maria's cheeks.

"He wants to talk to the boyfriend. Can you give me his name and a phone number or address?"

Maria dug around in a leather purse the size of a saddlebag, pulling out Kleenex, old grocery lists and white credit card slips. Finally, she pulled out a wrinkled pink receipt. She smoothed the paper against her knee.

"Brett Wilson, 2429 Birdsong, Gallup," she said slowly, as I jotted down the information. Maria clucked her tongue, shook her head and then folded the paper into a square before she stuck it back into her purse. She glanced at me. "Becca sent him flowers last month, on his birthday. Charged them to me. We had a big fight."

I was beginning to doubt Rebecca and Brett had really broken up. More likely, Becca staged the breakup for Maria's benefit. I slipped out of the car and hurried back into the office to leave Brett's name and number with Sheriff Clay.

When I slipped back behind the wheel and started the car a few minutes later, Maria stared out of the car's front windshield, expressionless. My heart was heavy. If Maria could not convince *me* someone had kidnapped Rebecca, I doubted she could convince anyone else, either.

"Maria? Do you have a place to stay? I can help you find a motel."

Maria looked at me with huge red-rimmed eyes. She covered her mouth with both hands and shook her head slowly back and forth. "I make mess of my life, Jamie," she said through her hands.

"What do you mean, Maria? It's not your fault if Rebecca chose to run away."

"She didn't run away. But, who am I to blame her if she did? I have not been a good mother."

I had never imagined this side of Maria. The woman had always seemed so sure of herself, as if the world belonged to her because of her beauty and her Latina heritage. This dismal, morose woman did not look much like the Maria who had made Ben's life miserable.

"I am not a good mother," she repeated. "I am selfish. I divorced Ben, married Eduardo. Such selfish things."

I had heard the story from Ben. Maria had conducted an affair for two years behind Ben's back. Ben's love for Maria had been replaced with tolerance for the mother of their child. So now, Maria felt remorseful. *A little late.*

"Eduardo is like me. We make each other crazy. We are divorcing." Maria sounded resigned to the facts. "If I get motel room, Eduardo – he'll think I came here to be with a man. He kill me if I with another man."

The hairs on the back of my neck bristled. "He's threatened you?" I turned the corner into my neighborhood.

By the light of the streetlamps, I saw the color drain from Maria's face. She picked at the fabric of her blouse with her fingers. "He'll kill me, someday. I know it." Maria stared blankly through the window again. "He has threatened to do it so many times. Everything wrong was my fault. He beat me. Cut me."

My arms broke out in gooseflesh. "Maria, have you filed a restraining order, told any of this to the police in Gallup?"

"You think they can stop it from happening? I deserve it. I make him crazy."

I drove the SUV into my driveway and turned off the motor.

"Maria, you are not responsible for his emotions. I can't believe I am hearing this." My heart and my head pounded. I bit at one fingernail. "You must divorce him, Maria. For your safety and peace of mind."

"I am afraid."

"Of course you're afraid. You must move away from him. That is better than feeling terrified he might come home any minute and hurt you." I rubbed at my temples, where the headache beat a staccato rhythm. "Maria, you are staying here with me."

I bolted out of the car and grabbed the evening paper from the sidewalk. My heart raced; I wanted to get Maria into the house.

A car engine revved down the street. Seconds later, the tan-colored sedan I had seen last night as Kate and I unloaded the car, roared past. As I looked up at the noisy car, the driver smiled through the open window. I caught a glimpse of dark hair, a full moustache and wide-set eyes in deep sockets.

The driver looked like my ex-husband.

I hurried us both into the house, my legs trembling beneath me. It had been a long, full day. My brain was playing tricks on me, imagining what was not there. All this talk of safety and peace of mind . . .

I carried Maria's bag up the stairs to the guest room. She dragged herself up behind me, the long straps of her heavy purse slung across her torso. "Make yourself at home. I'm going to take a quick shower." I closed her door behind me as I stepped out into the hall, and then stood, listening.

"My Becca. Where are you?" Maria muttered behind the guest room door.

I would probably have that same thought hundreds of times a day until Rebecca returned.

I glanced out the window of my bedroom and into the still, starry night. Small branches wiggled in the breeze, catching the moon glow. I lifted the window a few inches, letting in the breath of fresh, nighttime mountain air. Somewhere nearby, an owl hooted. Crickets chirped.

The driver of that car could not have been my ex-husband, Rob. *I had imagined it, hadn't I?*

Unable to sleep, I rolled out of bed and slipped on my robe. I trudged downstairs and curled up on one end of the living room sofa.

Maybe Sam was only a dream. As I sat in my living room in the darkness, he seemed so far away. I could not sense him. Ben's ghost filled the house.

How could I maintain a relationship with Sam when I was living with Ben again?

The despair I had felt when Ben died filled me up, ran out my mouth and ears and eyes. I had lied to Sam. I had told him I loved him, encouraged him to love me. I had been wrong. *So wrong.*

I had no idea what I would say to him the next time we talked on the phone.

My heart skipped a beat as I acknowledged an even bigger worry in my life, one that was now shadowing my every thought: *What had happened to Rebecca?*

CHAPTER 8

Wednesday, August 16

The mouth-watering smells of bacon frying and coffee brewing woke me. I lay in the darkness and squeezed my eyes shut; I must be dreaming. Ben sometimes made breakfast on the weekends, spoiling me with a feast of eggs, pancakes, bacon and fresh coffee, but never this early. Those mornings, after Alison and Matt had both left for college at the University of New Mexico, had been some of our most special times. I let the bittersweet memories wash over me.

Something crashed in the kitchen. I sat up. This was no dream. Someone was in my kitchen, cooking. The bedside clock's face glowed 5 a.m. Black night still hung behind the curtains on my windows. I pulled on my robe, grabbed my glasses and tromped downstairs to the kitchen.

"Buenas dias!" Maria called when she saw me. She had pulled her neatly combed hair into a bun at the back of her neck and dressed in a flashy silver and black running suit. Maria turned to the skillet of bacon and flipped a slice with the spatula. "It is almost ready. Grab a plate, Jamie."

She had already heaped platters with pancakes and bacon, filled glasses of orange juice and set a carafe of coffee on the kitchen island. Two place mats and silverware settings covered one end of the adjacent bar. Maria scooped more bacon from the skillet and added it to the pile on the platter.

"I eat big breakfast. Not know when I eat again. Sit." She

motioned to the barstool beside her as she hoisted herself up on the cushioned seat of the stool.

"Maria, this looks wonderful. But remember, I told you last night I'm starting a yoga class this morning. Six o'clock. I can't eat this heavy and then do yoga." I imagined myself attempting the Downward Facing Dog yoga position with a stomach full of pancakes and bacon.

Maria shrugged then slathered butter on her pancakes and poured maple syrup over the stack. "You can try." She cut into the pile of pancakes with her fork and stuffed the first bite into her mouth.

I perched on the stool and took a sip of coffee. Had to admit, I was tempted by the thick stack of pancakes and the crisp bacon. "Maybe just one bite."

Forty-five minutes later, I trudged out to the car, one hand on my stomach. I had eaten far too much. The breakfast had been delicious and Maria had been pleasant company, unlike yesterday when the woman could not stop crying.

"Rebecca will come back," she had said as we ate our pancakes. "She will. You see. I had a good dream last night. My baby is okay."

"I hope so, Maria. Maybe, wherever she is, she has just lost track of time." I wondered how that could possibly be true, even though I had just said it. If it was true, my stepdaughter was far more self-centered than I'd ever imagined.

"Yes, she will come back. She will be here for the start of school. She will."

I sipped my coffee. This bright, optimistic Maria was quite a change from yesterday. I wished some of her optimism would run off on me.

"She will be fine. No one harmed her. I am sure of it." Her smile widened and a dimple popped into each of her cheeks.

"I hope you are right, Maria."

"Si! I am. Today, I go to the University. I talk to those girls in the dorm. I look at Becca's things. I will find out where she went. You will see." She had bustled over to the sink, wiping out the skillet, and then filling it with soapy water. Outside the kitchen window, the night sky had softened to early morning gray.

"The police have probably already done those things, Maria." Probably right after Maria reported Rebecca missing on Monday, just before I had seen Jonah Clay on campus.

"I will find something new. Something they missed. You will see."

"I hope so," I had repeated. I dreaded her return to the house this afternoon if her search turned up nothing.

I backed down the driveway into a world waking up to the day. The sky brightened minute to minute. I punched the radio to a satellite oldies channel.

As I pulled into the street, I noticed the now familiar light-colored car sitting beside the curb several houses down.

I peered at the car, and then turned the steering wheel in the opposite direction. As I drove away, I glanced repeatedly in the rearview mirror.

It was so weird to see someone who looked like Rob right after Maria had told me of Eduardo's abuse. The power of sug-gestion? Of course, I felt empathy for any woman whose spouse was verbally and physically abusive. Once my marriage to Rob ended and we lived in different cities, my life became mine again. I regained my self-respect. I hoped that Maria would be able to do the same thing.

It seemed ironic. When I met Ben here in Las Vegas, my divorce recovery finally became complete. Ben had made me whole again. Right on cue, the first few bars of Nat King Cole's hit, "Unforgettable" played on the radio. It had been playing the night we met, and had become 'our song.' I hummed along with the radio.

Kate stood on the sidewalk outside the women's gym on the north end of the strip mall.

"You made it," she exclaimed.

"You seem surprised."

"Nah. I knew you could do it. You have always said you were a morning person. And 6:30 a.m. yoga is more morning than most people can take." Kate grinned.

Her pink sweatshirt and matching sweat pants brought out the rose in her cheeks, and her blue eyes lit up with energy. I wished I had not eaten that third pancake.

Forty minutes later, I wiped a thin layer of sweat from my forehead with a small blue hand towel and followed Kate to the juice bar inside the gym.

"Wow," I said, stretching to touch my toes. I grabbed at my side, where a muscle protested the stretch.

"Don't you feel great?" Kate beamed.

"Um, I'm not sure right now." My core muscles quivered.

"You will, believe me. Let's have a smoothie. You haven't eaten, have you?"

I did not want to admit that I had had a full breakfast and more, courtesy of Maria. I waved off the Drink of the Day, an apricot banana smoothie with extra flaxseed. The three other tables in the small refreshment bar area filled with yoga class members and gym patrons.

"Are you headed to work now?" I asked.

Kate stirred her thick beverage with a spoon. "Later this morning. I've got a few things to do first." She winked.

"Hmmm, there must be a man involved. I'll be nosy and ask, who?" Kate and I had not had enough time Monday night to catch up on her personal life, and now I wanted the skinny on all of it.

Kate's smile turned into a smirk. "As I told you the other night, I'm not really seeing anyone. Technically."

I raised my eyebrows. "But something's going on. What?"

She took a long draw of smoothie through her straw and looked around at her yoga classmates before turning back to me.

"I've signed up for an internet dating service," Kate explained. "Some people don't call it dating. But to me, if you spend hours on the computer, chatting, it's the same as hours on the phone or talking at a bar somewhere."

I nodded. "Okay. I figured you might do that eventually."

She sucked more smoothie through her straw and then wiped her mouth with a paper napkin. "I've been matched up to three guys already this week. Now I'm trying to decide which one I want to meet." She shrugged. "I'm trying to pump myself up for the face-to-face part."

"I have one question about internet dating. How can you know if what the person is telling you is true?" I thought about all the crime stories she had covered as an investigative reporter. Many of them involved single women targeted by criminals. "Is this risky behavior?

"What's the difference if you're hearing their story as they type it online, or hearing it from them on a date? Anyone can lie, anytime. Bottom line is that you have to listen to your gut, you know?"

I could not argue with that. Last spring, Sam Mazie had said, "you never really know anybody." He had been right. Neither of us had imagined someone we knew would try to kill me and almost succeed.

"I have decided Joshua McDaniel is actually kind of cute." Kate suddenly gushed. "I mean, cute in a scholarly kind of way."

I pushed back from the table and grinned. "I thought from what you said the other night that you didn't like him."

"Guess I've changed my mind. He came by the newspaper

office yesterday afternoon. Said he was in the neighborhood. He acted like a completely different person. He made me laugh, and he seemed very interested in my life." Her eyes sparkled.

"Did he ask you out?"

"Not so much asked as told me he 'expected' to have dinner, or at least a nightcap, with me this weekend. I haven't decided which expectation to meet." She stirred the icy remains of the smoothie with her straw and then tipped it up to her mouth.

I glanced at my watch. "I really want to know how this turns out, but I have to change the subject. Have you heard anything else about the other two missing women on campus? Could those incidents be connected to that trafficking ring you are investigating?"

"The curfew has put a damper on late night prowling at the university. There's nothing new with the campus investigation and no *indication* of ties to human trafficking." Kate fiddled with her empty glass. "But I'm not discounting it."

"I hope you're right that there is no connection. The dean hopes you are right. Maria is going to campus today to talk to Rebecca's suite mates and look at her things. Maybe she'll find some clue they missed."

Kate's eyes widened. "I don't have to tell you what statistics indicate about kidnap victims after the first 48 hours."

I grimaced. Kate did not need to remind me.

Both the street in front of my house and the house itself were empty when I returned home. I showered and plodded downstairs to the kitchen while towel drying my hair. Thoughts of Rebecca roared in my head. Where was she? What had happened? No more messages from Monday night's weird caller. Had that call only been a prank from someone who knew my stepdaughter?

The doorbell rang. I assumed it was Mildred, seeking more information about my emotional houseguest. Well, I had questions for her as well. She had been friends with Ben, but her reaction to his daughter's disappearance seemed out of character. I wanted to know why.

I pulled the door open. Paul Everson had rolled up his shirtsleeves and draped his sport coat over one arm. The morning air and the scent of a woodsy aftershave rolled into the house with him.

"Paul! I'm surprised to see you."

"We agreed I'd stop over today to help unpack those boxes, didn't we?" He stepped past me into the house. I cinched my robe tighter and squeezed my hair with the towel. "Looks like I came a little too early. I thought we might as well tackle it before I head to campus."

I had to agree; since Paul was here, we might as well unpack the boxes. I motioned at the stack along the hallway.

"Some of the boxes might hold resources you or Joshua could use in your classes. You're the best judge of that." I pointed toward the dining room table. "Bring them in here. Excuse me for a minute. I'll be right back down." I hurried upstairs.

Ten minutes later, when I returned to the dining room, Paul had emptied all the boxes. He had strewn the contents across the table; some papers had fallen to the floor. Two boxes sat upended near the table, and four others were stacked below the window. Sweat circles darkened Paul's shirt below the armpits and his forehead glistened.

"Wow. You work fast. What a mess."

Paul swiped at his forehead with one arm. "Thought I'd give it all a quick once-over, see what I might be able to use. . ." He reached for a stack of papers. "My assistant called, and I have to get to campus for an emergency staff meeting."

"Something about the disappearances?"

"Who knows? Be great if they had a lead, but I'm not expecting good news."

I thumbed through the piles Paul had assembled on the nearest end of the table. A stack of magazines with tabs attached to some of the pages contained mostly articles written by or about Ben in various alumni, regional and national magazines. Other loose pages appeared to be journal articles.

Another stack included copies of student papers marked "Exceptional" or master theses from other southwestern universities.

Paul pitched some papers into the two upended boxes. "I might be able to use these. What about these books? Are you keeping them?" Books towered in a stack on the table.

"Can you use these for classes or in your research?"

He shook his head. "Not really. Ben probably kept them for reference, but they are not important sources." He pitched a few magazines into a box. "I don't see Ben's laptop anywhere. You got it back, I hope?"

"Yes. It's tucked away." I cradled half of the book stack in my arms. "I'll make room in the living room for these if you'll help carry."

Paul grabbed the remaining volumes and we carted them to the living room bookshelves.

"I appreciate your help." I smoothed my hair away from my face as I arranged the books on the shelves.

He slid his books onto the shelf as his look focused on my face. "My pleasure. Sorry I have to rush off. I had hoped we could talk a bit about the event at the Fort."

"Another time." I crossed the room toward the front door.

"I'll grab those few things I wanted . . ." He hurried to the dining room, then back out to the hall carrying two full boxes. "How about having dinner with me tonight? Nothing fancy, maybe down at the Plaza Hotel."

"I don't think so, Paul. But I appreciate the—"

"It's only dinner. As friends. We'll discuss the agenda for the fall celebration."

I reconsidered. It would give Maria some space and allow me to follow through on my promise to help with the upcoming event at the fort. It did no good to spend every minute worrying about Rebecca when, personally, I could do nothing.

"Six o'clock?" I suggested.

I took one of the boxes from him and together we carried them to his car.

Not twenty seconds later, as I walked back up to the porch, Maria's blue Chevy screeched up to the curb. She jumped out and dashed across the lawn, hair swirling like a black cloud around her head. Black mascara skid marks trailed down her cheeks.

"Another girl is gone. Oh, mi Dios."

I slid my arm around Maria's shoulders and pulled her into the house. Her entire body was shaking.

"When?"

"Last night." Maria clutched at my arms. "Becca's roommate – Lindsey – she was crying. The sheriff and all his deputies are there." Her voice broke. Maria sank onto the bottom step of the stairs. She clasped her arms around her knees and rocked. "Oh, Jamie. Where is my Becca? What has happened to her?"

Maria burst into tears.

CHAPTER 9

"There's been another disappearance, Kate." I spoke softly into my cell phone as I drove to Robertson high school for another session of preparing my classroom and the lab. "Have you heard anything?"

"Maria probably heard the details on campus." Worry hung on Kate's words. "And the worst part about this, things are really heating up in the area as far as women trapped in this trafficking ring." Kate paused, and I could hear a song from her car radio playing in the background. "The FBI raided one of the traffickers' dives last night in Albuquerque. Two of the females they picked up were only fourteen."

"I didn't hear anything on the news today."

"The raid is under wraps. It's an undercover operation. My editor is telling me the FBI may hold up my article. They are not ready to reveal anything to the public. More raids in the works, I guess."

"That's a good thing, right? It means more opportunities for them to rescue more victims."

"The discouraging thing is that so many of those victims turn right around and get into some other kind of trouble. Sometimes something even worse."

I could not wrap my thoughts around the fact this criminal ring might have kidnapped Rebecca. Now a fourth girl had disappeared. The sheriff was no doubt conducting another press conference right now.

"It's so weird that Rebecca has vanished. Almost like Ben knew it would happen," Kate said suddenly.

"What makes you say that?"

"My investigative report was the result of something Ben said to me a day or two before he was diagnosed. He had researched missing women in the state. But after he told me, I got sidetracked with other assignments and didn't start doing my own research until after he died."

The aged newspaper articles I had found indicated Ben began his investigation two decades ago. He had suggested the subject to Kate as a possible investigative story. A thought pricked at my heart. *Why had he not shared his investigation with me as well as Kate?*

"I've got to run, Kate. I'm at the school now, and I have a ton of things to accomplish today. I'll call you later." I disconnected, parked in the half-filled teacher's lot and hurried up the sidewalk and into the high school.

Al Winters met me at the top of the second floor stairway.

"I saw that you placed your chemical order. Everything else ready for class?" Principal Winters asked.

"I'm working my way down my list. Yesterday was our deadline for ordering science materials, wasn't it?" Although Winters was beginning his third year at Robertson High school, he was still rushing the teachers' preparation procedures.

"It was." He walked beside me down the hallway toward the biology lab. "Be sure you didn't overlook something."

"Why do you say that?" I stopped. "We can order throughout the semester, can't we?"

He brushed his hand over his balding scalp and cleared his throat. "I heard about your stepdaughter. Can't be easy having a missing child, even though she is an adult."

I unlocked the lab door and stepped in, flipping on the lights as I turned to face the principal. "It's worrisome. Her mother cannot convince the police she has not run away. Rebecca has made that mistake in the past, I'm afraid."

He smiled. "Hard for a leopard to change its spots."

"I don't think my stepdaughter ran away."

"So, what do you think happened to her?"

"Someone kidnapped her. I don't know who or why, but Maria is convinced, and so am I."

Winters picked at the door jam with a fingernail. "A random kidnapping you think? For ransom?"

"No one has asked for a ransom. And then there's human trafficking to worry about."

He looked at me sharply. "Human trafficking? What do you know about that?"

"Enough," I stammered. I had promised Kate I would say nothing about her investigation, but it was fresh on my mind. Didn't a high school principal need to be informed that human traffickers were working the area? "I know enough to wonder if Rebecca might have been taken by some sex trafficking ring working around here."

"Have you mentioned this idea to the police?"

Had I? I shook my head. "Not specifically. But I have a friend who is connecting the dots."

Al Winters shrugged, turned on his heel and stalked away.

When I returned home later, I found Maria kneeling on the floor of the living room, her hands folded around her rosary, fingers working as she prayed. I tiptoed down the hallway to the kitchen.

What if my own daughter, Alison, disappeared into thin air like Rebecca had? My stomach clenched. Memories rolled through my head: Alison's birth, her crab crawl, her first steps. My mind began to replay all the little snippets of memories imprinted on my brain.

What if memories were all I had left of my daughter?

My gut wrenched. Similar thoughts must fill Maria's mind.

My own memories of Rebecca began when she was about five years old, a year after Ben's divorce. We had started dating, and it was Ben's weekend for Rebecca to visit. A beautiful little girl, Rebecca had been shy at first until the three of us had sat on the floor together and played a game of Candy Land. After the game was over, she had scooted over against me and given me a hug.

"Thank you for playing with me," she had said in a soft voice.

I had glanced up and caught Ben's sad smile. He had explained later that Maria rarely played like that with Rebecca. He passed it off as learned behavior; Maria's parents had never played with her.

"And what about you? Did your parents play with you?" I had asked Ben, wanting to learn all I could about the man I was falling in love with.

"As I remember, they did. I was five when my dad died. Mom married again a few years later. My step-dad taught me how to ride a bike, play baseball and football and talk to girls."

"Good memories."

"Yeah. My mom and my step-dad died in a car accident when I was in the seventh grade. I moved in with my mom's sister. Lived with Aunt Jean and Uncle Roy in Mora until I graduated from high school."

I had kissed his cheek and snuggled close. At the time, I had been unable to imagine losing either one of my parents. To lose both at once must have been an overwhelming horror. "I'm so sorry, Ben. No child should ever lose both parents at such a young age."

Ben's eyes had reflected his sorrow. "You take what comes and do the best you can. My stepfather taught me that, too."

My other memories of Rebecca were not as poignant. After Ben and I married, she'd come for the weekend at least once a month and spend a good portion of it alone in her bedroom. Rebecca never spoke to me about her stepfather, and talked to Ben about him only in monosyllables.

"Jamie? I didn't hear you come in." Maria interrupted my

thoughts when she stepped into the kitchen, blotting under her eyes with a tissue.

I looked up at her from my perch on one of the stools at the island. "I finished my work at school and came home early."

"I go up to my room now, Jamie. I need to pray. At least I can do that. I not come down for dinner."

"I'll be praying, too, Maria."

I did not tell her I had plans for the evening. I would leave a note when I went out, in case she wondered where I had gone. I heard her climb the stairs and then heard her bedroom door latch click. The house fell silent.

Just as well that I had made dinner plans, I thought. I did not want to spend the evening alone with my thoughts and with Ben's ghost.

CHAPTER 10

The sun beamed from the treetops when Paul and I walked down the porch steps to go to dinner. Traffic zoomed past on the street as my neighbors returned home from work.

"Let me tell you again how nice it is to have you back in town," Paul said as we buckled our seat belts after climbing into his Pathfinder.

"Thank you, Paul. It's good to be back." I glanced at Paul as he drove. Taller than Ben, the top of his head was only an inch from the roof of his SUV. Smile lines fanned out from the corners of his eyes. The line of his jaw and the shape of his ears reminded me of Ben.

He smiled when he glanced over and caught me studying him.

"I heard another disappearance was reported today," I said. "Was that what your morning faculty meeting was about?"

He nodded. "Some of the female students are talking about withdrawing for the semester. The dean called a second emergency faculty meeting this afternoon. Wants us all to cooperate fully with the police. As if we wouldn't." Paul glanced at me. "Anything new on your stepdaughter? Did her mom make it to town?"

"She's staying with me. Maria went to talk with Rebecca's roommate this afternoon. Both the girl and Maria are hysterical again after this latest disappearance."

He checked the rearview and side view mirrors as he drove.

"It's a terrible business. I hope they catch whoever is responsible soon, and that these young women are found uninjured."

We fell silent. I was thinking of all the horrible things that might be happening to the girls. I imagined Paul was, too.

Minutes later Paul Everson turned the car into a parking spot on the town plaza. As we walked past the gazebo and across the tree-filled park, I scanned the facades of the old buildings facing the plaza. Some shop windows were empty or covered with plywood. Signs in other windows advertised active restaurants or businesses. Several of the buildings housed antique stores with windows full of memorabilia and everyday items used long ago.

We crossed the street to the Plaza Hotel. A car crept by, its radio blaring heavy metal rock. The booming beat of a mariachi band played from another car.

After the cars had passed, the plaza grew quiet. I looked up into the first floor windows of the old hotel. Lace curtains hung to the floor, and in the lobby, people in period costumes greeted restaurant patrons. Time stopped. It could be any decade, any year.

I could be here with Ben as we so often were during our years together.

I glanced up at Paul as we climbed the worn concrete steps into the hotel lobby. He took my hand, and his touch brought me back to the present. I reached for the doorknob.

"Welcome! Table for two?" a voice boomed. The maitre d' bounded around the restaurant's check-in podium with menus in hand. His bushy handlebar moustache and long sideburns were from the same era as his mutton-sleeved white shirt, striped vest and trousers. He led us into the dining room and over to a table by the window.

I settled into my chair and glanced out at the spacious lawn and enormous trees of the town plaza, pulled in a deep breath and let it out slowly. Unpacking Ben's things, trying to relate to Maria, and worrying about Rebecca and the campus disappearances had tied the muscles of my back in knots. I glanced at the menu and then once again through the wide plate glass window.

Paul cleared his throat. "Did you and Ben come here to eat often?"

"Yes, especially when we first started dating. This was one of our regular haunts. I love watching the lights twinkle around the plaza."

"I'm still something of a newcomer here. Starting my third year as a professor."

"Where was it you taught before you came here?" As I glanced at the menu, I recalled which entrees I loved. My stomach rumbled. Breakfast, although huge, had been more than twelve hours ago, and I had worked through lunch. "I probably knew the answer to that question once. I'm afraid I've forgotten."

"I don't mind telling you again. You will have to answer questions, too. Ben probably told you about me once," Paul said with a sly grin, leaning across the table. "But you were his wife and not available. I didn't store the information."

Available? He was mistaken. Sam Mazie's face filled my mind. I stiffened.

Paul leaned away from the table. "I'm sorry. That was presumptuous of me." He cleared his throat and took a long drink of ice water. "I hope we can be friends. I'd like to get to know you better." He smile and the little creases at the corner of his eyes deepened.

His eyes are the same color that Ben's were. The realization startled me.

"Ben and I went to high school together, remember?" he asked. His eyes narrowed. "Did he ever say anything about that?"

"If he did, I don't remember." However, I did remember Ben not being happy when Paul joined the faculty as a history professor at Highlands.

"High school, and then we both attended UNM although we didn't see much of each other." Paul looked into my eyes as he talked, and I tried to focus on what he was saying. He had stirred my memories again, and I felt I was listening to Ben speak, not Paul. "We did our graduate studies in different places, and then I had various teaching assignments, mostly in Arizona and Utah. It was good to see him again when I took the position at Highlands."

As I recalled, Ben had not been so glad to see Paul. Back then, I had tried to pry details from him, but Ben was evasive, avoiding my questions, telling me he was tired and wanted to go to bed. Over that year, we saw Paul at faculty gatherings. He had also attended the departmental dinner we had hosted at our home before Ben became so ill. I did not recall that I had ever seen him and Ben have a real conversation at those events.

"And you?" Paul leaned across the table again.

I pulled myself back into the conversation. *We had been retelling history, hadn't we?*

"High school in Albuquerque, college at Colorado State, Masters' from New Mexico University. Got married, had kids, divorced and moved here to Las Vegas for a teaching job. Ben and I met at an education fundraiser." I glanced out the window. The dappled shadows of early evening hid the details of the people lounging across the street in the beautiful green park.

The waitress bustled up to the table to take our order.

"Are you okay?" Paul peered at me. "Why do I get the feeling you're someplace else tonight?"

"Sorry. Too much going on. Rebecca, the disappearances." I ran my fingers through my hair. "I'm listening. Let's talk about the celebration. How can I help?"

Paul launched into his ideas about the upcoming event. He had already decided he wanted me to not only help organize the agenda but also handle onsite logistics the day of the celebration. He made a steeple of his fingers and leaned toward me. "You know, I had expected to find more of Ben's research on Fort Union in his papers. Then it occurred to me it might be on his laptop or somewhere in your home. Have you located anything else?"

"No." But I had to admit to myself that I had not searched everywhere. Upstairs, Ben's closet still remained untouched. A row of shoeboxes lined the upper shelf. Some contained memorabilia from high school and college, things Ben had shown me when we were dating. He did not like to talk about those days. I felt certain that notes from research on Fort Union were not in that closet.

"If you find anything else useful about the fort, let me know. I'll be happy to drop over and pick it up."

The waitress slipped two plates of steaming food in front of us.

Streaks of pink, orange and blue smeared the sky when we left the restaurant an hour later. A still, late summer night hung over the plaza and the old-fashioned metal street lamps cast pools of yellow light on the sidewalks. Patches of shadow settled in the spaces between the lampposts.

Paul took my elbow and steered me down the sidewalk. A tan car rolled past and honked. Paul lifted his hand and waved. The driver grinned through the window at us and waved back.

My heart pounded. It looked like the same car that had driven past my home last night. *The one with the driver who looked like Rob.* "You know that man?"

"He's a security guard on campus," Paul said. "Seems like a nice guy."

I peered at the taillights as they grew smaller and farther away.

Was Rob working security on a University campus? *That was the last place on earth someone with his temper should be employed.*

I let myself into the dark house quietly, tiptoeing past the lamp on the hall table where I had left my note for Maria. It was still there, one edge tucked under the base of the table lamp. It didn't look like she'd read it. I crumpled the note and carried it with me down to the office. The message light on the phone flashed TWO. I punched the PLAY button.

Sam's voice split the silence. "Hello. Honey, it's Sam. Miss you. Period. I know you are busy. Hated to bother you on your cell. Have you had any news about Rebecca? How is it going with her mother? Call when you can, Jamie. I love you... Oh, Queenie barks hello. She misses you, too."

I closed my eyes. The muscles of my face relaxed. My heart swelled. I was reaching to punch in his number as the second message played.

"Your stepdaughter wants to see you," the gruff voice said. "She won't be around much longer."

A chill tracked across my neck. The phone rang. I grabbed it. "Hello?"

"Jamie, you haven't checked your cell messages tonight. Where have you been?" Kate asked.

"Oh, my God, Kate. I just listened to another creepy phone message about Rebecca." I rubbed my upper arms and sank into the leather desk chair.

"What did the caller say?"

I repeated the message.

"Crap," Kate said under her breath. "Did the caller ask for anything? Make a ransom demand?"

"No."

"He wants something."

"What? And why is he contacting me and not Maria?"

We both sat, silent. I shook off another chill. "You said you'd called earlier on my cell. I didn't hear it ring during dinner. Did you need something?"

"Wanted to chat, check the status of your muscles. Are you sore from yoga? Oh, and I also wanted to ask if you'd look for any research Ben might have done on trafficking when you go through those boxes from Ben's office."

"I've gone through some of the boxes. Paul Everson stopped by and looked for course-related materials. And, I did go through Ben's briefcase. Nothing about human trafficking. Just those articles on women who have disappeared. You want those?"

"The FBI has all that information, and they are Cold Cases anyway."

"Yeah, they are."

"So, call the sheriff. Maybe they'll put some tracing equipment on your phone. Then when the guy calls again, they can figure out where he's calling from."

"Good idea."

After we hung up a few minutes later, I huddled in the smooth leather chair.

I should call Sam. But, I had no news. And I felt so down.

Thoughts of the anonymous call buzzed around in my head like a horse fly. The caller's message provided no clue as to where Becca was, if she had run away or been kidnapped. I had no way of knowing if the caller actually knew Rebecca's whereabouts. Was there a tie-in between Becca and the disappearances on campus? Were these latest disappearances in any way connected to those Ben had tracked throughout the years? These puzzle pieces did not seem to fit together.

Why even bother to tell Sam any of this? He couldn't add any insight. Many miles now separated our lives. The present swamped my memories of the summer.

Were my feelings for Sam real?

Our relationship felt like a summer camp fling, and now I was back at home where Ben and I had lived. I was living my life as before, but this time with Ben's ghost peeking over my shoulder.

CHAPTER 11

Thursday, August 17

The morning paper carried the story about the latest disappearance on the Highlands University campus. Apparently, the sheriff and the administration continued to believe Becca was a runaway. The reporter had mentioned her only in a brief paragraph at the end of the article, and listed her as a student who was believed to have left campus on her own. Maria and I were the only ones who counted Rebecca among the missing.

I tucked one foot beneath me as I read and sipped my coffee. According to the girl's roommate, the most recent victim had left her dorm room to meet an internet friend. She had never come back. Same story as the other girls. I folded the paper and laid it on the table. *Is that what happened to Rebecca?*

My mind chugged away. How were these young women lured from the safety of their rooms? This latest victim knew she should be careful. What had enticed her?

Maria dragged into the kitchen, her eyes dark and her face pale without makeup.

"Buenas dias," I greeted her. Where was the Maria of yesterday, the woman who had bounced around the kitchen, making breakfast? Somber reality had struck.

Maria grumbled something in Spanish.

"You okay?" I asked.

Maria poured a cup of coffee and then added milk from the refrigerator. "My daughter is missing. Another girl is gone. I awake all night. Today, I will go to the sheriff. I will make him talk to me."

I pictured Sheriff Clay during my last visit. If Maria were discouraged now, she would be even more so after talking with Jonah Clay. I did not want to tell her about last night's call. I could hear her asking the same question I was, 'Why did they contact you, and not me, her mother?' But, I did need to let her know about the tracking device I had asked the sheriff to install this afternoon.

"You already talked to the sheriff. It is time I go and – you know – 'light a fire' under him?"

Maybe Maria was just the person to do that. Every passing day without word from Rebecca made the situation more serious.

"I've been wondering what these young women have in common," I said. "They go alone to meet someone. They disappear. I wonder if Sheriff Clay has tried to make connections. Are they all from the same area, all studying the same thing? Does Rebecca fit some sort of profile?"

Maria's face crumpled. She sniffed. "I ask him. I make him tell me. I do anything to find my Becca." She hurried out of the kitchen holding her coffee cup. Coffee splashed over the rim and down onto the floor, but Maria surged on. I cleaned up the spill.

Maria wanted to do this alone. I could insist and tag along, or I could wait and see what Maria could find out without me.

I carried a tote bag of supplies I had gathered for my classroom out to my car. Classes would start Monday. I still had so much to do. Now I had something else to check on at the University. *Had* they hired a new security guard? *Was it my ex-husband?*

"Jamie!" Mildred hurried across the lawn, head down, her body forming a forward-slash mark with the ground.

"Morning, Mildred." I tossed my bag and purse into my SUV

and turned to her. I had not seen Mildred since her hurried exit Tuesday after learning of Rebecca's disappearance. Would she open up and tell me what had been on her mind that night?

"I need to talk to you." The white-haired woman rushed up, hands on her hips. Her eyes looked huge behind the thick lenses of her glasses. Her brows arched. "It's about that car."

Both of us glanced toward the street where Maria's blue car sat next to the curb.

"How long is it going to sit there? Looks trashy. A blue trash hunk and a tan one down the street. Trashy cars don't help the looks of the neighborhood."

I followed her pointing finger down the street to where the tan car was parked.

"When did that car show up?" I asked.

"Earlier this summer. The man started sitting in the car a lot this week. You know him?"

My stomach clenched. "No. " I glanced down at the edge of the lawn. Black ants scurried in a line across the driveway.

"Could be he's watching you. He isn't watching me or any of our neighbors. The Carters on your other side are the typical yuppie family with two kids and a dog. Mr. Bates across the street is a scrawny old appliance repairman whose idea of excitement is the daily crossword. The Conways and the Taggees are married couples with high school kids. Unless one of them is having an affair and that guy is a private eye taking pictures, that leaves you, the single woman on the block. He has to be watching you."

"It's a coincidence, Mildred. There's no reason for him to be watching me," I said, but worry crept into my voice. I worked at sounding nonchalant. "And don't worry about Maria's car. She is not staying permanently. Only until Rebecca comes back."

"Ppffhttt. As if that will happen tomorrow. The girl has high-tailed it away from her mom if you ask me. Boyfriend or something. She'll crawl home pregnant in a few months, mark my words. You think her mom will stay with you that long?" She shook her head and tapped one foot on the driveway.

"I honestly don't know. I couldn't let Maria stay in a motel. Rebecca is Ben's daughter, you know."

"I wouldn't be too sure from the looks of her. He did not divorce that woman because of her looks. Maybe Rebecca wasn't even his!"

"Mildred, I've got to get to work."

I got into the car and drove away, leaving Mildred standing on the driveway, hands on her hips, staring out at Maria's blue car. *Crazy old busy body.* This was all I needed today. Now I had to wonder if I had a stalker.

And, another thing. *Mildred had a lot of nerve to suggest Rebecca was not Ben's daughter.*

I sat at the corner stop sign for a full minute. The route to the University led to the left, the route to the high school to the right. I turned right only because the start of school and my classroom prep weighed on my mind. I could always call the University to check on the security guard.

I placed the call to the University's human resource director's direct line as I neared the high school faculty parking area. Dave Anderson's answering machine picked up.

"Hello. You've reached Dave Anderson. I am in meetings all day today, Aug. 21. Please press zero to reach Margo or stay on the line to leave a message."

I disconnected. In person, Dave would not ask why I wanted the name of Highlands' newest security guard. However, his assistant Margo would treat that information as an official state secret. I would call back again after I finished at the high school.

In the science lab, I unwrapped the packaging from a beaker and set the glass piece on the top shelf of the cabinet.

Something caught my attention on the counter beside me. A trail of enormous, black ants snaked up the side of the cabinet from the lab floor and across the counter. The beaker fell from my hand and shattered.

Damn. I kept a can of Raid for the rare times when flies swarmed in through open windows during the spring and fall. I rushed to the closet and grabbed it, as well as a roll of paper towels, then returned to coat the line of ants with the foamy spray. The ants curled up and jerked on the counter.

I wiped the remains from the cabinet with a wad of paper towels. "Yuck!" I muttered as I cleaned up the chemical residue.

"Mrs. Aldrich."

I bumped a lab stool; it overturned.

Trey Woodard stood in the doorway, a grin stretching across his face. "Didn't mean to scare you," he snickered as I picked up the stool and set it back on its legs.

How long had he been standing there? He had probably seen what happened with the ants. At least it hadn't been a spider. If it had, he would have seen my deeply seated revulsion and fear. My life could become a miserable succession of spider adventures, all at the hands of this student.

"Trey." I tossed the paper towels into the closest trash can.

"Need any help getting ready for next week? Thought I'd volunteer my services. It is part of my plan to shine as a school aide this year. Looks good on the resume, you know."

I opened a drawer and grabbed a box knife, then used it to slice open another container, this one full of chemicals. "I've got it under control."

"Like you had those ants under control? 'Yuck!'" he mimicked.

Damn. "I'm finishing up here. Do you need anything?"

"No. See you next week, if not before." Trey nodded toward the door adjoining the lab.

"Have a nice weekend." I watched the tall young man as he stepped back into the hall.

A shiver tickled my spine as I absently stocked a drawer with the chemicals.

CHAPTER 12

Mildred was rocking in her front porch rocker when I drove past her house later. I had been short with her this morning and now I regretted it. With Ben gone, I might be the only friend she had on our little street. I was sure Mildred missed him.

"Hi, Mildred," I called as I pulled my school bags from my back seat.

"Hello," she responded. Her voice did not carry its usual enthusiasm. Instead of taking my greeting as an invitation to come over and talk, which was her usual response, she bolted from her chair and darted into the house. The Mildred I had known for all these years would never pass up a chance at conversation. Something was wrong.

I set my bags on the porch and crossed the yard. Mildred pulled her front door open before I could knock, greeting me with red irritated eyes and a puffy face.

"Are you all right, Mildred?"

She blinked. "I hope that girl comes back. Her mother— whatever she was or is ..." Mildred swallowed hard. "No one deserves not to know what happened to their children. No one." She covered her mouth, but not in time to muffle a soft sob.

"What's wrong, Mildred?"

She retreated inside. I followed.

"Ben didn't tell you."

"Tell me what?"

"He was an honorable man." Mildred stopped in front of her fireplace to pluck a framed picture of a young woman from the mantle. "Ben and I talked about my daughter often that last year, before he got cancer. I had hoped he would find out what happened."

I took the picture from her. The girl looked like a young Mildred, especially around her mouth and chin.

"Your daughter?"

"Jodie would have been thirty-eight last July 15th." Her fingers rubbed her jaw line, and then grabbed the picture back.

"She died?"

"Vanished. On her way back to UNM after Christmas break twenty years ago."

Mildred's face was the color of an unripe honeydew melon. "Jamie, I have to tell you something. Ben didn't share this with you because I told him not to. I didn't want your sympathy and I didn't want his, either. However, Rebecca – her disappearance – is so similar to what happened to my daughter. For the life of me, I do not understand how that could be. It was so long ago." Mildred closed her eyes. "The police call it a cold case. The few leads they had did not pan out. Ben had been doing some research for me."

The old newspaper articles I had found clipped together in Ben's briefcase now made sense. One of the women who disappeared was Mildred's daughter. I waited for her to continue, my mind reeling. I sat on the stiff cushion of a wingback chair.

"It was right after she graduated from high school. Several state schools had accepted her. Jodie was making her decision. She went off for a weekend visit to one of the campuses with her best friend. The pair never returned. Disappeared without a trace."

Mildred opened her eyes; they swam with tears.

"I'm so sorry. I didn't know." I touched her hand.

Mildred staggered into the next room. Condolences did not mean much after twenty years. I followed her through the dining room and into the kitchen.

She pushed out a breath and started again. "Three years ago Christmas I was feeling blue. You had gone to see your daughter for a few days. Ben was alone. He came over to talk."

My memories skimmed through to that last Christmas before the doctors had diagnosed Ben's illness. I had spent several days between Christmas and New Years in Albuquerque with my family. Ben had taught an intersession that year and couldn't go with us. I remembered it all very well because later I wished for a 'do over' on that Christmas. It was the last normal one Ben and I could have had together.

"He got the story out of me. He was always so sympathetic."

"Yes, he could be." Sympathy was not something Ben had ever expressed to me, but then I had had no need for it.

"He wanted to help. He was more concerned than anyone else had been in recent years. He researched the disappearances. I know he had an interest long before he knew about Jodie. He had collected articles about young women who disappeared around the state. Jodie and her friend were the first case."

I did recall the earliest case when two women had disappeared together. Neither of the women had the same last name as Mildred. She read my mind.

"Jodie's dad left us the year before our daughter disappeared. Afterward, I took back my maiden name. Stayed in the same house, always hoping she would show up or the police would find something. Seven years passed. Nothing. I had no reason to stay in Ruidoso, so I moved here. Now it's been twenty years since she disappeared."

She peered at me. "I know I sounded harsh about Rebecca. It is too hard to think Ben's daughter is missing now, too. If he had lived . . . if he had found the answers . . . maybe this never would have happened."

Mildred was assuming the two cases were somehow connected. I still wanted to believe the cause of Rebecca's disappearance was closer to home. As in the boyfriend, or maybe even Eduardo.

I wanted *my* assumption to be correct. Heaven forbid Mildred had the correct answer. In that case, it was unlikely any of us would ever see Rebecca again. I felt a stab of despair. What could we do? We had to find her. *I* had to find her for Ben.

I stomped across the yard, grabbed my sacks from the porch and unlocked the house. In the living room, Maria sat watching the news on one of Albuquerque's Spanish-speaking channels. In the kitchen, I dropped the sacks on the island, dug out my cell phone and stepped out onto the deck.

The late afternoon sun bore down. In minutes it would sink behind the peaks of the Sangre de Cristos. Two ravens called to one another as they flew over the yard on their nightly trek back to the mountains. Inside I felt cold and overwhelmed. I maneuvered one of the deck chairs to face the sun. *Why had someone targeted Rebecca?*

I stabbed the familiar number into the telephone. My daughter answered on the third ring. "Hello, Alison,"

"Hi, Mom. What's up?"

She sounded happy. At least there was good news there.

"I thought I should confirm our weekend plans. Are we still on?" I asked.

"Sure. That is, if you're not too busy."

"Never too busy for you. Plans coming along? Are you feeling all right?"

"Things are hectic. Wedding planning while working a 60-hour a week job is hard." Alison coughed and then cleared her throat. "I'll feel better after we get your dress."

"Me, too." I thought about everything happening around me here. My daughter and I needed time to talk more than we needed to buy this dress. Rebecca's disappearance had made me long for time with my own daughter, time to talk about her wants and needs and fears.

"Something wrong, Mom?"

Alison had always been good at reading my voice. "Getting ready for school to start. And other things." I would not make the same mistake my family members had made by not sharing the negative things in their lives. Were they trying to protect themselves or me? It was wrong to keep the negative things secret. Even if my family could do nothing to help, I needed to share both the good and bad with them.

"Did you get Ben's office cleaned out?"

"Yes. My friend Kate helped me. We moved Ben's office things here. I haven't unpacked everything yet." I fingered the necklace I had made of my wedding ring after Ben's death. During my last hours with Sam in Pawhuska, I had debated tucking it away in the bottom of my jewelry box but the thought had not crossed my mind since my return to Las Vegas.

"What else is going on?" Alison demanded. "There's something in your voice . . ."

I launched into the story of Rebecca's disappearance and the other missing female students at the University. When I told her that Ben's ex, Maria, was staying with me as the investigation continued, she laughed.

I felt the grimace on my own face. "Maria hasn't changed, but at least the two of us are united in our purpose this time, trying to find Rebecca."

As I hung up after making small talk for a few more minutes, I thought about the investigative report Kate was working on. Evil people were out there, and always had been. They did horrific things. I prayed that my daughter Alison would never experience true evil.

CHAPTER 13

Maria and I worked quietly together in the kitchen preparing dinner. Outside, a monsoon thunderstorm raged. Lightning flashed, and thunder rumbled, sounding like a boulder rolling across a wood floor. She blended a red chili pepper enchilada sauce and her special recipe of Spanish rice, while I made my own recipe for tortillas and grilled a dozen in the tortilla maker.

"How did the day go, Maria? Did you find out anything new?"

Maria put up one hand and shook her head. Inside me, irritation built up. How could I help Rebecca and Maria if Maria refused to fill me in on the investigation?

We were eating dinner when Maria finally decided to speak. Rain pelted the windows.

"You ask me to learn connections," she said as she picked up another tortilla, folded it and dipped it in the salsa before she took a bite. She chewed. I waited.

"I asked the sheriff. He would not tell me." She swallowed. "But I found out. The other girls are Latina or Native American. Two are named Alvarez and Torres, another is named Moya. Freshmen. All with dark skin and hair like Rebecca."

Here in New Mexico many women of all ages had Latina or Native American backgrounds. Why would a criminal want to target girls of this heritage on the Highlands campus? Rebecca fit the apparent profile. A beautiful freshman girl, ready for fun and ready to meet someone new.

My mind flashed back to the picture of Mildred's daughter, Jodie. She was not Native American. Not Latina. Most likely, there was no connection between the missing women whom Ben had investigated and Rebecca. That left the human trafficking ring. Were those characteristics typical of the women those criminals targeted?

After we had rinsed dishes, filled the dishwasher and cleaned the kitchen, I shut myself into the office and pulled out the articles Ben had collected on missing women. The oldest article was the one about Mildred's daughter and her friend. Twenty articles. I scanned each of them, studied the photographs, checked my desk atlas for the exact locations where the women disappeared and their hometowns. I listed the particulars of each disappearance.

I wondered if Sheriff Clay was familiar with these cases. Had he reviewed these files when Rebecca or the other Highlands University students went missing?

My cell phone rang.

"Jamie, I know you're getting ready for classes, but aren't you going to come down here at least once before school starts?" My mother asked. "I had actually expected you to come today. I stayed in all day, waiting." Her voice held disappointment as well as an accusation. *I was not being a good daughter.*

"Oh, Mom. I am trying to get my classroom ready for school on Monday. And I had to clean out Ben's office."

Excuses, excuses. Why was I still making excuses to my mother when I had grown children of my own?

On the drive back to New Mexico from Oklahoma, I had promised myself I would stay in touch and call Mother every few days. The series of medical tests she had undergone while I had been in Pawhuska revealed no serious health problems. Now Mother continued her life as if she had never had a health scare. She butted into everyone's business and offered unwanted advice.

However, I had learned life was tenuous. I had vowed to be more tolerant. No one knew when the clock would run out on the life of someone you loved.

"I'm meeting Alison in Albuquerque on Saturday. Would you like to join us? Or we could stop by for some coffee on the way there or back."

"No time for me, I hear you saying. At least your sister makes time. I can count on Ellen."

I interrupted her before she could continue with the guilt trip. "One bit of news. Ben's daughter, Rebecca, came here last week to start the semester at Highlands. Now she's missing."

"Becca? She's old enough for the University?" Mother's voice raised an octave. "Where'd she go? Did she run away again? Good thing you never did anything so juvenile."

"We don't know what happened, Mother. The police are investigating. I don't believe she ran away."

"You mean someone took her?"

"I think so. Yes."

Mother gasped. "I doubt that's the way it went. However, I am sure Maria is hysterical. She'll come to town and stir things up."

"Actually, Maria is staying here with me."

Another gasp came, followed by silence.

"It's fine, really," I added. "Hopefully, Becca will be home soon, and Maria will go back to Gallup."

"She's in your house! Well, I had thought about having Ellen drive me over for a visit tomorrow, but not now. Hell will freeze over before I intentionally put myself in a room with a woman who would treat our darling Ben like she did."

I doubted Ben had told my mother much about his ex-wife. Mother had filled her mind with suppositions, as I sometimes had.

"There's no time this weekend anyway with school starting,"

I said quickly. My mind raced. Why had I ever imagined my relationship with my mother would ever be anything less than difficult? Thank goodness, Sam was coming Thursday to spend the long Labor Day weekend. *I needed him.*

The phone ringing at 1 a.m. woke me from a sound, dreamless sleep. Startled, my first thoughts were of Alison, Matt and my mother.

"Hello?"

No response. I sat up in bed. Shadows from the light of the full moon stretched across the green walls of my bedroom.

"Who's this?"

"Jamie?"

Even at a soft whisper, I recognized the voice.

"Please come get me, I –" The click was loud in my ear.

"Becca? Hello? Becca?"

I immediately phoned 9-1-1. The operator told me to call the nonemergency line. At that number, a bored attendant took my information and promised to pass it on. Sheriff Clay, Deputy Ross and other investigating officers would be in the office the next morning.

"But the Sheriff's Department put a trace on my line. And I have had a phone call I want traced."

"I show no trace equipment on your line at this time. Someone will be in touch with you tomorrow," the attendant said.

When the phone rang again at 3 a.m., I was lying in bed wide-awake, reliving the sound of Becca's voice and hoping she would call again. I'd opened my window, and the cool, rain-heavy breeze breathed into the bedroom. This time, I glanced at the caller ID before I answered. Unidentified Caller.

"Hello?" I sat up and swung my feet over the edge of the bed.

Deep breathing. Then a soft raspy voice said, "Checked your place for ants lately?"

Definitely not Becca. Probably Trey. I threw back the coverlet, turned on the bedside lamp and then pulled my feet off the floor. The phone clicked in my ear. I checked the floor, and then ripped the covers off the bed. I looked under the dresser and inside my closet. No ants.

I did not want to deal with Trey the entire semester. Surely, I could get him transferred into another class or make some kind of a deal to have his last semester's grade deleted.

When I climbed back into bed, I fluffed my pillow and pulled the covers up to my chin.

I did not expect sleep and sleep did not come. The breeze played with the curtains the rest of the night.

CHAPTER 14

Friday, August 18

The road to Montezuma and the Armand Hammer United World College climbed out of Las Vegas and into the foothills toward the Santa Fe National Forest in western San Miguel County. Through my open car window, I breathed deeply, putting into practice what I had learned in this morning's yoga session with Kate.

Deputy Ross had phoned not long after sun up. During his thirty-second call, he did not offer an explanation as to why the tracing equipment was not in place. He had been courteous, but barely. The sheriff had put me on the back burner and was using Ross to keep me there.

Kate's suggestion that we drive to the Montezuma Hot Springs after yoga for a hot soak had sounded like a perfect way to finish a relaxation routine. Meditation during yoga had not erased my worry over Becca's call. Instead, my mind fuzzed and did nothing more than blur the worry.

Despite my deep breathing, as I followed Kate's car up the climbing road, my heart rate accelerated. Not because of the phone calls, Rebecca or the sheriff. I had been avoiding the springs. My last visit here had been with Ben in March before he died. That sunny spring morning with the temperature hovering at forty degrees, the hot mineral springs had invigorated both of us and given Ben's graying cheeks a rosy cast. It was the last time I had heard him laugh.

The springs nestled in a grove of trees off the road beyond the old town of Montezuma and across the Galinas River from the World College. I swung my car in behind Kate's on the wide parking shoulder next to the road, gathered up my towel and stashed my purse under the front seat. Kate walked up to my car, talking on her cell phone.

"That's what I'm thinking," she said as she tried to suppress a wide grin. "I'm looking forward to it." She punched the phone off and winked. "I'm taking it to the next level. A face to face."

I slid out of the car and locked the door. "You sure that's wise?"

"I'd have to be stupid not to meet him. Sounds like he is in demand, but I am the one he wants to get together with. Saturday night, baby!" Kate did a quick dance step, lifting her arms to snap her fingers.

I bit my lip to keep from saying something negative. She was excited about her date; she would not heed any warnings that her internet boyfriend might not be who he claimed to be. I followed Kate down the hillside on the winding dirt path past thorny mesquite trees, clumps of brown-green grasses, and blooming yellow broom weed. Across the Galinas River, we could clearly see several tree-shaded buildings on the hillside. Towering above them on the slope, sat the former Montezuma Hotel, circa 1890, restored and now serving as the administration building for the only United States campus of The Armand Hammer World College.

We reached the concrete pad surrounding the largest of the steaming hot springs, but Kate kept walking, following the trail past an ancient cottonwood tree with a four foot diameter and then farther down the hillside toward the river. We saw no other bathers and heard only the motor of an occasional car on the road above.

The second concrete pad, hidden behind mesquite and cedar trees, surrounded several steaming pools of water. Kate dropped her jeans and pulled her t-shirt over her head, revealing a bright pink tank. She dropped down to sit on one side of a square, steamy opening in the concrete and then slipped her legs into the water.

"Ooooh, feels great."

I left my jeans, work shirt and towel on a dilapidated park bench beneath a monstrous tree, adjusted the bottom of my suit, and then hurried over to Kate. A rotten egg smell wafted up from the springs on a cloud of steam. I slipped one foot into the water of the pool, and then jerked it out.

"Too hot? Try that one over there." Kate pointed to another steaming opening several yards away.

At the second spring, I lowered myself into the water, letting the hot water slowly creep up over my navy blue tank as I dropped deeper. The water felt like an almost-scalding bath. When I was finally submerged up to my neck, I felt the pool's stonewall behind me. A shelf jutted out from it where I could sit. I relaxed onto the shelf, closed my eyes and let the heat seep into me.

A few minutes later, Kate padded over from the first pool and dropped down on the cement beside me. Her legs flushed bright pink.

"I think I'm cooked. Is this one any cooler?" Sighing, Kate extended her legs and then eased down into the water. She found the stone bench opposite mine and relaxed onto it.

"You know, if the sheriff won't do his job the two of us are going to throw ourselves into this investigation," Kate said. "Let's come up with a plan."

I had already told her about last night's phone calls, and the 'courtesy' call from Sheriff's Deputy Ross.

Kate sank farther down into the steaming water and closed her eyes. I did the same.

After a few minutes Kate asked, "You and Ben came here a lot, didn't you?"

Heat rose in my cheeks. "Until he got really sick. We thought about getting a hot tub for the house but decided it would not be the same. Out here you're so close to nature."

"Yeah. Ben was a nature kind of guy," Kate glanced at the river; her look swept up and down the vegetation near the bank. "Why was he so fascinated with the frontier fort? And that last piece of research, about the laundresses doubling as prostitutes?" She laughed. "Leave it to Ben to dig up some dirt, aside from the earthworks that were already there."

"It was part of his research for Fort Union and an oddity about the old West," I explained. "The military hired laundresses and some of them moonlighted as hookers. Sometimes, these 'laundresses' were gays in drag." *So, Ben had talked to Kate about this research, too.* I bit back the jealousy that rose up in my throat. Kate was my friend and she had been Ben's friend, too. When he was alive, I had not been jealous of their relationship; I was not going to let myself feel jealous now. "The earthwork tunnels were interesting, though. Who would have thought that the army repurposed sections of the Civil War era fort for storage when the government abandoned the fort? Maybe the tunnels are still there."

"And maybe they caved in long ago. Wouldn't someone mention them if they were still being used?"

I shrugged.

"Why is it men are fascinated by whores, women in servitude, tunnels and illegal trade?" Kate flicked at a bug crawling on the concrete near the hole.

"You're talking about *your* investigative piece now, right?"

"Yeah. But, I am including Ben and his fascination with those missing women. The whole idea of human trafficking turns my blood cold. Many human cultures keep slaves even now. Maybe people in general aren't capable of being nice to one another." She shook her head. "Actually, I'm pissed because my editor is considering holding the piece. I get the feeling he is checking my research. He has some nerve. Have I ever lied about a source, or made up facts?"

"I hope that doesn't happen. The whole trafficking scenario sounds like something the public should know a lot more about." I closed my eyes again. *Had Ben really been fascinated by those disappearances? Why had he never said a word about them to me?*

Then another thought struck me. *Could Ben have had some kind of premonition that something similar might happen to his daughter?*

Beads of sweat rolled down my face; I had been in the hot springs long enough. I emerged into the cool morning air and reached for my towel.

"So, tell me about your date tomorrow night. Is it here, in Las Vegas?" I asked.

"We're meeting in Santa Fe for an early dinner," Kate said. She pulled herself out of the water. "I have some shopping to do first. If the two of us hit it off, we'll meet closer to home for the next date. I don't know where he actually lives."

"Shouldn't you let someone know this man's name? For safety sake, if for no other reason?"

Kate laughed. "You *are* a mother hen! Okay, I'll leave his name, email address and so forth on my desk at the newspaper office, okay?"

I agreed, but a seed of worry grew in my heart. Some criminal was out there, preying on Highlands' students. Kate might not be a student but she could probably pass for one.

"So, what's our plan for getting this investigation moving?" I asked as we pulled on our clothes.

"Get Maria to talk. Ask about Eduardo—and the boyfriend. Leave no stone unturned. If you want me to come over Sunday to talk to Maria, I will. We can also go over those newspaper articles Ben saved. Then on Monday, you go back to school and I'll spend part of my day on the internet investigating these disappearances."

"Thank you. Trying to get Maria to reveal anything has been difficult. Maybe she would talk to you. I'll be in Albuquerque with Alison tomorrow, so Sunday would work." I led the way up the path. As I stepped over the low cable separating the vegetation along the river from the shoulder of the road, I saw the tan Buick parked across the road.

I stopped abruptly; Kate bumped into me.

"Something wrong?" she asked.

"That car was not parked there when we came. Did you see anyone around?"

Kate glanced down the hillside and then at the other spring sites. "No, but some of the spring openings are secluded, like the one down at the river's edge." Her look roamed the edge of the road and up the forested slopes. "It could also belong to a hiker."

It looked like the same tan car that had passed us last night and the same car that had been parked down the street from my house: the car with the driver who looked like my ex-husband.

Maria sat the kitchen, her hands wrapped around a mug of coffee. She huddled over the table as if it was much colder than seventy-five degrees inside and outside the house. Despair shone in her eyes.

"Come with me back to the University, please, for little while this morning," Maria begged. "I need to go to Becca's dorm room again. I need to talk to her roommate."

She was finally asking for my help. Sheriff Clay was already having a tough time taking Rebecca's absence seriously. Adding myself to the mix might not help the investigation. But, what could it hurt?

"Of course, I'll go with you," I finally said. Uncovering any information related to my stepdaughter's disappearance would be more than what the Sheriff had uncovered so far.

Mildred's revelation about her daughter's disappearance tugged at my brain. *There was no way these two disappearances, twenty years apart, could be linked, was there?* Linking the crimes would suggest someone had been kidnapping women for over twenty years in the New Mexico area. What were the chances?

Before Kate came over on Sunday, I wanted to reread the articles Ben had clipped. I also wanted to study my notes. Then it struck me that Ben had probably made notes as he had read through the articles written about the disappearances. *Where would he have stored those notes?*

Thirty minutes later at Highlands University, I followed Maria into the freshman dorm. Maria walked a few steps ahead, sidestepping students who passed us in the hallway. I looked at each face, especially those of obvious Latina heritage. *Were they potential victims?*

Maria stopped in front of a dorm room door and rapped on the doorframe. When no one responded in five seconds, she knocked louder. A blond girl stuck her head out from the room across the hall.

"Lindsey's not there. Gone for the weekend. Help you?" She sang out in a northeastern accent.

We turned toward the voice. "Already gone? It's not even noon." I said.

Maria stared at the young blond student.

"Who would want to stay here? I'm leaving in a few minutes. This place will be deserted." She pulled her head back into her room and shut the door.

"Do you want to talk to the dean? See about securing Rebecca's things?" I asked Maria.

"No. I will not move her belongings. She is coming back." Maria sniffed, her head jerking with each quick breath. She wrapped her arms around herself and clamped her eyelids shut.

The possibility Rebecca might not come back loomed in the back of my mind. Another week might pass before the housing supervisor requested we vacate her room.

"Maybe you should go home for the weekend, too, Maria.

There isn't anything we can do until the students return Sunday night."

"I will not go anywhere. I will wait for Rebecca." Maria's voice cracked.

As we neared the stairway, I stepped behind Maria when a man in a gray janitor's shirt turned the corner at the landing below and started climbing towards us. He cradled three two-packs of light bulbs in one arm. His disheveled hair spiked in the center. He smiled, smugly.

"Ladies," he said as he passed us.

He gave a wolf whistle. I glanced back. A petite brown-haired woman walked down the stairs behind us. Her cheeks dimpled in an embarrassed smile.

I recognized the man I had seen in the parking lot. *Craig.*

CHAPTER 15

"I have a headache," Maria announced when we returned to the house. She trudged up the stairs to her room.

I wandered into the kitchen and out onto the back deck, where I curled up in a deck chair. My worry about Rebecca and Maria, stress about the start of the school semester, and my concern about Trey at the high school were a stress stew ready to combust. My heart raced.

Last night, I had not called Sam back. Today, all I could think of was how much I needed to talk to him. I ached for him in a much different way from how I now ached for Ben. Sam had opened my heart again, when it had been clenched and unyielding, like the fingers of a hand curled into a fist.

Ben and I had a good marriage. We had always been open and honest with one another. Never had our relationship been anything except truthful and loving. I missed the easiness of our marriage.

I wanted to be able to feel such trust, such love, with Sam. I thought it was already developing. Was I imagining it?

A sobering thought popped into my head. How could I tell myself that Ben and I had always been open and honest? Ben had kept secrets from me, telling me only scraps about his life before we met. He had not told me about all of his interests. He had omitted his obsession with the missing women and the newspaper clipping collection he'd begun long before I came into his life and long before he knew one of the women was Mildred's daughter.

My thoughts moved in a new direction. *What if the clippings were a scrapbook rather than an investigation?* My mind reeled. I shook off the thought. I had watched too many detective shows. I needed to get away from these thoughts. Meditation and yoga had not worked, and sitting here in the hot afternoon air was making it all worse.

The hairs on my arm tickled. I flicked away a little ant and peered down at the floorboards where a long line of the little insects marched. My skin crawled.

A long drive might clear my mind. I dashed inside to grab my purse and car keys, and then hurried out to my SUV.

My cell phone rang as I slid behind the steering wheel. The caller ID flashed. Sheriff Clay was finally personally calling me back.

He got right to the point. "This call you got last night. Are you sure it was Rebecca?"

"Yes. She said, 'Come get me.' Nothing else before the call was disconnected."

"Any background sounds to indicate where she was?"

"No voices or traffic noises. No music. Nothing."

"Did she sound upset?"

"She was whispering. Maybe she made the call secretly."

"If so, she had access to the phone. No one is holding her."

"But I thought you were installing trace -"

"Contact Deputy Sheriff Ross if anything else happens. I have to concentrate on the girls we know are missing." The phone clicked.

The tone of the sheriff's voice confirmed my fears. He was not taking Rebecca's disappearance seriously. My face burned with anger. Instead of hitting the highway out of town, as had been my first thought, I drove to the high school. The ever-present teacher in my head needed to be prepared for class on Monday despite everything else I was dealing with. At least that anxiety was one I could do something about.

I unpacked the boxes of chemicals that had been delivered to my classroom, and then placed the items in the locking cabinet before checking them off my inventory sheet. When that task was finished, I moved from the lab to the classroom. Outside in the hallway, a janitor pushed the waxing machine across the linoleum floor. Floor wax was forever imprinted on my brain as the smell of school.

One by one I clicked off the remaining items on my 'to do' list. I had stocked the science lab and organized my class-room. I settled into my desk chair, pulled my class planner from my teaching satchel and reviewed the lessons I would begin Monday.

"Jamie?" Principal Winters stepped into the room. "Did you get your lab order?" He crossed the room and stood in front of me, his fingertips beating a staccato rhythm on the wood desk.

"Yes. The chemicals are locked in the cabinet."

"Good. And remember, I keep extra keys in my office should you ever get here without yours." He moved to the front row of student desks. One finger traced the edge of the marred wooden surface.

"Good to know." My mind jumped to a detail that was on someone else's To Do list. "Has anyone tested the vent hood exhaust, and checked the emergency wash and the fire extin-guishers?"

Al nodded. "I had the custodian check those. You are good to go."

"Have they sprayed for ants recently? I had an ant parade in the lab the other day."

"I believe the exterminator sprayed the foundation last week. I'll ask him to check inside the building." The princi-pal turned toward the hall door and then glanced over his shoulder at me. "Have things settled down between you and Trey?"

I felt certain Trey had called last night, but I had no proof the call had been from the senior. "I haven't seen him today."

"Trey will do his best to succeed in class this time. He has told me he wants a better grade. His mother has told me several times as well." Al's smile softened.

I got the message. My bachelor principal was dating Trey's mother.

On the drive home, I noticed Kate's white SUV parked in its usual place in the alleyway beside the newspaper office. I angled into a parking space on the street.

The buzzer on the door sounded as I walked in. I waved at the receptionist and turned down the hallway to the tiny newsroom where the correspondents' desks formed the corners of an open square. Ink and newsprint scents permeated the air and the distant thump of the now-computerized printing press thumped. Kate looked up from the only occupied desk.

"Where is everyone?"

"Here and there. Afternoon deadline has passed. I am still here because I am haggling with my editor Mark about Sunday's story. I swear I'll quit if he pulls it after all this research with the FBI." Kate tossed me a curious look. "Any Rebecca news?"

I settled into a straight metal chair with a plastic seat cushion. "It makes my blood boil that the sheriff is not taking her call last night seriously. Am I off base?"

"Don't know. She called you. That means she has access to a phone. She's not a prisoner."

"Maybe not, but something doesn't feel right."

Kate pushed away from her desk and put her feet up on the open drawer of a file cabinet. "Tell me again exactly what Rebecca said during that phone call."

"Not much to tell. She said 'Come get me.' I think she was going to tell me where she was, but then the call dropped."

"Maybe she's scared. Maybe she realizes that she's in over her head." Kate pulled her legs up under her in the desk chair. "Have to tell you, I don't think Becca is with the missing girls. Something different is going on in her case."

I moaned, resting my head in my hands.

"That should make you feel better, but obviously it doesn't."

"Kate, will you give me your honest opinion on something?"

Kate leaned toward me. "You know I will." She waited.

"Ben had been collecting those newspaper clippings I found about the missing women for years yet he never mentioned them to me. Do you think he was involved with those disappearances in some way?" I blurted.

The shocked look in my friends' eyes told me the answer before she spoke.

"You mean personally? Of course not. Whatever gave you that crazy idea?"

I looked up at the acoustic tiles in the ceiling and then back at my friend. "Mildred says he was doing research for her, that her daughter was one of the victims. His interest must have been more personal than that. He did not become interested because of Mildred's daughter. There was some other reason."

"Like what?"

"I don't know." My throat muscles ached. Kate reached across her desk and grabbed my hand. Anxiety jabbed like a spear into my stomach. My great Aunt Elizabeth had described me as naive before the attack that almost killed her. Elizabeth had been right. I had known nothing of my aunt's real existence, the humiliation and pain she had endured in a life molded by one giant secret. Now, I knew Ben had secrets. "I can't stop thinking about that possibility."

Kate's look challenged me. "You're letting all of this tear apart your memory of Ben. He was a good man, Jamie. One of the best." She shook her head at me. "Maybe you should back off. The thing with Rebecca is enough. You concentrate on finding her. Meanwhile, I'll look into these cold cases. I won't hesitate to let you know if I find a connection."

Her computer dinged and a message flashed up on the screen. "Damn it! They pulled the article. Indefinitely." Kate slammed her fist down on her desk. "The time is right to catch these guys, before they grab anyone else."

"I agree with you." I rubbed my forehead. "Sorry about your article. You worked so hard."

Kate grimaced. "After all this research, I have to admit I'm afraid any naive young woman could be a target." She slipped out of her chair and paced across the room, then back again. "I'm headed to happy hour. You want to come?"

I shook my head. I did not want a beer, or a drink of anything. I wanted Rebecca to come home. And, I wanted these thoughts about Ben's possible involvement in the cold cases to go away.

CHAPTER 16

Shadows were reaching long fingers across the streets when I left Kate's office. I hurried down the sidewalk and then jerked to a stop when I noticed an older model tan car parked beside my vehicle. The driver's door opened.

"Jamie. Long time no see." Rob's white teeth glistened beneath the thick dark moustache; his brows lifted above wide-set eyes. "Surprised to see me?" He rounded the front of the car, leaned against the hood and folded his arms.

I tried to speak but my throat felt frozen.

His grin widened. "I got a job with security at Highlands University. Too good to pass up. Then I found this garage apartment to rent and guess what? It's three houses down from you." He uncrossed his arms. "Maybe we can get reacquainted. Both of us single again. It's been a long time since we split up."

"Why did you come here, Rob?" I growled, finding my voice.

He smirked. "Free country last I checked. And like I told you, good job opportunity." He stepped toward me. "We've lots of good old times to talk about. Living in the same town will make things easier for our kids at the holidays. I haven't seen enough of them lately." He smiled that charming smile, the one I grew to hate during our years together. "How about going for Chinese? Tonight?"

I pushed past him to my SUV. "You may live here now but that doesn't mean we have to see each other. Don't watch me, don't follow me, don't call me." I slipped behind the wheel. Rob grabbed the doorframe before I could pull it closed.

"I'm trying to be friendly." He grinned. "We ended on such a bad note. I regret that."

I tugged at the car door, but he held it open. "Shut the door, Rob. I have to get home. I've got a house guest." I gritted my teeth and inwardly cringed remembering encounters from our marriage.

"Oh, that's right." His voice softened. "Nice looking woman. Maybe *she'd* like to go out for Chinese with me."

"Shut the door. Please."

He abruptly let go.

My fingers shook as I jammed the key into the ignition and then threw the gearshift into reverse. The car shot backwards.

Rob cursed and jumped back. He shouted something, but I turned the wheel and punched the accelerator. The motor roar drowned out his words.

After parking in my driveway, I grabbed my bag and ran for the house. Once in the living room, I peered through the sheer curtains. The light from the street lamp pooled on the concrete in front of my house.

My head ached. How could Rob have this effect on me after all this time? I gritted my teeth. I replayed our conversation; I replayed it again. He had not been rude; he had not been angry. In fact, he had been reasonable. *Was it possible Rob had changed his ways?*

As I stared out at the street, I realized Maria's car was missing.

I trudged to the kitchen. With shaking hands, I poured a glass of water.

My cell phone rang. I pulled it from my purse.

"Hello?" My voice cracked, I cleared my throat.

"Hey, sweetheart, did I catch you at a bad time?" Sam's voice cut through the tension in my body.

My breath whooshed out. "It's so good to hear your voice."

"You're still stressed."

I did not know where to start. "It hasn't been a real good day – or week."

"Has there been any news about Rebecca?"

"She called me last night and asked me to come get her."

"Did she say where she was?"

"No. The call dropped." I stepped over to the island and settled on a stool. "I don't think the sheriff thought the caller was really Becca. He thinks she left on her own."

"Hey, he's a sheriff. Isn't he supposed to take all his cases seriously?"

"I wish. It's not an election year."

Sam chuckled. "You still have some sense of humor left."

"I just want her to come back."

"What about the former boyfriend, or Maria's soon-to-be ex-husband? Has the sheriff questioned them?"

"I hope so." I pulled in my breath.

"What else is going on?"

"You sure you want to know?"

"You need someone to talk to, honey. I only wish I was there with you."

I launched into the saga of my day, beginning with my morning visit to campus and the latest campus disappearance. My frustration built up again as I talked. "And there's one more thing."

"Go on."

Sam knew all about Rob, we had talked about him one hot night as we lay on a blanket in Elizabeth's yard, staring up at the star-filled sky, fireflies flitting around the bushes and trees. I remembered how the muscles in Sam's jaw had quivered when I told him about Rob's verbal abuse and his failure to accept the responsibilities of parenthood. "You won't believe who's moved here. Rob."

"Really." Sam's voice chilled.

"For a job opportunity with security at the University."

"Seems more likely he would move to Albuquerque for your daughter." A lawyer-like tone crept into his voice.

"I agree. But he's here." An ache pinged from the back of my head.

The phone line fell silent.

"Let's talk about you," I suggested. "And what's happening there. Is Vera doing okay in the big house? Are she and Trudy keeping up with things? And Queenie's not missing me too badly, I hope."

"We all miss you. Queenie and I had a long talk on the veranda last night. She wants to visit you next weekend."

I laughed, picturing the basset hound's ears flapping in the wind while Sam's little truck roared across the mesa-strewn plains of eastern New Mexico. My spirit lifted. "Of course she can come, if you want to bring her. Next weekend?"

"Is that too soon?"

My face split into a wide grin. "Tomorrow wouldn't be too soon, except I'm headed to Albuquerque to shop for a Mother of the Bride's dress with Alison."

"Next weekend then. I'm taking an extra long weekend off for Labor Day. I'll be there Thursday evening. We can spend three days together before I drive home Monday."

"I can't wait to see you. Surely, we will know something about Rebecca by then. Maybe she'll even be back on campus." My spirits lifted.

Somehow, in the next few days, I would figure out where Becca was. I knew she was alive. Hope filled me.

Sam would be here next weekend.

The front door bell rang as I rinsed my dinner dishes. I peered through the peephole after flicking on the porch light, and made out a distorted face. Maria. I turned the deadbolt and pulled the door open.

Maria pushed into the hallway, her face a mask of anguish, makeup running, hair disheveled.

"What's happened? " I asked.

Maria shrugged off her jacket and pitched it so that it caught on the back of one of the living room chairs. She glared at me as she tried to smooth loose hair back into the bun at the nape of her neck.

I rephrased my question. "I mean, is there anything new?"

Maria stomped into the living room. "Nobody knows anything. I do not know what to do next." Maria worried the neck of her sleeveless purple sweater with her fingers.

"You talked to the sheriff again?"

Maria turned her back to me. "I talked to him. He talked with Becca's old boyfriend. He will try to find Eduardo, even though I told him Eddy had nothing to do with this. He will find nothing. I told him the girls all look alike, that they were brown like Maria. He says a million girls look like that in New Mexico." She dragged herself across the room to the sofa and threw herself down.

Outside, a car honked as it passed on the street. I grimaced.

"Who is that?" Maria asked.

"You'd think only an adolescent would honk in front of the teachers' house, but no. It was most likely my ex. I told you about him. Seems he's moved to town and is living down the street."

Maria's face paled. "If he comes here, I tell him to leave you alone. You will do the same if Eduardo comes, won't you?"

"Eduardo knows you're here?"

Maria shrugged. "He will put it together. The police ask questions. He knows Rebecca is missing. He knows she came here for school. He knows where I must be."

I did not like the idea of a confrontation with Eduardo. Maybe I should have insisted Sam come *this* weekend. "We should let the sheriff know he's dangerous."

Maria vaulted from the sofa, stomped down the hall and into the kitchen, calling back over her shoulder. "The sheriff knows."

I traipsed after her and watched as Maria pulled an egg out of the refrigerator, cracked it into a bowl, scrambled it and poured it into a small skillet.

She waved one hand at me. "I eat something, take a long bath, then go to bed. I need time to think what to do next." Maria bustled back to the refrigerator for an onion and chili pepper, sliced and chopped small pieces of each before adding them to the scrambled egg. "I think I put up Rebecca's picture. Maybe someone has seen her somewhere, sometime. What do you think?"

Posters. An excellent idea and something I should have thought of. I had been no help at all to Maria. "Great idea. I would be happy to help. Do you have a recent picture?"

"Her high school graduation picture. But, I like that one in the office of her with Ben at the Rio Grande Gorge. She was happy and full of life. Can we use that one?"

I remembered taking the picture. Rebecca *had* been happy that day. So had Ben. When I looked at the photo, grief squeezed my heart again. What would it be like to see the picture plastered in windows and on telephone poles all over town?

Maria dashed down the hall and into the office. She returned to the kitchen clutching the framed photo. "It is a good picture. People will see Ben, remember him, and want to help. Please, Jamie?"

Whatever it took to find Becca. "Of course we'll use the picture. I will scan it into the computer and create a flier tonight. I am driving to Albuquerque tomorrow, but I will post some before I go. You can put the rest up around town tomorrow. I'll gather some nails, tape and a hammer."

"That is wonderful, Jamie. Thank you, from my heart."

CHAPTER 17

Saturday, August 19

The sun had climbed above the tree line and a light breeze ruffled the leaves as I parallel parked in front of The Perk, my favorite morning coffee hangout. The forecast called for hot today with little in the way of clouds and the breeze was warm. I climbed out of the car with two "Rebecca" fliers.

"Jamie!" Kate rushed up to the car, a cup of coffee clutched in one hand and a wide smile on her face.

In that instant, I knew what I had to say, knew what had been bothering me ever since I woke up this morning. "I have to tell you something Kate. And you're not going to like it."

Her smile faded. "Okay. What?"

"You and your internet boyfriends. I do not want you to meet that person tonight for dinner. I've been unable to get it out of my head."

"There's that old mother hen, again."

"I have a bad feeling, Kate. Why does he want secrecy and why won't you even tell me his name?"

"I want you to stop making such a big deal out of it. It's my business, not yours."

I glared as I brushed past her and stepped inside the coffee shop.

"You missed yoga this morning." Kate fell into step behind me. "And you're all tense. That cannot be all about me. What's up?"

"I'm worried about you, Kate. Really." I joined the line of people waiting to order.

Kate stood in line beside me. "No, there's something else."

The man in front of us turned and looked at us both, frowning. I glanced around the coffee shop and recognized the men at a table near the end of the counter. It was Owen Mabry and a uniformed ranger from Fort Union.

"Open up, Jamie. What's wrong?" Kate badgered me.

"It's not safe. I don't know why you can't see that." I glanced again at Owen and Eric. Another person waiting in the line turned and glanced at us. *Why was Kate talking so loudly?*

"Safe? Life is *not* safe, Jamie. Haven't you figured that out by now?"

"Kate, please," I whispered. I ordered a cinnamon roll and large coffee and asked permission to tape my flier to the windows on either side of the door.

As I carried my order from the counter a minute later, Owen Mabry waved at me from his table. I detoured over to him.

"Hi, Owen. It's nice to see you here in town."

"I had a few supplies to pick up. Heard you met with Paul about the agenda."

Kate lingered beside me.

"Yes."

"Good. Paul has been a great help to the Fort in Ben's absence. At first I thought we were doomed and should cancel this celebration, even though it was a year and a half away, but Paul saved the day by taking on major responsibility."

"It will all go fine, Owen. Glad I ran into you."

I waved goodbye. Kate followed me to the front door where I taped two fliers to the side windows. "I'm headed to Albuquerque to meet Alison and I'm already running late. We'll talk tomorrow, okay?" I sipped the hot coffee and headed for my car.

"I wish you weren't so upset with me."

I shrugged. I did not feel good about it either, but she was not going to change her mind and neither was I. "Have a good day and have fun on your date." I slid into the front seat. "Still don't think you should go," I muttered under my breath.

She stared at me from the curb. "Yeah. You, too."

I set my coffee in the drink holder and fastened my seat belt.

CHAPTER 18

On a day when I should have been fully focused on my daughter's wedding plans, the events of last week distracted me.

Alison and I fought the traffic, traveling from department store to bridal store to the mall, looking at dresses and talking small talk about wedding details, colors, decorations and flowers. Right before lunch, Alison jammed a sage green beaded suit back onto the rack and then grabbed my shoulder.

"Mom, don't you even care what you look like? This is the biggest day of my life and you are not interested. I do not want you dressed in some frumpy outfit," Alison scolded.

"Frumpy?" I pulled myself out of my stupor. "Is that the way you think I dress?"

My defensive tone was the last straw for Alison.

"Did I say that? I want some input from you. I want you to show some interest. Why did you bother to come down here today?" she grumbled.

I grabbed Alison's hand and swallowed hard. "I'm sorry. There is so much going on at home. I'm ruining our day."

"Let's break for lunch."

She led me out of the store and down the sidewalk to a restaurant with an outside seating area. We settled into our chairs, setting our shopping bags at our feet. The waiter stopped to take our orders. Minutes later, he brought iced lattes and a basket of homemade potato chips to enjoy while the kitchen prepared our sandwiches.

"So, Mom, what's bugging you?" Alison asked as she sipped her drink.

I looked up at the blue cloud-streaked sky and sighed.

"Have you had bad news about Rebecca?"

"It's a tough situation, honey. Maria is staying with me. And the sheriff doesn't think Becca was kidnapped."

Alison gasped. "Why not? And Maria. At your house." She nibbled on a potato chip. "That is major."

"For one thing, after Becca's 'run-away' activities over the past few years, there's some doubt as to whether she disappeared against her will. Maria thinks she was abducted, and I do, too." I sipped my latte. "And then Becca called me late Thursday night but the call dropped before I could learn where she is." I wiped my mouth with a napkin. "She asked me to come and get her."

"So you're trying to figure out where Becca is?"

"Kate offered to help me dig into a few things. Another girl has disappeared since Becca went missing. That makes four, all freshmen, all girls of Native American or Latina heritage."

"Nothing like this has ever happened at Highlands before, has it?"

"No. But, women have been disappearing in the area for twenty years. That's the other weird thing. I found a collection of newspaper clippings about these disappearances in Ben's briefcase. He had been saving them since the first case, twenty years ago."

"That's eerie, isn't it, since now Becca is missing?"

"Exactly. I keep wondering if there is any connection between these cases and Becca's disappearance. Why was Ben so interested in these cases?"

The waiter set our sandwich plates on the table.

"And ... what else? There's something else." Alison studied my face.

"I can't help but wonder why he never talked to me about these disappearances," I confessed. "And it turns out that one of the victims was Mildred's daughter, our next door neighbor. Ben had promised her he'd look into her daughter's case two years ago, before he was diagnosed." I sliced my sandwich in half and then took a bite.

"Maybe he didn't want to worry you, Mom. Maybe he knew another of those women who disappeared years ago. There could be any number of reasons he didn't talk to you about it."

I glanced at Alison and a smile crept onto my face. "You are wise for someone so young and beginning a marriage. Where'd that come from?"

"Good teacher." Alison's face beamed. "Love you, Mom. Keep me posted on Becca, will you?"

Hours later, with a long, light coral chiffon dress in a clothes bag on my arm, I said goodbye to my daughter outside the shopping mall. Alison's eyes glowed.

"One more thing I should tell you before I head home."

Alison's face drooped. "What? Something about Grandma? Is she sick again?"

"No." I clutched the plastic bag tighter to my chest. "This is about your father."

"Dad? I haven't heard from him in a couple of months."

"Well, you may be hearing from him soon about your wedding. He has rented a place in Las Vegas a few houses down the street from me. I ran into him the other day."

"Why would he move to Vegas?"

"He's got a job with security at Highlands University."

Alison glanced down the busy street, but her eyes seemed unfocused.

"He looks good. He actually has a great job," I reassured her. "We'll have to rent him a car to drive to the wedding. I'm not sure his old clunker will make it and he's not riding with me."

Alison smiled. "Renting him a car is a small expense. We'll pick it out."

Darkness fell as I drove home. A few miles beyond Santa Fe, where I-25 curves to the south, I noticed a pair of headlights close behind me. *Too close.* I tapped the brake. The following car nearly scraped my bumper before dropping back; its bright headlight beams flashed.

I was driving the speed limit on a four-lane interstate. The driver could have easily passed me in the left lane, but instead it dogged my rear bumper, moving forward and then dropping back, headlight beams flicking between bright and normal. I slowed and moved my vehicle onto the shoulder; the car behind me slowed and pulled off, too. With a twinge of panic, I punched the accelerator and pulled back onto the Interstate. The other car followed, repeatedly flashing its bright beams.

I passed the NM 84 junction at Romeroville. My heart hammered in my ears. *Ten more miles to Las Vegas.* Instead of driving to my house, I intended to drive directly to the police station. I kept my eyes on the road, and flicked the rear view mirror up so I could not see the headlights behind me. I drove; the car followed.

At the southern edge of Las Vegas when as I turned north into town, I corrected the angle of the rear view mirror. The car was gone.

As I drove through town, I kept expecting the car to show up again, hugging my bumper while the driver flashed the headlights.

At home, I drove into the garage, grabbed the dress bag from the back seat and opened the car door. As I got out, I glanced at the street. *No one there.* The garage door descended and thudded shut. I raced through the breezeway to the back door.

Inside the house, the television blared from the living room. Lamplight blazed in the hallway and from each room.

In the living room, Maria was asleep on the sofa, my multi-colored crocheted afghan pulled up to her chin.

CHAPTER 19

Sunday, August 20

Footsteps pounded from the downstairs hallway. I pulled on a robe and house shoes and slipped down the stairs in the gray light of early morning.

Maria was fully dressed; her tall thick-heeled boots clunked as she paced the hallway. "Enough of this! It is driving me crazy. Where is Becca? Why are the police not doing something? What can I do? Where can she be?" Maria threw her arms up and then wrapped them around herself. Her hands trembled.

"Come in the kitchen. Let me make you some coffee." I had no answers for her. We were helpless in this situation, and could only wait for news from either the sheriff or Rebecca.

"I no want coffee. I want Becca. She has been gone a week. Never this long before. Never." Maria sank down onto the bottom step of the stairs, head lowered.

The phone rang. I picked up the extension in the living room. I glanced at the clock when I saw the caller ID. Barely six a.m. Not too early for Mildred.

"Jamie, have you had the news on?" Mildred gulped.

"No," I said, grabbing the remote control to flick on the television. "What's wrong?"

"Something horrible happened up at the Hot Springs last night."

I clicked rapidly through the channels until I found a news

station. An on-location announcer spoke, gesturing as the camera panned the roadway and hillsides of the Montezuma Hot Springs. A news helicopter flew overhead, its camera providing a bird's-eye view of the Armand Hammer United World College campus. Crime scene tape fluttered around the area, stretched across each pathway leading from the parking area to the springs by the river. The camera operator focused on the road's shoulders and then the mountains. A lone car sat to the side of the road.

My heart jumped into my throat. *It can't be.*

"The body was pulled from the springs early this morning," the reporter said. "The victim's identify is being withheld pending family notification."

The camera angle shifted to four men carrying a black body bag up the pathway to an ambulance. Behind them, several people in police vests combed the hillside.

"My God," I breathed into the phone. My throat closed.

"Who do you suppose it is?" Mildred asked.

"No." I choked on the word. *This was not happening. It could not be.*

"Who is it? Do you know, Jamie?"

"Oh, my God." My legs gave out and I sat. "She had a date last night with some guy she met on the internet," I mumbled. "They were meeting for dinner in Santa Fe."

"Who?" Mildred asked again.

I swallowed. "Kate Gerard."

"Your friend, Kate?"

"Yes." My voice cracked.

"Oh, my Lord," Mildred said. "I'm sorry."

My heart raced. I could not catch my breath. *I did not believe it. I could not believe it.*

"What in the world happened?" she asked again.

I did not want to know. My imagination could fill in all the blanks on its own. I covered my eyes. I needed coffee. I needed wine, or a beer, or scotch or something. *This cannot be hap-*

pening. Maybe if I go back to bed, I will wake up and it will all be a dream. Not a dream, a horrible nightmare.

"I told her I didn't want her to go on that date. I told her." A sob burst from my throat. This was so wrong. *Kate could not be dead.*

"Do you suppose the police will contact you?" Mildred asked.

"Why would they?" I choked out the words.

"You two hung out together a lot. You know how Sheriff Clay puts things together. "

I looked up and saw Maria in the living room doorway. I stepped past her, wiping tears from my face. I carried the phone with me and closed myself into the office. "Clay couldn't possibly think I had anything to do with this." My shoulders shook with barely-contained sobs.

"Is Maria still there?"

"Yes," I whispered.

"Can I come over?"

I heard something odd in her tone. "I need to get dressed."

Mildred's voice quivered. "Could there be a connection between Becca and Kate? And Jodie?"

"I don't know." I shuddered as I hung up the phone. The police would go to Kate's office. They would find her date's name on her desk. They would arrest the man.

Oh, Kate.

The photo of Ben and Rebecca rested on top of the few remaining fliers of the hundred we had printed yesterday. I studied Ben's face, his eyes, his hair, the curve of his smile. More tears trickled from my eyes. The strong ache lanced my heart.

I felt something else, too, some twist of uncertainty.

Kate was dead. My best friend was a journalist, pursuing a story Ben had suggested.

A soft tap sounded on the office door.

"Jamie?" Maria called. "Open the door. We must talk."

I swiped a tissue across my face, retied the belt on my robe and pulled the door open.

"Who is dead? What woman?" Maria demanded.

My throat closed up again and more tears threatened. I stepped past Maria and into the kitchen.

"Her name is Kate? She call here yesterday before I go out. Asked for you to call her. What happen to her?"

With shaking hands, I filled a glass with water from the refrigerator spigot. My hands shook even harder as I turned on the coffee maker. *Kate had called yesterday? And now she was dead.*

When I faced her, Maria lifted her chin; her brown eyes smoldered.

Tears spilled from my eyes. I started toward the stairs. "I have to get dressed, Maria."

Her shoulders rose and fell in a slow shrug. "Okay. I go to my room. Today is a waiting day for me. Yesterday, I posted fliers all day. Today maybe the phone will ring."

An inner voice nagged. *Rebecca has called. She called me. Shouldn't I tell Maria?*

I trudged up the stairs. Numbness dropped over me and with it came a sense of incredulity.

Surely, this is not happening. Surely, Kate is not dead.

Mildred appeared at my front door fifteen minutes later. The two of us had just stepped into my kitchen when the doorbell rang again. I rushed down the hall and jerked the door open. Sheriff Jonah Clay peered in and then glanced at Mildred where she stood at the kitchen door. "Morning, ladies."

He focused his intense look on me; my skin prickled. I swiped at my eyes, where tears pooled.

"I'll get right to the point, Mrs. Aldrich. We are investigating an unattended death. You were one of the last people seen with the deceased." He rubbed the back of his thick neck.

Blood rushed from my head, and I grabbed the doorframe as the world started a slow turn.

"Kate Gerard is dead," he continued. "Witnesses have called to report they saw the two of you arguing yesterday at The Perk. What about?" He fidgeted in the front doorway.

"She was my best friend. We did not argue. We were disagreeing about something." I sucked in my breath.

"And where were you last night?"

Tears filled my eyes again and slipped down my already damp cheeks. "I was in Albuquerque yesterday, shopping with my daughter. I drove home late, got home after dark. I had a snack and went to bed."

"Is your house guest still here?"

"Maria was asleep in the living room when I got home."

He glanced down the hall at Mildred. "Do you know why Ms. Gerard might have killed herself? Or any reason someone else might have taken her life?"

Suicide? Kate had never even said the word, never indicated any feeling of hopelessness. She had been discouraged when Mark Hamm placed her article on indefinite hold but there was no way she would commit suicide over the delay.

"She had a date last night with someone from an internet dating site. That was what our disagreement was about. I didn't want her to go on the date." I rubbed at my forehead, trying to make sense of what had happened to Kate. "She was an investigative journalist. She had written a piece about human trafficking. The story was on hold."

"Human trafficking," the sheriff repeated. "I'll check into both those things."

"She was my best friend. She would not have committed suicide. Somebody killed her."

His footsteps echoed on the wooden porch as he stomped away.

I eased down onto the living room sofa. "How can she be dead?" I covered my face with my hands.

"Well, she *is* dead. She either wanted to die or someone wanted her dead," Mildred said.

Her voice roared in my ears.

I sniffed and pulled a tissue from the box on the lamp table. "I don't know who would have done this. She got along with everyone, even her ex-husband. They didn't have any money or kids to argue about."

"Maybe one of her newspaper stories made someone mad."

Her investigative piece would have been in today's paper had it not been placed on hold. Did my promise to Kate not to talk about her article still count now that she was dead and the article on hold?

"This human trafficking story you mentioned to the sheriff. Could that have gotten her killed?" Mildred asked.

I focused my attention on straightening the books on the coffee table so that Mildred could not read the lie in my eyes. "Don't know anything except that the police weren't ready to show their hand yet. Kate thought it was time. They didn't agree."

"Pornography? Prostitution? Gangs?" she probed, punching out each word.

I shrugged. "The police will have to get all that information from her editor. I don't know any details."

"I want to be sure ..." She swallowed and choked. She cleared her throat and then cleared it again. "Surely nothing connects my Jodie and your Becca to what happened to Kate."

I stirred the thought around in my brain. *Could there be a connection?* It was possible. Mildred's daughter had disappeared so long ago. It seemed unlikely she could be connected to a human trafficking organization still at work today.

I glanced at Mildred. Her eyes seemed to be looking through the present and into the past.

"I don't believe there is a connection," I whispered. I clasped my hands together and tried to focus. "What did Ben tell you after he researched Jodie's disappearance? Had he come to any conclusions after reading about the women who disappeared?"

She shook her head slowly, like a metronome going back and forth, back and forth.

I had not found any notes detailing his conclusions. Maybe he had not gotten that far. "Mildred? Are you okay?"

"Not knowing what happened is worse than knowing. Where did my girl go? Is she still lying out there under some cedar? Or is she alive somewhere with no memory of me and her home?"

"Don't torture yourself." I would only admit to myself that I had those same thoughts about Rebecca. Would we ever see her alive again? Would we know that she was dead, if indeed she was?

Kate is dead. Guilt slid over me like a cellophane shroud. I could hardly breathe. I should have been more insistent that Kate not meet her internet Romeo.

Tires screeched up the street outside and the deep bass notes of an amplified car stereo system shook my usually quiet neighborhood. I leaped over to the window and pulled the drape aside, looking through the sheers as a black Honda Accord rolled down the street. The tinted car windows made it impossible to see who was inside. The car squealed a u-turn two houses away and crept back past my house. The back passenger's window rolled down a few inches and a hand reached out, all fingers but the middle one folded down. The finger shook in my direction before the tires screeched and the car peeled away down the street.

"Idiot teenagers," Mildred said from behind me.

Which one of my former or current students had that been? I wondered.

Rob's tan car pulled into my driveway. He hopped out and started for my front door, tucking his golf shirt into his slacks as he moved. His clothes looked brand new. Alison and Matt would be surprised at how good he looked. I certainly was.

"Who's that?" Mildred said into my ear.

"Hel-lo!" Rob called from the porch. "Jamie, I need to talk to you." Rob knocked once on the door, pushed the latch and walked in. He smiled at Mildred, his brown eyes sparkling.

"Not now, Rob. It's not a good time."

"That's not very friendly." He took another step into the house and looked quizzically at Mildred. "Does Jamie always behave like this?"

Mildred peered at me.

"Rob. Please go," I said. "I've had some terrible news and I can't deal with anything else right now."

The smile dropped from his face. "Terrible news? Nothing about family, I hope?"

I shook my head and turned away.

"Okay, then." He faced Mildred. "You live next door, right? I live in the garage apartment down the street." His smile slipped back on.

"I'm Mildred. I would say I was pleased to meet you, but I do not think I am. Jamie is not happy you live in our neighborhood. Now, if you'll excuse us, we *were* having a private conversation." She slid past him and grabbed the front door knob, letting the door swing open in front of her. She stepped aside and waved her hand for him to move out.

"See you another time, Mildred. When we have longer to talk." Rob swaggered across the porch and back to his car.

"That was your ex? He's a good-looking one, isn't he?"

She swung the door shut and then peered out the window as Rob drove away.

"He may be good looking but you don't want to mess with him. The voice of experience speaks."

Mildred sank onto the sofa. I turned the television on.

The television journalist recapped Kate's death as the top story in the hourly headline news. Beside me, Mildred peered at the screen. Unexpectedly, the cocked angle of her head reminded me of a vulture, ready to tear into a carcass. I shivered.

"Awful. Just awful," Mildred muttered.

I nodded in silent agreement. *My best friend is dead.*

When Mildred trudged out of the house a few minutes later, I was ready for her to go. I needed solitude. I heard Maria banging around in the kitchen.

"I've got to get out of this house. Will you be all right alone?" I called from the kitchen doorway.

"Si. I wait for calls. Someone knows something. They see the poster. They call. I wait."

Once behind the wheel of my SUV I drove on autopilot, not caring where I went, only guiding the car around corners, through intersections, obeying traffic signs and signals by reflex. My mind exploded with thoughts of Kate's death, Ben's death, Becca's disappearance. The missing women. Mildred's daughter.

I found myself on the narrow old highway to Mora. Tree limbs arched across the road, met and entwined at the apex, blocking the sky. Filtered light hardly reached the ground where undergrowth hugged the pavement. Seams in the pavement had separated, leaving cracks filled with dirt and grass clumps. As the tires flew over them, the jarring bumps shook the car.

I felt as jarred as the car. The frayed edge of my world in Las Vegas seemed to be unraveling. Mildred's daughter. Becca's disappearance. Kate's death. Were they connected?

The answer roared into my head. *Yes, they were. I was the central knot connecting all the strings.*

CHAPTER 20

"Maria?" I called into the house from the threshold of my open front door. "Hello?"

The hairs rose on the back of my neck. Had Maria forgotten to close the door or was someone else here?

My first glance down the shadowed hallway and into the visible rooms showed nothing out of place in the quiet house. "Maria?"

The house phone's ringer peeled from the living room and kitchen extensions. I zipped across the entry hall to grab the living room phone before the answering machine came on. "Hello?"

"Mrs. Aldrich, it's Joshua McDaniel. How are you?" His deep voice sounded concerned.

"I'm shocked at the news about my friend, Kate."

"So am I," Joshua said. "I'm so sorry. I can't believe it happened at the spring."

Ice clinked in a glass.

"Thank you." I glanced around the living room and then down the hallway. Shadows deepened as the afternoon sun dropped lower in the sky.

"The reason I'm calling," he continued, "– and I realize you may not have had time to go through the stuff from the office – but I was wondering if you have any of your husband's test files. I want to compare tests to be sure I'm writing my questions with reasonable expectations from the students."

Down the hall, I could see the office door slightly ajar. My pulse quickened. I had closed the office door this morning. I was certain of it.

"Are you there? This isn't a good time, is it?" Joshua asked.

"Can you hold on a minute?"

"Really, anytime in the next few days would be fine. You don't have to check now."

"Stay on the phone while I look, Joshua." I tiptoed down the hallway to the office and shoved the door open. The letters, magazines and books I had left neatly stacked on the desk this morning were now strewn across the floor. I gasped.

"Mrs. Aldrich? Are you all right?" Joshua asked.

"Someone's been in my house. The office is trashed." I surveyed the room as I circled the desk. Other than tossing off the items that had been atop the desk, nothing else seemed out of place.

"You should call the police," he suggested.

"Yes," I agreed. I continued to check the room. The closet door was open, and the hanging items pushed to one end. The floor-length folds of Ben's robes still covered the laptop computer in its case.

"I'll let you go."

"Wait." I noticed the two brown Expand a-file folders leaning against the side of the desk where I had left them. "Hold on, Joshua, I think I remember where the test files are."

I laid the phone on the desk. Inside the folders, neatly labeled manila folders identified the various tests and assignments used throughout the semester for two of Ben's courses.

"I found exams and assignments for his class on 'Southwest History prior to 1865' and 'New Mexico History after 1865.'" I stepped over the items scattered on the floor. "I'll look for more."

"If it's no bother, I'll come over to get those. In about an hour?"

I punched off the cordless phone and sank into the desk chair.

Most likely, Maria had been in here digging through Ben's things. I wanted to know why.

After I cleaned up the mess of papers on the floor of the office, I slipped into the kitchen and flicked on the small television. Kate's death was once again the lead story on the 5 o'clock news broadcast. The reporter said the police were waiting for the medical examiner's report; the death remained a suspected suicide. The police would not comment on the cause of death.

I turned the television off. My mental picture of Kate in the Hot Springs would not go away. The image of Kate laughing and smiling with Ben and me as we drank a beer on the back patio one hot summer night came unbidden.

On impulse, I returned to the office and to the closet, where I pulled the laptop computer case from beneath the robe. The computer powered up instantly when I hit the 'on' switch after placing it on the kitchen island. I typed Ben's password, *Americanhistory*, at the prompt. A fall campus scene at the University filled the screen. I clicked on the Documents folder, scanned the titles and then opened first one file and then another, looking for test questions.

As I searched, opening and closing documents and files, Ben returned to life. I felt he was looking over my shoulder. My heart ached. Ben had left secrets behind. It was hard to accept there were things he had not wanted me to know, things he had never told me. The answers might be on this computer. *Did I really want to go there?*

The next document in the lengthy list was "Journal8." Probably an outline for a new article he was considering for some historical or Americana journal, I thought. When I clicked on the file and the document filled the screen, I found the pages numbered and dated, beginning with August of the year before he died.

"August 14. Enrollment rosters out today. Full classes. Faculty meeting at nine. Dread seeing Paul. Hard to be in the same room with him. Jamie has no idea – and I won't tell her unless I have to."

I chewed at a fingernail. 'Jamie has no idea?' Of what? Ben *had* been hiding something. Paul knew what that was.

The front door latch clicked, pulling me back to the present and pulling my eyes away from the computer screen. "Maria?" I called. She dragged into the kitchen.

"Si." Her car keys clanked as they landed on the counter next to the sink.

She trudged across the room, then back to the hallway, her fingers combing through her tousled hair.

"Maria, did you leave the front door open when you left the house earlier?" I closed the laptop.

Maria clutched her stomach and sobbed.

"What's wrong?"

"What do you think is wrong?" Maria groaned. "You forget my baby is missing?" She closed her eyes and worried her bottom lip with her teeth. Dark circles marred the skin under her eyes and red blotches spotted her cheeks.

I had not forgotten about Rebecca. Kate's horrific death had overshadowed her disappearance for the time being. I could do nothing about Kate but I could pray for my step-daughter's return.

"Did anyone call who saw the poster?" I asked.

"Two calls. One man says, 'that's a pretty girl on the poster.' Does he think I put the poster up to get her a boy-friend? PSSSHHHT." Maria shook her head and her wild dark hair tumbled around her face. She clasped her hands together. "The other call was a hang up. I wait inside all day for phone to ring again. Finally, I can stand it no more. I get outside. And drive."

The phone rang.

Maria grabbed it. "Hola," she said. As she listened to what the caller said, her eyes widened. The color drained from her cheeks. She clenched the phone tightly. "Si. Si." Maria turned her back to me. She swayed and leaned against the counter. "Si. Si. Pronto." Maria slammed down the phone, snatched her keys from the counter and raced down the hallway toward the front door.

"Maria? Where are you going?" I sprinted after her, caught her at the threshold and grabbed her arm.

Maria jerked free. "I must go now," she cried. "Don't follow."

She dashed out to her car.

What was happening? I ran back to the kitchen for my own purse and keys, intending to follow her.

The house phone rang again.

I grabbed the phone and my purse at the same time.

"Hello!" Sam said.

My frenetic energy level took a dive. I sank onto a barstool. "Sam."

"How's everything, love?" Sam's voice was warm. Calm surged through me as my adrenaline rush dissipated.

"Crazy." The word caught in my throat.

"Tell me."

"It's horrible. I can't believe it." Tears surged, filling my eyes, and I sobbed into the phone. Finally, I pulled my emotions in check. "My friend, Kate . . . she's dead." I told Sam about the article she had been writing and about the date she had made with an online boyfriend. My voice quivered and a giant sob erupted.

"Jamie. I wish I was there to hold you."

"I wish you were, too." I covered my mouth to suppress another sob.

"And still no word on Rebecca?" He asked quietly.

"I helped Maria create some fliers and she posted them around town yesterday. Today, she is waiting for phone calls.

A few minutes ago, she got a call and rushed out. I should have followed her. I shouldn't have let her leave alone."

"Who called? Was it someone she knew?"

"It might have been her husband—soon to be ex—Eduardo. But she didn't tell me."

"Damn it, honey, I wish I could come out there now but I have hearings scheduled the next three days. I will be there Thursday evening, sooner if I drive through the night."

"Don't do that. I have to work Thursday anyway," I said, trying to brighten my tone. "You're busy. School starts tomorrow. I won't have time to think about all this." I grabbed a tissue and blew my nose. "Sorry."

"This article Kate was writing, could someone have killed her because of her investigation?"

"Possibly." If that was true, I could stop wondering if Kate's internet date had killed her. "As far as I know, the authorities are calling it a suicide."

"And what do you think? Was she suicidal?"

"Not in the least. She has been through a divorce and many disappointing relationships and circumstances but she never, ever gave any indication she would consider suicide." I took a minute to breathe deeply and gather my thoughts.

Sam waited on the other end of the phone connection.

"If she didn't commit suicide, someone killed her. Someone from the human trafficking ring." My mind circled back to her investigative reporting.

"Kate was also going to investigate Rebecca's disappearance, wasn't she?" Sam asked.

"Yes. We were going to talk about it today." I felt a new stab of guilt. According to Maria, Kate had tried to reach me Saturday afternoon. "We argued yesterday. She had a date with someone she met on line. I didn't want her to go."

I heard Sam's gasp. "Maybe there's an internet connection. Had any of the girls who disappeared been using internet dating sites?" he asked.

My body went still. Rebecca and the other young women had been talking with online friends. I could not imagine any student going to college these days without a computer. *Where was Rebecca's laptop?*

After our conversation ended, I opened Ben's laptop and jostled the mouse. The screensaver, a photo of the old Frontier Fort at Fort Union, flashed onto the screen. The user box appeared, showing Ben's screen name, ProfHist. I clicked to enter the password, but clicked on the User button instead. Two more possible user names popped up, Honeybone and Guest. *Honeybone?* Did Ben have a second email account? I clicked on *Honeybone* and found that the user had saved the password. The mailbox opened.

Honeybone had 141 new emails waiting to be opened, the latest dated last Thursday. I scrolled down the list.

Many of the emails were from sites selling prescription drugs, others linked to video-cam sites and online dating services. The few non-spam emails seemed personal; the subject lines did not indicate campus business. I clicked on the message 'Not Tomorrow.'

> *Hi. Can't meet you tomorrow night after all. Having dinner with suitemates. Maybe this weekend? Shawna.*

I clicked back to the email list and moved through it, checking dates. I clicked on 'sent' email. All of the messages, both to and from Honeybone, were dated over the recent summer months. More than a year after Ben had died.

My doorbell peeled. I closed the computer, stowed the laptop in the case and shoved it into the kitchen pantry.

"Coming," I called. My brain raced. *Honeybone could be Joshua.*

I glanced out the peephole before pulling the door open;

Joshua grinned and waved from the front porch. In spite of his height, his face was boyish and his thick hair hung in a lock over his forehead, projecting the innocent look of a ten-year-old.

"Hello," he boomed as I opened the door. "I promise to be out of your hair quickly. Don't want to be a pest."

"Come in and have a seat, Joshua. I'll get the files." I motioned toward the sofa in the living room.

"Sure. Take your time." He stepped into the living room. Joshua did not look like someone who would kidnap women or let someone drown at the hot springs. I did not want to believe he could be dangerous.

I hurried to the office and grabbed the two sets of test files I had found earlier before sprinting back to the living room.

"There should be more but this is all I have found at the moment." I handed the files to Joshua.

His head drooped. "You don't suppose he had any tests stored electronically on a computer, do you?"

A few hours before I might have pulled out the laptop and let Joshua search through it, unsupervised. *Not now.*

"I'll check tomorrow and save them on a flash drive if there are any."

"Super. That would be a big help." He leaned close to the fireplace mantle. "Nice family. Your daughter favors your husband." He nodded at a picture of Rebecca.

"That's my stepdaughter, Rebecca."

Joshua straightened and cleared his throat. "Rebecca." He turned toward the front door. "Thanks so much. You'll let me know about the laptop files, right?"

"Yes."

"Again, I am sorry about your friend Kate. She was a beautiful woman." Joshua leapt off the front porch and jogged to his car.

I shut and locked the front door. In the kitchen, I locked

the deck door, and did the same with the door that led into the breezeway and the garage. I turned the radio to the Hits of the 90s station, and filled a glass with water.

Finally, I pulled the laptop from its hiding place in the pantry.

"Sure would like to get together with you after you get to campus. Something about the way you write tells me we are compatible. We seem to have so much in common. Let's see if we really do!" from 'Sissy'

"So you'll be here Tuesday, right? It sounds stupid, but I can't wait to meet you! I sense that you and me would make beautiful music! Nerdy, I know, but then I guess I am nerdy. My ex-girlfriend thought so, but she also thought I was a good kisser!" from 'Honeybone'

Many similar emails and responses followed. This person was laying out the bait, sounding shy, a little insecure and so complimentary. At that age, I might have fallen for those lines. I counted eighteen personal messages from seven different girls, all freshmen and new to the University campus. After fifteen minutes, I could not stand to read any more of Honeybone's gushing compliments. My stomach twisted.

I switched back to user ProfHist, then searched through the computer files again until I found Ben's journal. When I turned the computer over to the police to review *Honeybone's* email, they would also have access to Ben's journal. These words were all I had left of him.

I went to the closet in the office and pulled the portable printer down from the shelf. After hooking it up and loading it with paper, I hit the print command on the laptop. All 63 pages of Ben's journal file spewed one by one out of the machine.

The printer hummed and kicked out pages while I scrolled through subject headings of the other folders and files on Ben's laptop. Some files appeared to be class-related lectures and notes as well as source files. I did not open each individual file even though some of them might have included the quizzes Joshua wanted. Before I turned over the computer to anyone, I would erase Ben's personal files and the journal. A computer geek could retrieve the erased files, but I did not want it to be easy for Sheriff Clay to read Ben's intimate thoughts.

When the printing was complete, I deleted the journal file, turned off the computer and stowed it back in the office closet beneath the long folds of Ben's black robe.

CHAPTER 21

"Hello, Alison." I cupped my hand around the icy glass of tea and hunched over the island, letting my feet rest on the rungs of the bar stool. Crumbs from my ham and cheese sandwich dotted the pottery plate and a few uneaten potato chips tempted me. I shoved the plate away and turned sideways on the stool.

"Hi, Mom. Any news about Rebecca?"

"Afraid not. Maria posted the fliers while I was in Albuquerque with you. She had a couple of calls yesterday and one this afternoon. I'm still waiting for her to come back."

"If it was a prank to upset her mother, Becca would have come back by now."

"Seems like it. She called me once, so I know she's out there somewhere."

"When you go searching, don't go alone, Mom. Promise me. You cannot go after bad people all by yourself. Haven't you learned that yet?"

I had learned it, but I still felt responsible for Rebecca. I did not want to let her down after her call for help. That would be the same as letting Ben down, and I had already spent the last two years struggling with my inability to help him at the end of his life. I sighed and prepared myself to tell Alison the worst news yet.

"And another awful thing has happened. Kate, my best friend, died at the Montezuma Hot Springs last night."

"How terrible." Alison's voice dropped to a whisper. "I'm so sorry."

"My neighbor called early today after she saw the news on the television."

"Was it an accident?"

"I don't think so. The police are calling it suicide but Kate would not do that. I would know if she had been considering it."

"Yes, you would," Alison agreed.

"It might have been because of an article she was writing about human trafficking. Kate wanted people to know the awful things happening here, now. The FBI has been carrying out sting operations. Maybe someone wanted to stop her investigation."

"Did Kate think Rebecca was kidnapped by the people in that trafficking ring?" Alison's voice rose.

"That would be my worst fear." I had convinced myself her disappearance was unrelated to the ring, something entirely different, but deep inside I was so afraid it was true.

"I remember what you said Great Aunt Elizabeth told you last summer, 'There is nothing worse than for someone you love to disappear and not know what happened.' She'll come back, Mom. I really think she will."

During the 10 o'clock news, Kate's photo and identification appeared on the screen at the beginning of the news story about her death. Her parents had probably arrived from Scottsdale to identify the body. The newspaper would carry an obituary with information about funeral arrangements in the next two or three days.

I remembered meeting her parents once when they visited Las Vegas. Would they contact me?

By 10:30 p.m., Maria had still not returned. I plodded up the stairs and got ready for bed. Rebecca. Kate. Thoughts of the two women circled in my mind as I prepared for bed.

The phone rang. No one spoke when I picked up.

I crawled into bed. An image of Kate superimposed itself over all my thoughts.

When would Maria come back? I kept anticipating the ringing of the doorbell or the house key I had given her scraping in the front lock. When I heard her come in I planned to go downstairs to ask about the phone call and where she had been all afternoon.

I watched the swirl of the fan on my bedroom ceiling, and lay frozen under a light woven coverlet.

Kate. What happened?

CHAPTER 22

Monday, August 21

I startled awake at six a.m. to my radio alarm clock. My eyes ached.

Stretching and yawning, I rolled to the edge of the bed. My fern-green cotton curtains fluttered in the cool morning breeze, sending whiffs of evergreen-scented air swirling through my room. I remembered being awake late into the night, watching moonbeams dance on my bedroom walls. I had not heard Maria come home.

I vaulted out of bed and across the room to the window. Maria's car was not parked at the front curb.

Then the realization struck: *Kate is dead.*

I completed my getting-ready-for-school routine—dressing and putting on makeup—on autopilot, fighting the mental haze from lack of sleep and shock.

It was hard to move, to think, to see. *My best friend is gone.*

I'd felt like this when Ben died. I remembered struggling to do simple things, wanting instead to lie in bed with my eyes closed and pretend I was dreaming. I could not let myself do that this time. Rebecca was out there somewhere. She needed my help, even more so now that Maria had vanished.

First on my list was a call to Sheriff Clay. He should check the hard drive on Ben's laptop. The emails from *Honeybone* might lead to the identity of an internet stalker on the Highlands University campus. Those emails might also provide clues to the kidnappings. I would ask the sheriff if the police had taken Rebecca's laptop computer from her dorm room. *Honeybone* might have emailed Rebecca. Maybe they were already searching for him.

I brewed a cup of hazelnut coffee and carried it into the office. The stack of pages making up Ben's journal sat in the middle of my desk. I would make myself read the journal tonight. All day I would work on steeling myself to discover Ben's secrets.

Someone pounded at the front door, then rang the bell. I glanced through the peephole. Sheriff Clay. He had saved me a phone call.

I jerked the door open, coffee cup in hand, letting in a rush of fresh air and the scent of spicy aftershave.

"Good morning."

"Mrs. Aldrich. May I come in?"

"Sure. I was about to call you." I glanced at my watch. 7 a.m. "I have to be at school, soon. It's the first day."

"What were you going to call me about?" He stepped into the front hall.

"I found something interesting on my husband's laptop. Someone used it this summer, at the University. They were sending emails using the name 'Honeybone.' Making dates with freshmen women."

"We'll need that computer."

I turned to retrieve the laptop, but the sheriff cleared his throat. Deputy Ross and another deputy walked through the front door. "But I'm here because I have additional questions for you. Can you give me a time for your trip to Albuquerque? As well as a list of people who saw you afterward and can confirm your whereabouts?" He removed his hat.

"You think Kate was murdered?" Even though I had considered this possibility, discovering the police thought that Kate had been murdered shocked me.

"You were seen arguing with the victim Saturday morning," he stated.

I led the sheriff into the living room where I sank down

onto the sofa. "We were having a conversation. Kate had made a date Saturday night with someone she had met on an internet-dating site. I did not want her to go. That's what we argued about."

The sheriff peered at me. He fingered the brim of his brown hat. "And your alibi for Saturday night again?"

"I was with my daughter all day Saturday. I left Albuquerque after an early dinner, returned home about nine. As you know, Maria Sanchez is staying here. She was asleep on the sofa when I got home. I went to bed."

"Can she confirm you didn't leave the house any time during the night?" His brown eyes drilled into mine.

"She's sleeping in my guest room. I did not leave the house." I rubbed my forehead, where a headache throbbed against my skull. "What did the autopsy show?"

"The autopsy and various tests are not yet complete."

"Tests for what?"

"Her death was not an accident—and it wasn't suicide." His stare was intense.

I shifted to the edge of the sofa.

"Preliminary blood tests indicate a foreign substance in her blood."

"Someone slipped something into her drink?" I imagined the scenario: the smiling couple beside the hot springs, sipping drinks as steam rose from the steaming cement pools.

The sheriff shrugged. "I'll deny it if you tell anyone I suggested this, but you should consult a lawyer."

My heart thudded beneath my ribs. The edges of the walls fuzzed. "Why?"

"A preliminary report notes that the drug found in Ms. Gerard's blood is the same one the medical examiner found in your husband's system after he died. The drug was used to hasten his death and more recently to cause Ms. Gerard's."

My body chilled. Ben had been taking so many drugs and painkillers. As far as I knew, the medical examiner had not blamed his death on any specific drug.

The sheriff glanced at the open door. Outside, car doors slammed and voices shouted. "Here's my team with the search warrant. This should not take long. Then you will be free to go on to school. That is, unless we find potassium chloride."

Potassium chloride.

Large doses of the drug could cause the heart to stop. That drug had not been part of Ben's drug regimen. Footsteps sounded across the entry hall.

I stared up at the photographs on the mantle.

Ben smiled out at the world from a sandy beach in Jamaica.

An hour and a half later, I parked my car on the far side of the lot at the high school in the last available faculty space. I stepped around to the passenger side to reach the pile of canvas bags full of student handouts.

Potassium chloride. The police had not found any in my home although they had turned it upside down. The detectives had gone through every cabinet, every drawer, every storage box. Every possible hiding space. In a little over an hour.

"Mrs. Aldrich. Something I can help you with?"

Startled, I glanced up at the blond teenager. The numbness enveloping my body this morning even extended to my feelings about Trey. "Good morning. You can help me carry some of these bags." Wide-eyed, he picked up two of the overflowing bags and followed me to the building. I tried to focus.

"Already sucking up, Woodard?" Someone called as the two of us walked into the building.

Trey did not respond and I did not look back at him. His expression probably said all he needed to say to his friend. I did not want to know what that was.

Trey accompanied me to my room without a word. As he put the canvas bags down on the floor by my desk, he grinned again. "It was a pleasure to help you, Mrs. Aldrich. You can count on me anytime. Just give me a shout. Morning, Mr. Winters."

I glanced up. The principal stood beside my desk.

"Good morning, Trey." Mr. Winters' look followed Trey as he sauntered out of the class. "See, what did I tell you? The ideal student. He's not going to give you any trouble, Jamie."

Trey did seem to be turning over a new leaf. Maybe Al Winters was right and I had exaggerated the teenager's anger toward me.

What weighed the heaviest on my mind was not an exaggeration.

Potassium chloride.

An office assistant interrupted my third hour class to hand me a note. "A man left this note for you and asked me to hand deliver it right away."

I unfolded the message.

"I know where Becca is. I go bring her back. Maria."

"Mrs. Aldrich? Am I doing this right?" a red-haired junior waved her hand at me as she pointed to a genetics problem in her biology book.

I stepped to the student's desk, pulling my mind off Maria and back to my work. I still had to get through the next hour with Trey Woodard.

The last fourth hour student left the classroom. Trey Woodard had been surprisingly quiet and cooperative during class. Maybe his little show last week had been all hype. Maybe he really was going to calm down and devote himself to doing well in Biology. I pulled out my cell phone. I had missed a call from the sheriff. I knew what he wanted from me. After the search concluded, we had both rushed off. I had not given him Ben's laptop.

I punched the 'call back' button. When he answered his cell, I tried to put aside the fact that he had searched my house this morning for evidence that I had murdered my best friend. Maria was gone to 'get' Rebecca. If she did not return, I was the only one who could push the sheriff to investigate my stepdaughter's disappearance.

"Sheriff, Jamie Aldrich. This morning I forgot to give you Ben's laptop after your men finished searching my house. Those recent emails on it could be related to the disappearances out at the University."

"The messages from Honeybone?" Clay boomed. "Yes. I need that laptop. Can you get that computer here right away, or can I meet you and pick it up?"

"My lunch break has started. I could run home and meet you."

"Meet me at your house in 10 minutes."

I grabbed my purse and snatched up the note from Maria to show Sheriff Clay.

CHAPTER 23

As I pulled into my driveway, I glanced next door and wondered if Mildred was watching from a window. I felt positive she would come over early this evening to find out why Sheriff Clay had been at my home twice today. What would she say when I told her about the potassium chloride used to kill Kate—and my husband?

I hurried to the front porch to wait for the sheriff.

A car roared into the drive. Sheriff Clay bolted from his cruiser and sprinted up the walk. Deputy Ross emerged from the passenger side and hurried after Clay.

I unlocked the door. "The laptop is back here, in my office."

The men followed me down the hall and into the small office. I opened the closet and pulled aside Ben's doctoral robe. The laptop case was gone.

I looked under the desk. "It was here this morning before your men searched the house."

The sheriff's forehead wrinkled as he peered around the room. He watched me dash into the kitchen, check the shelves and floor of the pantry, look under the table and in the cubby where I stored cookbooks and recipe files.

"It's gone. Someone else was here this morning," I announced.

Clay motioned to Deputy Ross. Hand on his gun, the deputy crept down the hall and cautiously up the stairs.

"Maybe you better start at the beginning." Clay spoke in

low tones. "You said this laptop had been in your husband's office since his death? And you brought it home when?"

I reminded him I had been moving Ben's things from the office a week ago when he stopped me to tell me Rebecca was missing. "I brought it home, but I didn't really look at files or emails until last night."

"Tell me about the emails."

I explained how I had found the additional user name on the email account and then reviewed the 'sent' files and the current unopened emails, some dated as recently as last week. "Someone's been using that laptop. They didn't know I was coming to clear out the office and bring everything home."

"So they stole the computer. Who knew you brought Ben's things home?"

"The Dean, Joshua McDaniel, Paul Everson, Kate. The entire faculty probably knew I had cleaned out the office within 24 hours of my being there. McDaniel moved right in."

"We have already spoken with the Dean, McDaniel and Professor Everson. They all have alibis for Saturday night as well as excellent reputations. I do not think we will find the kidnapper or the murderer among those men. Did Mrs. Sanchez know about the laptop?"

"She saw me using a laptop but did not know it was Ben's."

"Is Mrs. Sanchez here now?"

"No." I explained about Maria's hurried departure last night and the note delivered to me at school earlier today.

I glanced at the kitchen clock. "I have to get back to school. My students will be there in 15 minutes."

"We need that computer." His eyes were riveted on mine. "Does Maria Sanchez have a key to your house?"

"Yes. I gave her a spare key last Saturday, when I left town for the day."

Deputy Ross shuffled into the kitchen. "The house is empty. No one is upstairs. Did you notice anything else missing, Mrs. Aldrich?"

"It will take me a while to figure that out." I glanced around the house. Every inch of space was in disarray from the police search that morning.

The sheriff cleared his throat. "I should tell you that emails from Honeybone were on the computers of the three other Highlands University women who have disappeared. One had been corresponding with that person all summer, ever since she was here for the orientation session. She had planned to meet he or she the night she disappeared."

"Were similar messages on Rebecca's computer?" I asked.

He looked at me warily and then glanced at the deputy sheriff. "Yes," he said. "And also on Kate Gerard's computer. It's possible *Honeybone* is the screen name of the kidnapper and also the person who murdered your friend."

My heart sank. "It's someone on campus. Why did you search my house this morning looking for potassium chloride? Why make me think I am a suspect?"

Sheriff Clay's lips pressed together. "We've been working the computer angle, among others, for some time. We see connections. The bad news is that you seem to be a common denominator. I'd change my locks and get a security system if I were you."

The afternoon continued as a typical first back-to-school Monday usually did. Voices loud, the students trudged the halls, some talking on cell phones, some talking to each other. The cacophony of voices did not stop when the class bells rang. I resorted to flipping the lights on and off and slamming the door to get their attention. In a way, it was good for me to focus my effort on holding class; it left no time to think about what the sheriff had told me.

After school, as soon as my brain was empty of teaching, it filled to the brim with thoughts of Kate.

I called her home number, certain that her parents were in town by now and planning my best friend's funeral.

"Jamie, I'm so glad you called. Mick and I knew we'd hear from you," Kate's mother, Arlene Yates, said as soon as I had identified myself.

"I am still in shock. It is so hard to accept this," I said.

Their silence on the other end of the line was affirmation they felt the same way.

"I'd like to stop by tonight, bring in some dinner. Would that be all right?"

"Jamie, we would love to see you. Dinner is not necessary." Arlene's voice shook.

"I know it's not necessary, but I want to do it. Can I plan to be there about six-thirty?"

Arlene agreed. I would stop at the deli on the way home. I had to prepare myself to face their grief as well as my own.

CHAPTER 24

I sat in the driveway and studied my house. Off to the north-west, clouds rolled and merged into one another, their balloon shapes rising above the house as if someone was blowing them up as I watched. A raven, on my roof, cocked his head and uttered a brief squawk.

Someone had broken in earlier and found the laptop despite the topsy-turvy state of my belongings. If they had gotten inside once, they could do so again. Had the thief been *Honeybone*? I needed a locksmith and an alarm system, fast.

I glanced at my watch. I might be able to get the locks changed before I took dinner to Arlene and Mick Yates. Mildred would know the best local locksmith but if I went next door my neighbor would ask three things: what was going on with Rebecca, why the police had been at my house and why I wanted to change my locks. I did not want to retell any of it.

My head ached. I had not eaten all day. I could not stop thinking about Kate.

I pulled myself out of my SUV, uncertain how long I'd sat in the driveway.

"Jamie? Late day at school?"

Rob's voice sliced into my thoughts.

I slammed the car door and glared at him as he walked up the driveway.

"Got a minute? Let's go inside." He hurried past me on his way to the porch.

I grabbed my purse and school bags, and then joined Rob at the front door.

"What do you want?" I studied the face of this man who had been such a big part of my early life and was the father of my two children. Was he capable of kidnapping? Of murder? Did Rob's security clearance give him access to the professor's offices?

"Is your guest here?" Rob peered into the house.

"No. What do you want?" My stomach ached. Twenty-year-old memories of our last painful altercation seeped into my head. *How could his mere presence turn me into a quivering wreck so many years later?*

"Who is your visitor? Best looking woman in town, next to you." Rob pushed past me and into the living room. "Tell me her name. I'll arrange my own introductions." He grabbed a photograph of Rebecca from the mantle.

"Tell me what you want or leave."

He stared at the picture.

"Rob!" Sweat broke out on my forehead.

"Who is this?" Rob asked, insistent.

"My stepdaughter, Rebecca. Maria's daughter. Now please go!"

Rob carefully set the photograph down and looked at me. "We need to talk."

"Jamie?" A voice spoke from the open front door. "Interesting to find you here, Rowland. Am I interrupting?" Paul Everson asked. A sly grin played on his lips.

"Yeah. You're interrupting," Rob said. He placed one hand on my shoulder and squeezed.

I shook his hand off and stepped away. "Rob is leaving."

Paul's eyes widened. "I didn't realize you two knew each other."

"She's the mother of my children." Rob gestured at the photo of Alison, Matt and I taken in front of the old mission church at Rancho de Taos.

Paul's jaw went slack.

"And he was just leaving. Good night, Rob." I said between clenched teeth.

"And you should leave with me, Everson," Rob said under his breath as he drew even with Paul on his walk to the door.

"Jamie, we need to talk about the Fort Union celebration agenda. Five minutes?"

Rob sauntered through the front door, leaving it open. I watched him take the steps two at a time and dash across the lawn. I turned to Paul. "This is not a good time. I've had a horrendous day." I stalked to the front door, grabbed my purse and work bags, then carried them to the kitchen. Paul trailed behind.

"So your first day back at school was rough?" Paul fingered a banana from the fruit bowl on the butcher-block island.

I grabbed an apple as well as a paring knife from the knife block and sliced off a chunk after a quick wash in the kitchen sink. 'Rough' did not come close to describing my day.

"Committee meeting, tomorrow at 4 o'clock, city library," Paul announced. "We need to kick around some ideas."

"You'll have to do it without me."

"I was counting on you." He settled onto one of the bar stools. "What's wrong?"

"I've changed my mind."

The stool screeched against the tile floor as he shoved it back and stood. "You could at least tell me why."

"I didn't know how to say no when you asked. My step-daughter is missing and my friend Kate has been murdered," I blurted. I set the knife and the apple on the counter and wiped at my eyes with the side of my hand. More tears threatened.

His face froze. "Kate Gerard?"

"Yes," I sighed. "Saturday night. Haven't you heard about it? It's been all over the news."

"Damn. I'm sorry. I've been so busy . . ." He ran one finger across an eyebrow.

"It's horrible. I'm on my way to take dinner to her parents, who are in town to handle things."

"I don't know what to say."

"Well, I don't feel much like conversation." I picked up the knife and sliced the apple.

"Again, I'm sorry. I'll let myself out." His footsteps sounded in the hallway; the front door latch clicked.

I paced the hallway to the front door; silence boomed in my ears. The hair prickled on the back of my neck.

I wished I had brought Queenie home with me. I needed the dog's protection. The basset-mix pooch had saved my life in Pawhuska earlier this year. When Sam visited this weekend, I would ask him to leave her with me.

The locksmith. I called the first company listed in the yellow page advertising section of our small local phone book. The locksmith agreed to be there within thirty minutes.

I eyed the stairs to the bedrooms, but did not make the climb. To confirm the laptop was the only item that the thief had taken would confirm *Honeybone* had been in my house. I walked out on the front porch with an iced cola and lowered myself to the top step.

I pulled out my phone. I needed to talk to Sam. It was an hour later in Pawhuska, but I knew it was likely Sam was still at his office. When in the middle of several cases, he sometimes worked until nine or ten o'clock. I glanced up and saw Mildred marching across the yard.

"Nice day," Mildred observed a minute later as she sank onto the step beside me.

I tucked my phone back into my pocket and sipped my drink.

"You okay?" she asked. "Did the police find out who killed your friend? Have they found your stepdaughter?"

From which window had Mildred been watching? All of them, in rotation, most likely.

Mildred cocked her head.

"The police think Kate Gerard was murdered," I said. "They searched my house this morning."

"Your house? Why the hell...? All the ne'er-do-wells in the world and they suspect you? What is that sheriff's name? I've half a mind to give him a call." Mildred slapped one leg and moved her hands to her hips.

"The missing Highlands students, my stepdaughter and Kate were all corresponding online with someone who was using Ben's office laptop. Might be the kidnapper and Kate's murderer."

"The laptop from Ben's office," Mildred stated. Her look shifted to the street.

"Someone stole it this morning. No sign of a break-in. Did you see anyone here after I left for school?"

"Damn. I had my annual pokes and prods at the doctor's office. Gone all morning."

"I'm changing the locks."

The locksmith pulled into the driveway.

The empty spot at Kate's dining room table shouted through the quiet of the dinner as I ate with Kate's parents. After greeting one another with tearful hugs, we said all the usual condolences. Now, it was time for the difficult conversation.

"Will you hold the funeral service here or at home?"

Mick Yates reached for his wife's hand and patted it as he spoke. "We think a memorial service here on Thursday and then when they release the body--" he coughed. "When they release the body we'll take Kate back home for burial."

Arlene looked at me with teary eyes. "Who could have done this to Kate? And why?"

"I don't know. The sheriff is working the case. I hope he'll have answers, soon."

"Was it that piece she was writing, about the human trafficking ring? Do you think those people killed her?" Mick asked.

I formed my words carefully. "It could have been them."

I did not want to tell them her murder might also be connected to an investigation my husband had suggested.

Later I paced from one end of the house to the other, waiting for a call from Sheriff Clay, or Maria, or simply for the doorbell to ring. As I paced, my thoughts churned.

Someone had poisoned Kate and Ben.

The sheriff had once threatened me with an assisted suicide charge after Ben's death, but it had only been bullying. A mental curtain had dropped over my memories of the week following his death.

All I knew was that my husband had come home from the hospital to die. The Hospice staff had spent hours here, caring for Ben, relieving me so I could sleep or shop for necessities. Neighbors and friends from the University and the community had stopped in for short visits. I had kept a guest book for visitors to sign and sent 'thank you' cards after the funeral.

The name of whoever had given Ben a large dose of potassium chloride would be recorded in the visitor's book on that last day. Those signatures belonged to people Ben and I had known well.

I had stuffed the book, copies of the obituary, sympathy cards and small florist cards from bouquets and green plants into a box and stored it after sending out the thank you cards. Had I put the box in a closet, the attic or the garage? I did not remember.

It didn't really matter. I couldn't tell from those signatures which person had given Ben the chemical compound.

My mind jumped to Ben's journal. Would it explain why someone had killed him? Another thought echoed in my head. Maybe someone else had been able to do what I could not. *Help him die.*

I prepared myself for the roller coaster of emotions I would experience as I read the journal. I checked the new lock on the front door and trudged down the hall to the office. Then I pulled the journal pages from the desk drawer and settled into the chair.

Beautiful August day here. First day of class so all the freshmen act interested in my subject. Hopefully, they'll learn something.

I heard Ben's voice as if he were speaking. *This was going to be hard.*

I scanned rather than read Ben's journal. The fall semester was under way. I keyed in on names.

My scan screeched to a stop when I saw *Kate.*

Kate stopped by today to talk to me about her research project. Why did she come to me? Coincidence, or does she know something? Paul would not have said anything. He would be too worried about implicating himself. I think I'll discourage her from pursuing this any further the next time we talk.

I moved on, scanning the lines.
Jamie.

Jamie and I picnicked at the springs Saturday. I cannot stop thinking about it. I love her so much. I wish I felt like I truly deserved her love. I don't—and never will.

My heart thudded. I nibbled on the end of my fingernail. The song I had always thought of as 'our song,' "Unforgettable," played in my mind. I closed my eyes and savored the melody. Then, I forced myself to read on.
Mildred.

Thank God I have Mildred to talk to. That old woman

keeps me from cracking. She listens but keeps her thoughts to herself. The other day I came close to telling her all of it except what I think happened to Jodie. It is speculation anyway. If I say it aloud, I'm afraid the whole universe will suddenly know my secret.

I reread the entry. *The whole universe.* What secret? My imagination whirled. Ben had taken his secret to his grave, unless . . . Could I uncover what he had taken such trouble to keep hidden?

My thoughts flowed like the current in a stream, and then abruptly stopped.

Earlier this year my great aunt Elizabeth had nearly died because of something she knew. Was it possible Ben had died because of the secret he was keeping, and not from the cancer?

My mind shifted into a new line of thinking, one I had suppressed previously many times.

What if Ben had survived the cancer and gone into remission? What would we be doing together, today?

I could not process the possibility. I stuffed the pile of journal pages into the desk drawer.

Mildred. A good listener? How about an eccentric, cynical busy body? Ben had seen a softer side. Their relationship had gone much deeper than I ever knew. He'd seen the mother who had lost her child. I only knew the neighbor who played weekly bridge and gardened. The rest of the time, she sat at her windows watching the neighborhood.

Why hadn't Ben talked to me instead of Mildred?

I rubbed my eyes, aware of how heavy my arms and legs felt, and how much energy I would need to pull myself out of the chair.

I'd barely eaten a thing when I was with Kate's parents.

I dragged myself into the kitchen and checked the refrigerator. A quick cheese omelet would have to do since I had only bought food staples since returning home. I cracked two eggs into a small skillet and stirred.

The phone rang with the opening measure of a Bach fugue. With a sigh, I punched on the phone.

"Jamie, is Maria still there? Is that woman driving you crazy?"

"Hi, Mom." I pulled in a deep breath and sat down at the island. "You know, Maria has reason to be upset and I'm glad I can help. I am concerned about Rebecca, too." I added some shredded cheese from a zip storage bag to the bubbling omelet. Egg-scented steam rose into my face.

"I haven't seen the girl since Ben died," Mother grumbled.

"We need to try harder to maintain a relationship with Becca. Ben would be disappointed in us." Mother sat silent on the other end of the line. "Rebecca hasn't returned and there are no leads on where she might be."

"Have you seen your brother since you got back?"

I cringed inwardly. *Here we go with the guilt.* "I haven't had time yet. With school starting and all . . ." I closed my mouth. I was falling into my mother's trap, letting her get to me. I did not need to make excuses. She knew I was busy. I flipped the omelet over, folded it and scooted it from the pan onto a plate.

"Seeing family and friends is his only attachment with reality in that hospital." My mother's voice quivered. She sniffed.

"I'll get down there soon." I stepped into the pantry and pulled a jar of salsa from the shelf.

"Hmmm." Her disapproval hummed through the phone. Then, she launched into an account of her latest visit with my sister Ellen. If she followed her usual conversation routine she would soon move on to the latest news from her best friend, then her neighbor and . . .

Minutes ticked past as I listened. I had no opening to tell her about Kate's death or Rob's local residence and job. It was probably for the best. I did not need her input. It would include many dramatic innuendoes. Besides that, my mother's worry-plate was already full. I ate my omelet and listened, inserting an occasional 'really' or 'right.'

When the conversation ended, I returned the phone to its charge station and sat at the island, finishing my glass of milk. I stared out the kitchen windows at the back yard but my mind registered nothing.

Kate is dead.

It was impossible to believe. I wanted to punch her autodial number and hear her answer the phone in the usual way, "What's up?"

I rinsed my plate and slid it into the dishwasher.

The phone rang again. This time the caller ID read, Vera. I *wanted* to answer this call. I hurried to the living room so I could get comfortable as we talked. Outside the front windows, the evening light fell golden; shadows darkened the yard.

"Vera." I smiled as I answered the phone. It was the first time I had felt like smiling since I had learned of Kate's death.

"Hello, Jamie."

"It's good to hear your voice." I collapsed into Ben's old leather chair. "How are you?" My spirit lightened.

Only this past spring had I learned I had an extended family on my mother's side. They had become as important to me as some of the relatives I had known all of my life.

"You know I'm getting tired of hearing Sam say how much he misses you," she whined, and then laughed. "But really, he's not the only one. We're all suffering. And he's headed there for the weekend, right?"

"Yes. I cannot wait. But I have to tell you, I miss you all, too."

"So, how are you?" Vera asked.

I gave her an abbreviated version of my life in the week since I returned to New Mexico. She listened without interruption. Finally, she exclaimed, "You've come home to an ant's den, getting ant bit at every turn. How are you holding up?"

I took a deep breath. "The worst of it is my friend's death, and then the terrible fear about what has happened to Rebecca."

"I am so sorry."

"But there's something else, Vera. I told you about my husband Ben's death, the cancer and everything. I recently learned that the actual cause of death was a drug named potassium chloride. My friend Kate, despite the burns from the boiling springs, died because someone gave her the same chemical."

"She was drugged?"

"Apparently. Before she was dropped into the hot springs."

"How awful." Vera paused and I could imagine the wheels turning in her brain. "Do not tell me the sheriff suspects you?"

"I think he did at first."

"What?"

"The drug that killed Kate was the same drug that ended Ben's life." My voice broke. "Someone killed him before the cancer could. Assisted suicide. Or murder." I fought back tears.

"You did what you could to ease Ben's pain." Vera soothed from six hundred miles away. "But, you did not give him the drug that ended it all. Someone else did."

"I don't know who would have," I said. "He was in such pain those last days. Anyone who saw him would have thought about it. I kept hoping there would be a miracle." My voice dropped to a whisper. "The miracle came when he was no longer suffering. Now I know the truth. Somebody gave him something."

"If the police found the drug in his system, why didn't they make an arrest last year? They were posturing as if it 'might' have been assisted suicide when they knew it was."

"They were probably closer to arresting me than I ever knew."

"Maybe they had other suspects."

"So many people were in and out of this house that last

day. Any evidence would have been circumstantial." I looked up at the picture of Ben and me on the mantel, pulled in a deep breath and then let it out. "It's a weird connection between Ben and Kate. The same drug."

CHAPTER 25

Tuesday, August 22

I lingered over my second cup of morning coffee, watching the minute hand creep toward 7:15 and my usual departure time for school.

Even without annoying phone calls, my sleep had been restless. I could not stop thinking about Ben's death, or Kate's. Having new locks and dead bolts installed had not made me feel any safer. Someone had been in my house and taken the laptop. It was the only thing gone. No electronic gizmos, no jewelry, no valuable old books. I hoped the thief was Maria. The thought that she had *not* been the one in my house sent shivers up and down my arms.

As I rinsed my cereal bowl, I thought again about calling Sam. *Damn. He was probably already in court. Thursday evening could not get here soon enough.*

The doorbell peeled. I rushed to the front door hoping it was Maria. One glance through the peephole proved me wrong.

"Got a minute?" Sheriff Clay shifted the box he was carrying and rested it against the front door frame. "Mrs. Sanchez back yet?" He peered over my shoulder and down the hall.

"No."

"Still no idea how to reach her?"

"I'm hoping she'll check in with me."

"Then you can pass this information along when – if – she does. Rebecca has used her credit card at a shop in Los Angeles. One of my men called the store and talked to the clerk. He said that a young Latina woman used the card there last night with a photo ID. She matched her picture. The young woman was alone and according to the clerk, she did not seem frightened or nervous. We have dropped the investigation."

I had been prepared for the worst possible news: a body. Instead, the police had tabled their investigation. Had Maria gotten the tip that Rebecca was in Los Angeles? Was that where she had gone?

"The Dean would like for you or Mrs. Sanchez to stop by the dorm and pick up Rebecca's things in the next day or so. He will release the information that Rebecca was sighted in California at our press conference this morning on campus." He nodded at the box he held. "These are the items we took from her dorm room during the investigation. I'll release them to you."

He hefted the box again and carried it into the house.

Anger bubbled in my stomach. Rebecca was in Los Angeles. How could she have caused her mother—and me—so much worry?

"Have you found your missing laptop?" Clay asked. He handed me an evidence release form and pointed at the signature blank.

"No." I led the way into the living room. He set the box on the coffee table, and I signed the form.

"Too bad. It could have told us a lot. Plus we might have been able to get fingerprints." He reached into the inside pocket of his jacket. "I brought you a copy of the theft report I will file. It needs your signature."

I took the report, signed it and then glanced at my watch. "I'll swing by the university after school to get Rebecca's other things from the dorm."

"Sure." He rubbed one hand across the back of his head. "And, so you know, we are working on the investigation into your friend's death. We found some helpful information at her home and at the newspaper office. We'll announce her death as a homicide at another press conference this evening." Clay nodded at me, stepped out the door and closed it behind him.

Rebecca was in L.A. She had used her credit card. If Maria had known her location, why didn't she tell me?

I gathered my things for the school day. My cell phone rang on my way to the garage.

"Is this Jamie Aldrich?" An urgent voice asked.

"Yes."

"This is Sheila Parker at Alta Vista Medical Center. We admitted Robert Rowland a few hours ago. His ID card lists you as the emergency contact."

She paused, and I stopped in mid-step.

"Rob Rowland?" My ex? "What happened?"

"I can't release any information other than to tell you he's in intensive care and is listed in critical condition following emergency surgery here."

I rushed to my car.

"There was a 9-1-1 call off the Plaza," the I.C.U. nurse said as she walked with me down the hall toward the unit. "Paramedics picked him up. The caller left the scene. The victim's wallet ID listed your name and number in case of emergency."

"Was he drunk? What happened?"

"Hit and run, apparently."

"Have the police been called?"

"Yes, ma'am. The detective asked me to give you his card after you got here. He'd like to talk to you."

She handed me a business card.

"Can I see Rob?"

"He's unconscious and on life support. The prognosis is not good. He had severe head trauma and extensive internal injuries."

I processed the information. "Should I call his children?"

"I would. It is likely he'll pull through. The next 24 hours will tell." The nurse tapped the large red entry button outside the unit. The ICU doors swung open. She gestured toward a curtained cubicle on the left.

Rob lay in the bed, his face ashen. Tubes and wires criss-crossed his body and snaked up his nostrils. Other tubes disappeared under the sheet covering him. Monitors beeped rhythmically around the small curtained room. Low voices and moans seeped into the cubicle from the surrounding ICU patients. Bile rose up in my throat; the room was stifling.

Unbidden, a buried memory surfaced. Our wedding reception, cake smeared around Rob's mouth, his eyes bright. How handsome he was, and so full of life.

His bruised and swollen face was unrecognizable. Bandages swathed the top of his head. His left arm and left leg were both elevated and in casts.

Seeing him this way would not be easy for Matt and Alison.

A hit and run. The Las Vegas police were at work to determine the type of vehicle involved. Were there any witnesses?

The image of Paul's angry face last night zipped into my mind. He had not been happy to find Rob at my house or to learn Rob and I had once been married. Still, I did not believe Paul could have done this.

I wondered again if Rob was *Honeybone*. Had he lured the girls to the kidnappers?

My mind swirled around the possibilities. I reined in my overactive imagination and pulled myself back to reality. Rob had let his children and me down. He had abandoned us, disappeared for weeks on end and then verbally abused us when he was at home. Despite that history, I did not want *Honeybone* to be Rob.

I stopped in the waiting room to call Matt and Alison. Each of them should make the decision as to whether they would come to Las Vegas. If their father was dying. . .

Too much death.

I called the high school. The secretary promised to pass my message on to Principal Winters. She also offered to contact the next substitute on the Las Vegas school district list. My mind would not be on my classroom work at school, even though I was not exactly the grieving wife.

I confirmed my cell phone number with the nurse, looked in on Rob one more time and then left the hospital.

The personnel department at Highlands University was housed in the Rodgers Administration building, at the end of a long hallway. Through the window in the door, I could see the secretary hunched over her desk, working.

"Corrine? Can you help me with something?" I asked

The elderly woman looked over her half-glasses and shoved back the chair as she stood up. Her brown skin gleamed; she had tamed her long, kinky gray and white hair into cornrows and pulled it back into a ponytail.

"Why, Jamie! It is good to see you. What brings you in here, anyway? Looking for a job?" Her white teeth sparkled. "We have an opening in the science department."

I smiled. "I'm not looking for a job. Still teaching high school science."

She faked a frown and let out a sigh, but her eyes glinted.

"I have an odd request about an employee. He's been critically injured." I sat on the chair next to her desk. "His wallet ID lists me as his emergency contact, but I can't be the only one. Could you check his file?"

She raised her eyebrows. "You're *not* an emergency contact? You don't know him?"

"I know him. We were married a long time ago. I suppose he listed me because I live here. Please, could you look it up? Robert Rowland."

Corrine pulled her chair closer to her desk and fingered the computer mouse, clicking several times as she searched. "Let's see. Here it is. Started work in June. Security Services." She moved the mouse to review the entire document. "This lists three contacts: an Alison Rowland in Albuquerque, a

Matthew Rowland in Dallas and you. That's it." She took her hand off the mouse and tapped the desktop with a long finger-nail painted red, white and blue.

"Where was he employed before coming here?"

She glanced at the computer screen again. "Looks like Diego Security in Espanola, three years. I am sure we checked his references. The Regents are strict about that. Alison and Matthew are your kids?"

I nodded. "What is his local address? I should tell his landlord what's happened."

"241-B Summer, here in Vegas."

I knew exactly where '241 B Summer' was. As Rob had said, it was down the street from my house.

"You have a tenant renting the garage apartment? Robert Rowland?" The elderly man who answered the doorbell looked familiar to me although I did not know him by name. He had come to a few of the neighborhood Fourth of July picnics and often worked in his flowerbeds next to the street.

A short fringe of white hair circled his head but his white brows were unruly and long. He had zipped his blue poly-blend coveralls all the way up to his neck.

"Rob? Yes." He peered through the barred security door. "Don't I know you?"

"Yes, I'm Jamie Aldrich. I live a few houses down. We've met at the barbecue." My neighbor sized me up. "Rob's been in an accident. He's in the hospital."

"Now that's too bad." He scratched his head. "He gonna be okay?"

"He's stable." I was faking the worried look on my face. I was worried but mostly about how Alison and Matt would handle their dad's death if it happened. They both had unre-solved issues with him. "Could you let me into his room? I need to take a few of his personal items to the hospital so he'll have them when he wakes up."

"I'll grab the keys." He disappeared into the back of the

house and reappeared in a few minutes with a small ring of keys. "This way." I followed him across the driveway and up the stairs to the apartment over the garage.

After he had unlocked the latch, he stepped aside and then stationed himself by the open door. "Get what ya need. I'll wait. Aldrich, is it?"

"Yes, sir. I live in the cottage, three houses down and across the street."

I surveyed the small apartment. A sofa covered in faded green chenille and two straight back chairs were grouped in front of a flat screen television set on a small table. Water rings and cigarette burns marred the surface of the lamp table beside the sofa. Its straight legs were dark with age and grime.

I crossed the room, detouring around a couple of piles of newspapers and magazines. The linoleum top of the dinette table next to the tiny corner kitchen held a stack of mail and a letter opener as well as another pile of magazines. An open door led to the small bedroom and bath. One glance through that door showed a neatly made double bed and a pair of jeans discarded on the floor.

I stepped into the little bathroom and opened the medicine cabinet. Bottles of over-the-counter medications, shaving cream, after-shave lotion and eye drops filled the shelves. Under the sink in the vanity cabinet, I found an empty shaving kit. I stuffed the toothbrush, toothpaste, nail clippers, razor and comb into the kit. Rob had little need of them uncon-scious, but when he woke up . . . If he woke up . . .

Back in the bedroom, I studied the dresser and nightstand. A quick glance toward the living room assured me the property owner could not see what I was doing. I opened the dresser, searched through the few items of clothing and then opened the nightstand drawer.

The drawer contained only gas receipts and a few old bills from Espanola with PAID written across them. I peered under the bed and saw only dust bunnies. The top of the tiny closet contained a small suitcase. There was no laptop or desktop computer in the apartment. If Rob had emailed those girls, he did it from campus. *On Ben's computer.*

I stepped back into the living room, holding the shaving kit.

"Get what ya needed?" The old man glanced at the kit and then pushed open the door.

"Well, give Rowland my best," he said as he followed me down the stairs. "Let me know how long he's gonna be in there. I'll watch the place."

"Thank you."

As I climbed into my car, I glanced down the street. Maria's car was parked at the curb in front of my house and a second car had parked close behind it. I started the motor and backed into the street.

Seconds later, as I pulled into my driveway, Paul Everson raced across the lawn and slid into the second vehicle.

"Paul? Wait!" I called, vaulting from my SUV and running toward him. The tires of Paul Everson's car squealed as he u-turned onto the street. The car roared away.

On the porch, Maria slumped against the doorframe, her purse clutched to her chest.

CHAPTER 26

I dashed up the front steps. "What's happened?"

Maria wailed. "My little girl is dead to me. I no see her again." Maria sniffed. "We go get her things, now. You go with me."

"Of course I'll go with you, but first tell me what's happened. Where have you been?"

"Please, let's go now."

Not a speck of the usual makeup covered Maria's blotched face. She wore the same wrinkled clothes she had been wearing when she left the house two days ago.

"Maria, talk to me."

Maria grabbed my arm and pulled me down the front steps and out to the driveway. She slid into the passenger's seat of my car and snapped her safety belt. Her gaze locked on something outside the window that was not there.

"Who called you Sunday?" I asked as I backed into the street.

When Maria did not respond, I tried again. "Was it Eduardo? What did he say to you?"

Silence.

"Maria, did you find Rebecca?"

No response.

I drove to the University.

At the dorm, we parked in the loading zone in front of Rebecca's building and then checked in at the residents' desk in the entry hall.

"Room 289. The Dean said you'd be coming by," the student desk clerk said politely. "Here's the key and a couple of empty boxes. Sign here, please." He held out a pen but neither of us reached for it. He glanced from Maria to me. I took the stick pen and signed the form.

Becca's roommate Lindsey answered the door. She looked at our boxes, stepped aside, then stood in the doorway, arms crossed, eyes downcast.

"Are you all right?" I asked.

"Sure. Why not?" The girl sighed and looked out into the hallway. "Hate to rush you, but I have class in fifteen minutes." She perched on the side of her twin bed.

"No problem." I glanced around the small room. It would not take long. Maria and I piled photos and knick-knacks into the boxes the clerk had given us.

We filled the two suitcases from under the bed with clothes from the closet and drawers. A deep frown distorted Maria's features as she grabbed items and tossed them into the bags.

Minutes later, the two of us made our way back down the hallway with the full boxes and suitcases. As we loaded the suitcases and boxes into the back of my SUV, Maria began to cry.

Only Maria's sniffs broke the silence during the ride back home. My mind raced from thoughts of Rebecca to thoughts of Rob to thoughts about the drug found in Ben's system and Kate's death. Were any of these things connected?

"Why was Paul Everson at the house?" I asked, remembering how he had raced away from my home without even a glance at me.

Maria stared straight ahead with watery eyes.

"Damn it, Maria. You have to talk to me. How can I help if I don't know what's happened."

"Rebecca was your stepdaughter when you were married to her father. Now, her father is dead. She is nothing to you."

Her words had the effect of a stun gun. What else could I say?

"I go home tonight with Becca's things. I no bother you no more." Maria kept her head turned toward the window, where trees and houses flashed by.

"I care about Rebecca," I insisted. "I care what happens to her."

Maria's shoulders moved in a quick shrug.

Suddenly a black Chevy cut in front of our car. I stomped the brakes and hit the horn. The tires squealed and my car stopped inches from the Impala. The driver opened his door and stuck his head out, glaring at us. The tall, brown Latino man's glare turned into a leer.

Maria ducked her head. She grabbed my arm as I started to blast the car horn again.

"Be still. He will go on."

The man closed his door, drove through the intersection and then pulled to the curb. "Who is that?" I asked as we passed his vehicle and drove down the street. In the rear view mirror I saw the Chevy pull back out onto the street.

A few blocks later, the black car followed when we turned onto my street.

"He's following us." I glanced at Maria.

She shrugged. "He knows where you live."

My pulse quickened. "Is that Eduardo? How did he find you?"

"He knows Ben lived here."

"Have you been with him the past two days? Did you find Rebecca?"

She clamped her lip closed and shrank down into the seat.

I pulled into my driveway. The black car cruised past the

house. I pulled the hatch release and slid out of the car, then hurried around to unload Rebecca's belongings.

"I take everything," Maria said as she climbed out. She scurried to her car and opened the trunk. Together we carried Rebecca's boxes and suitcases to her car. Then, Maria turned toward the house. "I get my things."

I glanced over my shoulder at the street before I unlocked the front door. "Can I reach you in Gallup? What if Becca comes back here?"

Maria trudged up the stairs to the guest bedroom.

I waited in the hall, staring out the front window, watching for Eduardo. Maria was afraid of him and Rebecca did not like him. How could Maria expect Rebecca to return home if Eduardo was there?

Maria tugged her loaded suitcase down the stairs. "I go. Thank you for your kindness. I can never repay you. Adios."

She bustled past me and out the door. Maria Sanchez hurried across the lawn and stowed her suitcase in the trunk with Rebecca's cases and the boxes. The old blue car roared to life.

Maria was gone.

Behind me, my son's ring tone sounded from my cell.

"Mom. Why haven't you returned my call? What's up with Dad?" Irritation bubbled in Matt's voice.

"I'm so sorry. I've been involved with something else and I haven't had a chance to check back in at the hospital." I told my son what the nurse had told me and gave him the phone number for the intensive care unit.

"Should I catch a flight? Is he critical?" Matt asked.

I heard indecision in his voice. Dallas was a good ten-hour drive from Las Vegas, or a short flight from DFW to Albuquerque and then an hour-and-a-half drive. "I'll get an update. You check on flights."

I disconnected and then dialed the I.C.U. at Alta Vista.

"Robert Rowland's condition, please? This is Jamie

Aldrich." I carried the phone into the living room and sank down on the sofa.

"Oh, Mrs. Aldrich. Your daughter is here. I believe she spoke with the doctor a few minutes ago. I'll get her for you."

Alison took the phone. "Mom, I tried to call after I got here. Where are you?"

"Allie, I went to your father's apartment and then to the University to try to find out if there was anyone else we should contact. And, I talked to Matt. What did the doctor say?"

"Dad's holding his own. Is Matt coming?"

"Should he?"

"Dad looks awful, lying there. Seeing him like that makes me feel . . ." Her voice faded away.

"I know, honey." I could picture Alison chewing her lip. She would try to gauge whether Matt's reactions would be different from her own. It was difficult to be angry with someone when the person was lying in an intensive care unit hooked up to life-saving machinery.

"Maybe he should wait. Let's see how Dad is tomorrow. Tell his boss he might need to take a few days off," she suggested.

"I will call and let him know. Are you coming to the house for supper?"

"I'll check on Dad one more time, and then I'll be home."

I hung up, leaned back into the sofa pillows and closed my eyes. When my eyelids snapped open a few seconds later, I noticed Becca's box still on the living room table where Sheriff Clay had left it. I had forgotten all about it during the brief time Maria had been here to load her things.

I would have time enough to go through the box later, and then I would store it upstairs in the spare bedroom. I wanted so much for Becca to be safe and to return for her things. Would she? *Would I see her again?*

Matt did not answer his phone. I shuffled into the kitchen, filled the teakettle and set out a mug and a tea bag. I tried to reach Matt but had to leave a voice message to fill him in on his dad's condition.

Upstairs, I peeked into the guest room where Maria had stayed. She had pulled the sheets off the bed and left them in a pile on the floor next to the reading chair. The top of the dresser was empty and the open closet door revealed only a cluster of plastic hangers. I don't know what I expected her to leave behind. A note explaining where she had been? A thank you card? The faint scent of her heady perfume lingered in the air.

I patted the pillows, folded the coverlet and then checked the drawer in the nightstand. It was empty, except for a purse pack of tissues and my extra ankle/wrist bracelet, just like the one I usually wore when I went running. Finally, I gathered up the sheets and checked the bathroom for used towels.

My thoughts kept circling back to Rebecca's box. *Why was I obsessing over it?* I finally gave in and rushed to the living room to dump the contents onto the coffee table. A manicure kit, an art glass paperweight, a tiny stuffed dog, a small carpet, a throw pillow, a hairbrush, several books and her laptop computer. The police had probably checked everything for prints, even taken DNA samples. I was certain they would have booted up the laptop and gone through her files.

The small stack of books included two young adult novels, a college dictionary/thesaurus and a used English comp textbook. The fifth book—Rebecca's sketchbook—had no words on the spine or front cover. It contained only two pages of drawings, both dated last week, August 15 and 16.

August 15: 'What would Dad think about me being out here?' Rebecca had written the words under the sketch of a tree.

August 16: Rebecca had written, 'I can hardly believe I'm here and Dad is gone. I miss him.'

I recognized the subject of the sketch as the old Castaneda Hotel next door to the Las Vegas train depot.

Neither entry indicated Rebecca's intent to run away.

I punched Sheriff Clay's number into the phone.

"Clay."

"It's Jamie Aldrich. Something's happened—"

He interrupted me. "Rebecca's investigation has been dropped, as you know, Mrs. Aldrich." He sounded tired. "You can speak to Deputy Ross if you still need to talk. I have another news conference in a few moments to prepare for."

"But ..." The phone picked up voices, and then Deputy Steve Ross came on the line.

"Mrs. Aldrich? Is there something I can do for you?"

"Mrs. Sanchez came back. We picked up Rebecca's things from the dorm this afternoon."

"Glad to hear it. Did she know anything about your missing laptop?" He asked.

"She loaded up and left town." *Damn. I had not had a chance to ask her about the laptop.* "Eduardo Sanchez, her ex, followed us. She could be in danger."

"Sanchez?" the Deputy repeated.

"Yes. Does he have a record?"

Ross cleared his throat. "I shouldn't tell you this." He paused, and then continued. "Sanchez did time for assault and battery in the '90s. Police at Gallup had notations about 911 calls made from his home last year. Domestic disputes. Mrs. Sanchez later dropped the charges. Didn't she tell you?"

"No, and she's gone. You shouldn't have closed Rebecca's case. I fumed. "It's not over yet. Something's not right."

"All you have is a distraught mother. Unless she has proof that she'll share . . ." His voice trailed off.

There was no proof. I did not expect to hear from Maria again, even if Rebecca did contact her.

"Have you found out any more about Kate Gerard's murder?" I asked.

"The sheriff and the University are holding a joint news conference tonight. 5 p.m. I have nothing else to tell you right now." The deputy disconnected.

I carried my tea into the office. One move of my mouse and my operating system opened. Seconds later, an instant message screen popped up over the list of emails waiting in the in-basket. I did not recognize the sender's name, Sparky.

"I have some info you need."

Usually, I ignored emails from strangers, but there was no file to open. I typed in a quick response. "What info? Who are you?"

The response screen stayed blank. 'Sparky' was no longer in cyberspace.

When Alison arrived, I threw together a salad with chicken chunks and raspberry vinaigrette dressing. Neither of us had taken time for lunch. Despite the early hour, we needed to eat. We settled onto the bar in the kitchen. Both of us picked at the food, moving lettuce from one side of the bowl to the other and occasionally swallowing a bite. Eventually Alison laid down her fork and stared out the window into the hedged back yard.

"He's in a coma. What if he dies?" She rested her head in her hands. "Why don't I feel something?"

"It's shock, honey. It doesn't seem real when something like this happens."

Alison peered at me. "You don't have any feelings for Dad, do you? Are you the least bit sad this happened?"

"Yes, I'm sad that it happened to him." I pulled in a quick breath. "I wonder who ran him down, and why they didn't stop."

"You don't think it was an accident?"

"I'm not sure."

I slipped off the stool and went to the refrigerator to fill my water glass. I was not good at hiding my thoughts from my daughter. She would see in my eyes that I was not telling her everything. I did not want to tell Alison I suspected that her father might have been involved in the disappearances at Highlands University.

Chapter 27

I turned on the local news at 5 p.m. Alison and I sat on the sofa to hear the news conference I had been told about. Dean Stuart Russell from Highlands University and Sheriff Clay stood side by side, flanked by deputies and University dignitaries.

The camera focused on the sheriff as he stepped up to the podium where five or six different news stations had propped their microphones. Cameras flashed. Sheriff Clay cleared his throat and leaned down toward the mikes.

"Good afternoon. I am Sheriff Jonah Clay of San Miguel County. Today we received information that one of the students reported missing last week, Rebecca Sanchez, has been seen, alive and well, in Los Angeles, California." The sheriff paused; cameras clicked. "The investigation into her disappearance has been closed. However, we continue to investigate the other disappearances from Highlands University campus. We are currently pursuing several leads linking these cases and expect to have more information to release by the end of this week."

The sheriff retreated from the microphones and turned to Dean Russell.

"Thank you, Sheriff. I want to assure the community of Las Vegas, New Mexico that the University is cooperating fully with the sheriff's department and the Las Vegas Police Department to find these missing young women. I speak for the University Regents, and all members of the faculty in saying that we are so pleased to learn Ms. Sanchez has been located. We remain hopeful these other students will be found in good health as well and are eager for all of them to return to the University and continue their studies." He cleared his throat. "In the interim, I want to assure all students and their families that, as always, the University is focused on student security. We have a curfew in force. Our security force immediately investigates any reported unusual activity on campus. All students who see any such activity should immediately call campus security, the Las Vegas Police Department or the San Miguel Sheriff's Department Headquarters."

One of the reporters called out to the Dean. "If security is tight, how did these girls get kidnapped?"

The dean and the sheriff looked at one another. I leaned toward the television. *Good question.*

"This is an ongoing investigation," the sheriff responded. "I am unable to reveal details about the incidents. However, I can say that it is believed these students acted of their own free will when they left their dormitories at a late hour. Students are not locked in at night and are free to come and go as they please."

A few more questions were shouted at the two men but they ignored the reporters. The camera operator focused on the onsite news reporter and then eventually back at the podium where Sheriff Clay once again leaned toward the mike. "I also have an update in the matter of the death of Ms. Kate Gerard. Ms. Gerard was found dead at the Montezuma Hot Springs early Sunday morning. The coroner has determined that Ms. Gerard's death was not from natural causes. Her death has been classified as a homicide and is currently under investigation."

The room exploded with questions from the news reporters.

Clay shook his head at them. "That is all the information I have at this time. We'll update you later this week." He turned his back to the reporters. The entire group left the room.

"Is that true about Rebecca, Mom? Has she been found?" Alison asked.

I let out the sigh I'd been holding. "Supposedly. Maria took her things and went home. Except for the box I forgot to give her."

"You don't seem relieved."

"That's because I'm not sure it's true."

"You don't think Rebecca is in Los Angeles?"

I shook my head.

"You knew Kate was murdered, didn't you? You weren't the least bit surprised to hear that just now."

"The sheriff told me this morning."

About 8 p.m., after Alison had called the hospital one more time to check on her dad, she went upstairs to the guest bedroom. I flipped on the desktop computer in the office to check for emails in both my personal and my school inboxes. I read a short message from the substitute teacher about today's class sessions. The new message bell sounded. *"New Email"* flashed on the screen.

"Good. You're online," Sparky wrote.

"Who is this?"

"I've got info about Becca."

"What?" I typed. My heart pounded.

"I know where she is."

"In Los Angeles."

"No."

"Where?"

"Let's meet."

"Tell me where she is," I typed quickly, wishing I could reach through the computer and grab the person by the throat.

"We need to meet."

I shoved the desk chair back. For all I knew, Sparky could

be the person who kidnapped Becca. Meeting him, or her, was not smart, especially alone.

"You don't care much about Becca, do you?" The words popped up on the screen.

Becca was all that was left of Ben. Over the course of the week, I had learned how much I did care.

"How do I know you're telling the truth?" I typed. Maria and I had posted many fliers last weekend. Anyone who had seen one could make the connection between Ben, Becca and me.

"She was wearing a pink top and jean shorts last Sunday," Sparky wrote.

"You could have seen her anywhere that day."

"I want to help get Becca out of this fix. Let's meet," Sparky wrote.

"Give me something, so I know you're for real."

"The missing women all have Latina or Native American heritage. And no siblings."

No one had said anything about the girls each being the only child in their family. My fingers hung over the keyboard.

Sparky sent another message. *"Proof enough. Now when do we meet?"*

My brain raced. It was dangerous to meet until I had a chance to talk to the sheriff about this. *"Tomorrow?"* I finally typed.

The screen remained blank. Sparky had disconnected.

When the phone rang while I was drying my hair after a shower, I picked up the bedroom extension.

"Hello?"

No one answered. I listened to the silence on the phone. *Trey? Sparky? Rebecca?*

An owl hooted outside my window. A shiver tingled down my body.

I jerked on my robe and house shoes and padded down-stairs to the living room. Whoever Sparky was, the person knew something. Why did he/she insist on meeting me rather than simply telling me where Becca was?

Water gurgled through the pipes in between the first and second floors of the house. I flipped the stereo receiver to my favorite XM Radio channel and collapsed on one end of the sofa. "One of These Nights" from the Eagles, played.

I dialed Sam's cell number. His 'away from the phone' message played. "Hi, Sam," I said. "Miss you and can't wait to see you. Call if you can." I hung up. My heart ached.

The photographs on the mantel drew my eye. Ben. Becca. Alison and Matt. My parents in their wedding photo from 1955. A family photo from the Seventies, one summer in Pawhuska, with Aunt Elizabeth. All the people I loved. Suddenly, my look swooped back to a photograph Ben had taken of me at Fort Union.

Early in our marriage, Ben's fascination with Fort Union had taken us there most weekends. He took photographs and sketched the grasslands, which stretched for miles in all directions.

I grabbed the box of Becca's things, pulled it to the sofa and dug out Rebecca's sketchpad. I looked up at the photograph, then at the drawing. The tree Rebecca had drawn could be the one in the photograph taken at Fort Union.

I propped the sketchbook up on the mantel, next to the photo. *Was it the same tree?* When had Rebecca gone out to Fort Union? And, why had she taken the time to drive 30 miles to get there?

Where was she?

Sparky knew.

CHAPTER 28

Wednesday, August 23

I pulled my car into a space in front of the coffee shop. *Caffeine.* After another sleepless night, how could I ever get through today's classes? As I shoved open the door, the aroma of coffee brewing lifted my spirits. A bright red scarf caught my eye. I turned, smiling, my brain expecting Kate to have a table saved for us. But it wasn't Kate.

Of course, it was not Kate. *Kate was dead. She had been murdered.*

I waited in line to order and pay for coffee and a blueberry muffin. As I waited, I noticed Paul Everson and the Fort Union ranger sitting at a far table, against the wall of windows. What had Paul been doing with Maria at my house yesterday? Did he know if Maria had found Becca?

The barista called my name. I grabbed my coffee and small sack and then weaved between the small tables to the back of the shop. "Paul?"

Everson took a final swallow from his coffee cup and stood. "I'm running late. We'll talk another time, Jamie." He brushed past me, and then worked his way through tables and customers to the front door.

I scurried after him, pushing through the double door and out onto the sidewalk into the bright morning sun.

"Paul, wait. Did you talk with Maria Sanchez yesterday?" I called.

Paul sprinted toward his car.

"Where did Maria go?"

Paul Everson slid in behind the wheel, slammed the door of his SUV and gunned the engine.

At the hospital, I hurried to the ICU. Alison sat in the waiting area, her feet tucked up under her in the cushioned armchair. Her creased brow told me how worried she was.

"The nurse said his condition is unchanged," she said. "He's no better, but no worse, either. Are you going in to see him?"

I nodded and punched the button to open the wide doors to the unit.

Tubes and wires attached to Rob's arms and chest still connected him to various beeping machines and monitors. The wait-and-see mode continued.

I stood beside his bed for a moment. My memories played. How charming he had been when we first met. What an attentive dad he had been after Alison was born, offering to change diapers, getting up with her in the middle of the night to soothe her, lying on the floor with her for hours before she had learned to crawl. Why had he changed when she began to walk, and again after her brother was born? He had turned into someone I did not know – and did not want to know.

Who was he now? Was Rob involved in the kidnappings at the University or connected to the human trafficking ring?

"Mom? You've got this strange look on your face." Alison stepped up beside me and touched my arm.

"Memories. I'm wondering why things went so wrong with your dad and me."

"'Wrong' is a nice way to put it." She hugged me. "I think I'll drive back to Albuquerque and work the rest of the day. I'll call you tonight."

At the high school, the buzzer sounded as I sprinted to my classroom; students flooded the halls. I flicked the light switch and rushed to my desk. My class planner lay in my 'in box' tray. *What was I supposed to be doing today?* My mind was blank; my teaching schedule was the least of my concerns now. I stowed my purse in the bottom drawer and slid my backpack into the kneehole of the desk, then grabbed the planner and flipped to today's date.

Instead of the pages I sought, only ragged edges remained; all the pages containing reading references and experiments, test questions and related resources for the remaining August class days had been ripped out. I dropped into my chair.

Students filed in. I reached for the biology text. It was only the third day of school. Surely, I could wing it. The students could tell me what they did yesterday; we would review their notes and the experiment they had conducted. I would turn the class period into a review and then assign the students something to read.

"Good morning, Mrs. Aldrich. How are you?" Trey Woodard strutted up, a grin smeared across his face. "We missed you yesterday."

This was not his Biology class period. What was he doing in here?

"I'm sure you did, Trey." I smiled pleasantly. *I could be as fake as he was.*

"Watch for a surprise. Later." He winked and then strolled back out into the hallway as the desks filled with students.

A surprise? The missing planner pages were not a big enough surprise. Trey would have something worse in mind, something to embarrass me in front of the class.

For the next two hours, I winged it, using class time for review and clarification. I anticipated an unpleasant surprise. I felt as if I was waiting for a Black Cat firecracker to explode after the fuse had been lit and I had pitched it onto the driveway. I caught a couple of students making faces at one another as they sensed how off track I was.

By third hour, it was easier to follow the trail of the substitute from the day before. The material was a continuation of the genetics process I had begun Monday, with investigation into the father of genetics, Gregor Mendel. Trey fidgeted in his seat with a smug smile.

When the dismissal buzzer sounded after seventh hour, the students hurried through the doorway. I locked the classroom door. So much for Trey's 'surprise.' My tense muscles did not relax. Whatever it was, I needed to find it today, otherwise, I would be just as on edge tomorrow. I pulled open each of the drawers and looked through all of the cabinet storage spaces, including the shelves in my small closet. *Nothing.*

The more I searched, the madder I became. I was letting Trey get under my skin. He was yanking my chain and I was going right along with his teenage pranks. *Enough.*

I called Mr. Winter's office. Of course, he was already gone for the day.

"Mr. Winters. I need Trey out of my class. Let's talk about that tomorrow. The sooner the better." I set down the receiver and then turned off the lights. I returned to the desk and sat. Afternoon light filtered in through the windows. Overhead, the ceiling fans turned, pushing the air, flicking the corners of the genetic worksheets stacked on my desk. I scanned the room, looking for anything that seemed out of place. Nothing caught my eye.

If Trey had planted a surprise, it was not something obvious. Then, another thought occurred to me. What if Trey's 'surprise' was not something in my classroom, but something outside the school, or even at home?

I would have to take it an hour at a time.

Sam could not get here fast enough to suit me.

CHAPTER 29

When I left the building, my muscles tightened across my shoulders and the hairs on my arms rose. I scanned the trees and bushes surrounding the building as I walked to the nearly empty teachers' parking lot.

At my car, I found a note tucked beneath the windshield wipers. I unfolded the fluttering paper.

"Be on the internet tonight at 6. Sparky."

I peered at the row of bushes north of the parking lot and then around the campus. Sparky knew I worked here, knew my car. Sparky could be anyone. *Even Trey.*

I had no choice but to meet Sparky. I would be on the internet, waiting, at 6 p.m.

As I drove toward home, my thoughts churned, trying to narrow down the long list of Sparky suspects before the 6 p.m. call. My brain circled around a possibility I did not want to acknowledge. *I was the connection between Rebecca and Ben and Kate.*

I clicked through the people I knew at school, at the University, at the museum, parents of my children's friends, students, coaches, teachers, shopkeepers, neighbors. What about the years before I moved to Las Vegas? My mind bogged down. The list seemed endless. *Was I being paranoid?*

When I passed Rob's apartment an unfamiliar car sat parked outside the detached garage. I drove past my house and circled the block. The second time I rolled by a man was coming down the apartment's stairway. Hair slicked back, Craig Sanford still wore his maintenance uniform shirt.

If Rob was involved in the kidnappings, Craig could be his partner.

I pulled into my driveway. Next door, Mildred knelt by a flowerbed, a bucket of tools beside her on the lawn. She looked over, waved one hand and got to her feet.

"Jamie! Need to talk to you!" Mildred called.

I waited on the driveway, my mind still stewing over a possible criminal tie between Craig Sanford and Rob. Would Mildred be a good sounding board? Ben had thought so.

Mildred hurried across the lawn, pulling off her gardening gloves and slapping them together. Lumps of loose dirt flew off.

"I'm glad to see that car gone. Did your stepdaughter come back?" Mildred pushed her glasses up on her small, upturned nose. Her magnified eyes looked bright. "Good riddance, I say. The neighborhood doesn't need the riff-raff hanging around."

"I don't think of Maria as riff-raff." I frowned. Mildred had returned to her abrasive self.

"Well, think again. All the comings and goings when you weren't home. She had a regular clientele. I was truly afraid you were going to take her on as a roommate. You're not, are you? She's not coming back, is she?"

"People coming and going? When?"

"You have no idea." She clicked her tongue.

"Mildred, who was coming and going?"

"Latino men, black men, men in uniform, even that professor fellow from the University. In and out, anytime you were gone. Last week, this week. Was she selling something? What is her profession anyway?"

I tried to speak calmly. "Maria left Sunday night and didn't return except to pick up her things yesterday afternoon. She has hardly been here the past several days."

Mildred nodded. "But they came all the same. Constant

stream. Anytime you weren't home. What was she selling? Drugs? Her body?"

"Are you exaggerating?"

"It is not in my nature to exaggerate." Her eyes widened behind the thick lenses.

"You haven't seen anyone around here today, have you?"

Mildred licked her chapped lips. "Yes. Didn't go in the house since nobody was here but they stopped by all the same."

"Who? When?" I sounded like a scratched CD.

"That professor guy and someone else. A swaggerer with slicked back hair. And, of course, the mail carrier. Might have been more. I had to go inside late morning. Stomach's been acting up again. Too much spicy food, I'm thinking."

"Mildred," I interrupted. If Mildred started talking about her ailments, I would never get any more information from her. I had a lot to do before logging into the internet at 6 p.m. "Please answer. Was it this morning or this afternoon?"

"Both. First the professor, then some Latino. After lunch, the swaggerer. Might have been more." Mildred patted her stomach. "Tamales and chili don't set well these days."

"Will you let me know if you see anyone else hanging around or stopping by at odd hours? Call me. It could be important."

"Of course." She rubbed her hands together as if they were cold. "So did the girl come back? I saw the fliers. Ben must be writhing in his grave."

"You didn't see the news last night."

Mildred shook her head. "Never watch it. Nothing but misery."

"Rebecca used her credit card in Los Angeles. Supposedly. She's no longer considered missing."

"Ahhh. That's good, but you don't look happy."

"I don't believe it. I still think she's around here, somewhere."

"Hmmphh." Her eyes shifted away from me and clouded over.

"I'll have company coming in tomorrow for the holiday weekend. A friend from Pawhuska."

Her look jerked back to me. "Oh! One of your cousins?"

I could not keep the smile from popping up on my face. "No. My friend Sam."

Mildred jerked. "A boyfriend?"

Color rushed to my face. "Anyway, you'll see him around for a few days. We'll talk later, Mildred." I walked to the curb to pull the mail from the mailbox. The black ants marched in a long line into their grainy brown den near the grass. I crossed the lawn to the porch.

In the kitchen, I dropped the mail and sale circulars onto the table. If Mildred was to be believed, Paul had been to the house today and so had Craig Sanford. The man she described as a Latino could have been Eduardo. Why would he come here? Maria had left with him, hadn't she?

I flipped through the junk mail and then plucked out an envelope with only my name printed on the outside. I pulled a plain sheet of paper from the envelope.

"Rebecca—Gone. Maria—Gone. You—Next."

I glanced at the clock.

My only hope rested with Sparky—a stranger. Did he/she truly want to help me find Rebecca?

Another conclusion would be that Sparky did not want to help at all. Maybe he/she had written this note. Maybe he/she was following through on this threat. *I was next.*

Corrine, at the Highlands Personnel office, sighed into the phone. "OK, Jamie. Last time, though. You doing some kind of private eye work?"

I stretched out on the sofa in the living room and stared out the front window toward the street. "I need info about a maintenance employee. Craig Sanford. I know it's unusual, but could you pull his personnel file and read it to me?" I kept my voice light. "It's for a friend of mine. She thinks she might have known him in high school. Will you check, please?"

"Okay."

I was pushing her limits with this second request. In the background, Corrine's fingers clicked on her keyboard. While I waited for the information, I fingered the items in Rebecca's box. Finally, Corrine came back on the phone.

"Here's what it says. Craig Sanford. He's from Mora. Born in Black Lake. High school diploma. Associate degree from some two-year college in Kansas."

"How did he get the job at Highlands?"

"Sanford first applied for the job two years ago. He wasn't hired until last year. Looks like it took a faculty reference to get him on. The recommendation is from Dr. Paul Everson."

My mind whirled. Paul was from Mora. *And so was Ben.* The three of them had known each other in high school.

I pulled myself up from the chair and trudged to the kitchen phone.

"I know you'll be here tomorrow night, Sam, but I couldn't wait," I said when Sam answered. "I need you to talk me through this." Tears filled my eyes at the sound of his voice.

"News about Rebecca?"

I pictured Sam pushing his longish black hair away from his face, his brow furrowed and his eyes piercing the air as if trying to see all the way to New Mexico. "You could say that."

I told him about Maria's sudden return on Tuesday and her immediate departure. Then I told him about Rob's hit-and-run accident. Reciting it consecutively made it sound connected and ominous.

"I'm afraid Rob knows something about the disappearances. When he realized one of the victims was my step-daughter, he tried to intervene."

"You think Rob could be part of something like this?"

"He wasn't a criminal when we were married, but so many years have passed . . ."

"Don't cut yourself short. You're a good judge of character."

"I want to believe he had nothing to do with any of this."

Sam paused, and then, in the solemn Native American way I had often heard him speak, he said, "I will stand with you in hoping that is the truth."

I started to tell Sam about Sparky's note on my car as well as the threatening message I had received with today's mail, but I didn't. He would be here in less than 24 hours. Surely, whoever had threatened me would back off while Sam was here. If Sparky legitimately wanted to help me find Rebecca, and I met with him, my stepdaughter might be safe and here with me by tomorrow night.

The phone crackled.

"Are you there?" Sam asked. "Crap. Are you there?" Static broke into the connection, louder this time. "There's a thunderstorm coming, honey, and I'm losing you," he said, sounding as if he was speaking from the moon.

Static took over.

"Love you." Sam's voice was faint, broken.

The phone went dead.

The silent, empty house pressed in around me.

CHAPTER 30

The evening stretched long; Sam didn't phone back. My thoughts jumped from Rob to Paul, then to Craig Sanford, Ben and their hometown of Mora. *But how does Rob fit in?* My hands trembled.

Maria was from Mora, too.

I carried the phone out onto the back deck and punched in Maria's number. On the other end, the phone rang and rang. No answer. No answering machine.

My stomach churned.

I dashed down the hall to the office and connected to the internet. I typed Paul Everson's name into a Google search; up came an article about his employment at Highlands University and a list of articles from the universities at Arizona and Utah where he had previously taught. Next, I searched the name 'Craig Sanford.' Nothing. I tried Robert Rowland. Nothing, again.

Matt's ringtone pulled me out of cyberspace.

"Any change in Dad's condition, Mom?" he asked.

I rubbed my forehead. *I had not checked on Rob since this morning.*

"Not that I've heard," I said. "Are you coming home?"

"I'll be up Friday. My flight gets in to Albuquerque at 4:35 your time. Alison's coming to get me."

"Call me if there are any changes and I'll do the same. Sam Mazie, from Oklahoma, is also coming in for the weekend."

"The lawyer from Pawhuska?"

"Yes." Warmth surged through my icy fingers. "Sam and I went through so much together after Great Aunt Elizabeth's attack. I want you to spend time with him. How long can you stay?"

"My flight back is on Sunday. Whether Alison and I stay over with you on Saturday night will depend on Dad's condition and what Alison has going on Sunday. I'm open."

"I'm glad you're coming. I hope your dad is awake by then." My heart thudded. *Would he even be alive?* "See you Friday, son."

I dragged the kitchen step stool with me upstairs and into the master bedroom closet where the few remaining boxes of Ben's belongings were stored. I had been unable to find the heart to throw it all away. The box of yearbooks was tucked beneath a pile of thick sweatshirts for cold winter days.

Using the index in the back of one of the Mora high school yearbooks, I located Paul's name in the book from the year Ben was a sophomore. I flipped to Paul's photos. They included Chess Club and Volleyball Team. Ben had pictures under Baseball, the Law Club and Student Council. There was no entry for Craig Sanford.

I opened the volume for Ben's junior year. Again, photos for Ben and photos for Paul. No Craig Sanford.

Ben's senior yearbook was last. Heavily looped writing scrawled across the entire inside front cover. Some of the words were in Spanish, and underlined. I recognized the Spanish words for Heart and Love and Eternity, as well as phrases describing Ben as Handsome and Strong. The signature at the bottom of the entry was "Maria."

I knew Ben and Maria had an off and on relationship before

marrying after he graduated from UNM. Until this moment, I had not known the relationship extended all the way back to high school.

Maria had not signed her last name, so I could not look her up in the index. I looked at photographs on pages listed for Ben and Paul. This time I found Craig Sanford, too, with the sophomore class. Little in the photo reminded me of the man I knew as Craig Sanford. Maybe the eyes were the same but the hair seemed darker and longer, and his face much thinner than the man I had seen flirting with female students at Highlands University.

I flipped again through the yearbook, looking at the candid photos taken by yearbook staff.

My eyes stopped at a photo of students at a basketball game, cheering from the bleachers. I recognized Ben instantly as well as the beautiful Latina woman next to him. Maria. Behind them sat Paul Everson. Next to him was the person identified elsewhere in the book as Craig Sanford.

I flipped through the pages, scanning autographs and short entries until one in particular jumped off the page. The person had drawn a skull and crossbones around the entry.

"I love M. Don't fight me. Remember R? P."

No last name, but I didn't think I needed one. Questions surged into my mind about this love triangle: Paul, Maria and Ben. *Who was R?*

I closed the yearbook. Ben's journal pages were still stuffed in the drawer downstairs. Would the answers to my questions be among those pages?

As I clomped downstairs, I switched on lamps and even the porch light. In the office, I opened a window to let the night breeze in and then pulled the journal pages from the drawer before settling into the chair.

Ben's first few entries seemed mundane; comments on students, class sizes, and an occasional mention of a student who seemed especially promising or in too far over their head. I scanned through, watching for a name I recognized.

I read on. Most of Ben's journal entries carried no emotion, containing information about conferences, meetings or community events. When he mentioned Alison or Matt, one of them was usually visiting for a weekend, or holiday. Often when Rebecca was the topic, he was upset about some shenanigan she had pulled or concerned over Maria's husband Eduardo and that man's influence on his daughter.

It was mid-November of the year before he died before he mentioned Paul Everson in the journal. At the same time, the tone of Ben's journal entries changed.

Paul better back off. He seems to have forgotten I could put an end to his career at Highlands.

I reread the entry. Had Paul done something illegal? If Ben knew his secret, why would Paul want to be here where Ben was? His professional move to Highlands University seemed the opposite of what most people would do.

I read on. Ben's cancer had manifested itself and his body had become its own enemy. Some days his writing was sullen; other days, it was argumentative and angry. I could pinpoint the very date his diagnosis came in. The two of us had been so overwhelmed there seemed to be no time for anything but clinging to one another and the people we loved. The six-month time span attached to the diagnosis made living day by day and moment by moment a reality. In the end, he had lived only four of the six months he had been given. Now I knew it was not cancer that had shortened that period of time.

I blinked back tears. In the journal, every sentence he wrote radiated his anger, although I had not seen this anger when he and I had been together. The usual subject of his tirades was Paul Everson. He did not think Paul should receive tenure. At the same time, Ben was worried about 'consequences' if he told what he knew about the man.

At first I thought 'consequences' referred to the University but as I read on I sensed something different. Ben was afraid.

He had written:

How can I speak up when it might tear my life apart?

What would an accusation from Paul do to Jamie and her children?

If I don't speak up, would I ever forgive myself for keeping quiet?

The next short entry chilled me from head to toe.

Would Paul kill again?

Cold air wrapped long bony fingers around me. I stuffed the pages back into the drawer.

I paced the hallway. *What had Paul done?*

Ben's parents were deceased and he had no siblings. He had never attended a reunion or kept in touch with anyone from Mora. The only person who might know what Ben's entry in the journal had referred to—other than Paul himself—was Maria.

I rushed into the kitchen, picked up the phone again and tried Maria's number in Gallup for the second time that evening.

"This number is no longer in service," a recording said.

I dialed directory assistance. The operator could not find a new number for Maria and no forwarding information had been entered into the system.

I shivered in what seemed like a sudden blast of cold air. Why had Maria disconnected her phone? *How would Rebecca contact her?* The most likely answer was that Maria did not expect to hear from her daughter again.

I snatched Rebecca's laptop from the box in the living room and toted it down the hall to my office. I powered up both my computer and Rebecca's laptop. Becca had stored her internet password. I clicked on email and her mailbox opened with 137 old messages stored.

Reading them seemed pointless because I didn't know

Rebecca's friends or their screen names. How could I tell if any of the messages were from strangers? I began to open and scan the messages, anyway. Friends detailed arguments with parents and boyfriends, new clothes, their excitement or nervousness about going to college, roommates or just good old gossip about friends from high school. Nothing seemed relevant to Becca's disappearance.

I clicked on the 'sent' messages folder. Becca's last message, sent the day she disappeared, was to someone with the screen name Tyk4439dat.

> *I want to make my dad proud. I miss him so much.*
> *Wherever he is, maybe this will let him know I love him.*

That email did not sound like a message from someone who intended to run away. Ben would not have been proud of a run-away. Ben would have been angry beyond words.

Was this proof Becca had not left campus willingly? I clicked on the 'read' messages file, looking for other messages to Becca from Tyk4439dat. There was only one in the computer's current memory. The message had been sent and opened the day she disappeared.

> *Same place about 6? I'm so glad you are here. T.*

I didn't remember anyone coming forward to tell the police they had met with Becca earlier the day she disappeared. *Who was T?*

A ping from Becca's computer startled me. *'You have an IM'* appeared on the screen.

I clicked the message open.

"U r here." The sender was Sparky.

My thoughts rolled. Obviously, Sparky knew Becca's email address. He also knew I had her computer.

"Come and get Becca. She's ill."

"Where is she?"

"I'll tell you when we meet."

"Tell me who you are."

"Tomorrow. I'll send another email with details about when and where. To YOUR computer."

Sparky went offline. I slumped in the desk chair, my heart thudding. *Why tomorrow and not tonight? If Rebecca was ill, she needed help now.*

Someone pounded on the front door.

I pushed up out of the chair and rushed down the hall. A key scraped in the door's lock. The dead bolt clicked but did not slide open. A heavy pounding shook the door.

"Open the door. Now." A voice yelled. The fist slammed into the door again.

I dialed 9-1-1 from the living room phone and gave my address. The pounding continued along with shouts in Spanish. Suddenly, the noise stopped.

I darted down the hall to the kitchen and leaned against the wall. *How long would it take the police to get here?*

A fist hammered the glass of the deck door, inches away from where I stood. "Where is Maria?" the man shouted. An angry face stared through the window. "Let me in!"

"I've called the police!"

"Maria is in danger. She needs your help." He kicked at the door.

I backed into the hallway. *What kind of game was he playing?* An arc of light streaked through the front windows of the house, brakes squealed on the driveway. Red and blue lights flashed across the front yard.

"Police," someone shouted from my front porch.

I hurried down the hallway and glanced through the peephole. A trio of uniformed police officers waited, hands poised over holstered guns.

"He was at the back door a few seconds ago," I said as I opened the door.

Two of the officers took off, one racing in one direction, the other running the opposite way.

"Can you describe the man?" the remaining officer asked.

"Big, over six feet tall. Hispanic I think. Dark hair and eyes. Muscular. I believe it was Eduardo Sanchez."

"How do you know this man?"

"I had a house guest, his estranged wife. But she's no longer here." It was impossible to turn the events of the last few days into a ten-second sound bite for this police officer. "Sheriff Clay knows the whole story."

"We'll comb the neighborhood and alert your immediate neighbors to be on the lookout," the officer said. "If this man is still in the area, we'll find him. And we'll post a watch on your house tonight in case he comes back."

"Thank you."

Sanchez said Maria was in danger. *What did he know?*

No sooner had the officers left than the phone rang.

"Jamie? What happened? Is somebody else dead?" Mildred's voice shrilled.

"Nobody's dead. Somebody was here, trying to get in."

"I saw the man in your porch light. He was here before. When that Maria was staying with you."

Maria would never have let Eduardo in the house, not if what she had told me about him was true. "Are you sure?"

"Last weekend. Saturday, I think."

"Saturday?" I had gone to Albuquerque to meet Alison. *And Kate had been murdered.*

"Maria let him into the house?"

"I'm not saying that. I'm saying he was here. Big Latino guy. Maria left with him."

This didn't make any more sense than the pages from

Ben's journal I had been reading. What was Maria hiding? She seemed to hold the key to Ben's secret.

"Jamie, I'm coming over. You and I need to talk. I'm no butt-in-ski usually, but this time ... we need to investigate some things."

"Mildred, it's late, and—"

"I'll be there in thirty seconds."

The phone clicked in my ear.

CHAPTER 31

Twenty seconds later, a loud bang shook the front door. When I pulled it open, Mildred pitched into the house carrying a cardboard box full of books and folders. Mildred dropped the box onto the hall floor as I reached for it. She peered at me with her magnified eyes.

"You don't know how many hours Ben spent at my house when you weren't home." I helped Mildred maneuver the box over to the living room coffee table.

I bit my tongue. I wasn't sure I wanted to hear what Mildred had to say but I had never discovered a way to shut her up when she wanted to talk.

"Ben didn't talk to you much about Rebecca, did he? Well, he had to talk to somebody. Guess it was me. I never even met the girl." Mildred's eyes flitted from me to the box and back again. "To tell the truth, I looked forward to those talks. Evening time, I would see you drive off and I would go sit on the porch. Within a few minutes, Ben would make his way over." She cleared her throat.

"Can I get you a glass of water, Mildred? Or some tea?"

"Water, yes. Entirely too late for tea. Caffeine, you know."

I hurried down the hallway to the kitchen, filled a glass and then returned to the living room with her water. I lit the cinnamon candle on the coffee table. The scent soothed me, and I had a feeling I would need soothing when I learned whatever it was Mildred wanted to tell me.

"Our conversations ran the gamut," Mildred continued. "I especially enjoyed talking about Highlands University. You know I spent a good many years there as the provost's secretary before I retired. Some of the faculty I worked with are still there." She took a long drink of the water. "It's all about tenure, now. Having that safety net. Not that a safety net is bad. In today's world, one needs all the safety nets one can have." Mildred nodded and tilted her head. "Ben talked about safety nets. I remember the specific conversation, on the day he brought this box of books over, several months before he died." She tapped the box with one finger. "He said, 'This box links me to my past.' He asked me to keep it for him."

I had no idea where Ben had kept this box before taking it to Mildred's house and no idea what it contained.

"The box has been in the bottom of my coat closet for nearly two years." Mildred pulled a box knife from the front pocket of her slacks and slit the packing tape, which held the flaps of the box closed.

"Ben said, 'After I'm gone, take them over to Jamie.' I suspect he wanted to forget his past, but he couldn't bury it. That wasn't the way Ben was."

"Something tells me you are the same way, Mildred. You can never forget anything." My look met hers and held.

"You're right. But I can't keep it all in my head, either, Jamie." Mildred's eyes flashed. "I keep records, you know. Without a neighborhood watch, someone has to keep an eye on things. Hard habit to break. I have notebooks full of license tag numbers and a dozen notepads stacked in the drawers of my work desk in the den. Never know when someone might ask, 'did you see a Red Ford LTD in your neighborhood on the night of February 17, 2001?' When the question comes, I'm prepared."

"Yes, you are." I really knew so little about my neighbor. *Records of license tags?*

"Well, you have to agree it's a better use of my time than watching the damned television, except for "Law and Order" and its spin-offs. People in those other shows, sitcoms and realities, are stupid. No wonder the world is in such a mess. If I can help by having some useful information tucked away when it's needed, it is certainly worth the time it takes to observe and write down the facts."

I nodded, took a long sip of my hot tea and watched her over the rim of my teacup.

"License tags aren't all I write down." She blinked her owlish eyes at me. "I note the make, color and approximate year of manufacture. I describe the driver and the precise length of time he or she sat parked in front of whoever's residence."

"Wow." I could see the value of her notebooks to anyone investigating the comings and goings of me or my neighbors. At the same time, it was creepy to know she kept these records.

"The notebooks are far from complete. I do have to occasionally go to the grocery store, fix a meal or have a conversation. Can't be helped. There are fewer gaps now than there were when Ben was alive." She drained the remaining water from her glass.

I pointed to the box. "So he brought you this after he'd learned he had cancer. Was he worried about Rebecca, afraid someone might harm her?"

Mildred's look shifted around the room. "He talked about her stepfather. Far be it from me to pass on hearsay but Rebecca did not like him much. Ben thought she came for weekend visits primarily to get away from him and her mother. He could not see any other reason a teenager would want to continue spending every other weekend and half the summer break with you two. I told him it was because she loved him and wanted to be with him, but Ben didn't think that was the only reason." Mildred shivered. "He was worried about kidnapping."

"Why?" My body felt Mildred's chill.

She shrugged. "Ben knew someone who had kidnapped somebody years ago. The girl was released and the person never charged. People said it was a prank. No malice intended."

I slumped deeper into the chair's soft cushions. "Go on."

"Ben tried to forget about it. But as the years passed, he saw newspaper articles about women in this region who had disappeared." She traced the deep lines in her forehead with her fingertips. "Like my Jodie."

"If he thought there was a connection to this earlier kidnapping, why didn't he go to the police?"

"Ben was afraid of putting one of you in danger," she said slowly.

I pulled myself to the edge of the seat cushions.

Mildred looked up at the ceiling. "The person kidnapped Maria before she and Ben were married."

A stunning thought occurred to me and Mildred smiled as if she had read my mind.

"I did the math, Jamie. Rebecca was born a full year after Ben and Maria married. Not a product of the kidnapping. Could have been a product of something else, though. Far be it from me to make an assumption."

"So Ben read about these disappearances and saw a connection to what had happened to Maria?"

Mildred leaned over the box. "Maybe."

"Looks like I've got some digging to do." I pulled open the box flaps and glanced in at more books, photographs and newspaper clippings.

"Yes." Mildred stood up. "And I'll go on home."

I walked with her to the front door. "Thank you, Mildred, and not just for the box. Thank you for being such a good friend to Ben."

I stood in the doorway and watched her trek across the yard and back to her house. The street was quiet, no traffic, no parked cars except for the black and white police car across the street. The moon, nearly full, glowed in the sky.

Sam would be here in less than 24 hours. A lot could happen in that time. What would the contents of this box tell me about Ben, Maria and Paul? Would I find clues that would help me find Rebecca without Sparky's help? Maybe this whole episode with Rebecca would be over soon.

Then I had another realization.

Somewhere out there, the kidnapped University students were hoping for rescue.

If they weren't dead, like Kate.

CHAPTER 32

Thursday, August 24

I rubbed my eyes and shook my head, trying to fend off the desire to sleep. Somehow, five cups of coffee hadn't done it. I had the gist of what had happened all those years ago. I glanced at the scattered magazines, newspaper clippings and yearbooks on the floor. My notepad lay on the coffee table.

The earliest article of an assortment of magazine articles Ben had clipped together was from a now defunct regional magazine. The printout looked to be from a library microfiche machine.

"Kidnapped woman found alive; tells strange tale." Ben had attached a page of notes, citing specifics from the article. "Cave . . . blindfolded . . . hands and feet bound . . . Food and water." At the bottom of the page, he had written, 'Not raped. Spoke in whispers. Background music. Man or woman?'

Neither this magazine piece nor any of the others he had saved mentioned arrests, suspects or connections between the victims. I wondered about the one thing that Sparky had told me that connected the victims of the disappearances at Highlands University: they were the only child in their families. *How did Sparky know that?*

Despite all the reading, I was no closer to knowing where Rebecca—and possibly Maria—might be. I had no idea where to begin to look for them. This last piece, the draft of a letter, with words crossed out and arrows indicating sentences to be moved, might be a clue.

> *I have concluded it would be in the best interest of the university to expend the funds for a security investigation. I can provide adequate evidence to substantiate the need for this inquiry. For the University to employ a faculty member who, in all probability, has committed crimes is not prudent. Please take my recommendation to heart, and undertake an investigation.*

Had Ben ever sent the letter? He had folded and tucked the letter into *Kidnapped*, the book about the Lindberg's kidnapped and murdered baby.

The digital clock read 6 a.m.

I reread the draft of the letter to the Dean. Ben suspected Paul had committed crimes. Even murder. He had requested an investigation and questioned Paul's hiring as a professor. Did the University ever follow through?

I padded to the kitchen for another cup of coffee. Mildred had reacted emotionally to Becca's disappearance over a week ago because it brought back horrible memories. I thought of all the times I had shut Mildred down when she had tried to start a conversation with me. If I had not always been so brusque with her, I might have learned about her daughter long before now. Perhaps I might have even been able to prevent what had happened to Becca.

I worked my way through the box again, expanding my notes. An hour later, my mind buzzed. What had happened with the investigation Ben had wanted? The clock read 7 a.m. I had to be at school in another hour. Was it too early to call Dean Russell?

On the third ring, the dean answered his office phone. He

sounded tired. Rather than the usual, "Dean Russell speaking," he merely said, "Hello?"

"Dean, Jamie Aldrich. I have found some records Ben kept. Could someone at Highlands be responsible for the disappearances of these young women?" I asked. "Ben saved years of newspaper and magazine articles written about kidnappings in New Mexico. With the articles was a draft of a letter written to you requesting a staff investigation into a faculty member."

The dean audibly sighed. "Professor Aldrich made that request." He cleared his throat. "Some members of the Board of Regents were concerned about Ben's state of mind due to his illness." The dean paused. "Then, there was an incident late this spring in Santa Fe. Young woman kidnapped. She turned up a week later in Red River unharmed with an odd story. We hired an investigator." He cleared his throat again. "Jamie, you have to understand we were unaware of any connection between you and Rob Rowland. He came to us well recommended as an undercover officer. Very well recommended. He started the on-campus investigation in July."

"My ex." I straightened and clutched the phone tighter to my ear. My mind spun. My former husband wasn't the criminal I feared he had become. He was an undercover investigator working for the University.

"Yes. We've been concerned that his undercover identity had been blown after he was so badly injured earlier this week," he said. "But, the incident appears to be unrelated to the investigation."

"How do you know?"

"The two suspects he was investigating have airtight alibis, according to Sheriff Clay."

"They could have paid someone to run him down," I said.

"I suppose. Rowland's investigation on campus is now on hold. Students are still missing, and we have no leads." His voice sounded heavy with despair. "At least your stepdaughter was found. I'm glad for you she is no longer among those missing."

"I don't believe the information about the sighting in California was correct. Several things have happened since, Dean. And now her mother is missing."

"You can't get in touch with Mrs. Sanchez?"

"No. Her home phone has been disconnected."

"I'm sure she's fine. Disgusted with her daughter. So much effort goes into parenting and in the end, you never know how your children are going to turn out."

My teeth clenched. I felt sure he was wrong about Rebecca and Maria. Nothing the dean said would convince me that neither Becca nor Maria was in danger.

I perched on a stool at the kitchen island and mulled over this strange, new fact. *Rob had been working undercover investigating Paul Everson.*

CHAPTER 33

The IM popped up on my computer as soon as I opened my mailbox minutes later.

"*Maria is with Becca.*" Sparky, again.

"*Where?*" I wrote back.

"*U need to go get them.*"

"*Where are they?*"

"*I'll IM when and where after school today,*" Sparky wrote.

"*I'll be at a memorial service early this afternoon, and then at school. Home about 4.*"

Sparky signed off without leaving another message.

I knew meeting Sparky could be dangerous. The only way this could happen would be if he agreed to meet me in broad daylight in a public place. I would refuse to go anywhere with him, and I would notify Sheriff Clay so the deputies would be watching.

I tapped my foot in exasperation. Where were Maria and Becca? If Sparky was indeed an informant who wanted to help, I had to listen to him.

I stopped by the hospital before heading to school. Rob remained in a coma. I stood beside his bed and studied his still swollen face. I traced the line of his jawbone with my finger.

"I'm sorry, Rob, for thinking so badly of you," I whispered, blinking back tears. "Come back to us. Alison and Matt need for you to set things right with them."

The medicine cart rattled behind me as a nurse entered his cubicle.

I hurried to the nurse's station.

"His two kids will be here tomorrow evening," I told the nurse. "They need to see him."

"Good. Visitors seem to help. He seemed to rally yesterday when his friend was here. Got restless, and I thought he might wake up. Since then, though, his vitals have been constant."

"He had a visitor?" I could not imagine who that would have been.

The nurse shrugged. "Guy said he was Mr. Rowland's only friend in town. He wanted to see him. I told him I would have to call you to get your okay since he was not approved family. He seemed confident you would approve but I stuck with our policy and made him wait while I called you. When you didn't answer your phone, he left." She picked up a pen and began to review some paperwork. "I'll get his name and number on the visitor's log sheet if he comes again."

"Please do that," I said. "And call me when he's here. What did he look like?"

"Jeans, denim shirt. Dark hair and a baseball cap." She didn't look up as she spoke.

Sanford.

I was preoccupied with thoughts of Craig Sanford as I walked up the steps and into the high school. What did the sheriff know about Sanford? I pulled out my cell phone and punched in his office number. His secretary said that both he and Deputy Ross were out of the office; I was welcome to leave a message.

Irritated by the delay, I gritted my teeth.

"Sheriff, Jamie Aldrich. Craig Sanford tried to visit Rob in the hospital yesterday. And he was also at Rob's apartment." The answering machine beeped and the sheriff picked up.

"Ms. Aldrich? What about Craig Sanford?"

"Is Sanford involved in whatever Rob was investigating for the University? The dean told me my ex-husband was conducting an undercover operation."

Clay cleared his throat. "Well, you have dug your way into this after all, haven't you? Yes, Sanford is being investigated. You say he visited your ex-husband? Interesting. Now that your Rowland is in a coma the investigation is at a standstill."

"Maybe not." Quickly, I told Clay about Sparky and the recent emails. "Sparky will send me instructions about meeting him later this afternoon. I'd like for you to arrange for some officers to be there and to follow me when I go after Maria and Rebecca. The other missing women may be at the same location."

"You should let us handle it."

"I am already involved. Sparky wants to meet me. He didn't call the police."

The class buzzer sounded and a din of voices erupted in the hallway outside.

"I have to go, sheriff. I'll call you once Sparky has sent details this afternoon."

I sat down at my desk and tried to collect my thoughts. My brain pounded. Sam would arrive today and I had not slept in 36 hours.

Third hour, preparing for a biology experiment in the lab, I unlocked the supply cabinet and pulled open one of the drawers. I froze. Red ants teemed over a package in the drawer. The box label read: *potassium chloride.*

I shoved the drawer closed and scurried to the window, trying to calm myself before Trey Woodard and his classmates entered the room. Minutes passed. Students filled the seats. The second buzzer sounded.

"Good morning, Mrs. Aldrich."

Trey spoke behind me.

"Hey, Trey. How are you?" I moved toward my desk without looking at him.

Trey fell into step beside me. The voices in the classroom quieted. I scanned the room, taking in the boys with hair hanging over their eyes, girls with multiple facial piercings and students whose clothing looked slept in. All of them watched Trey and me.

"Everything all right?" Trey asked.

"Noticed I have some friends in the supply cabinet." I nodded at the cabinet and did my best to keep my voice even. "Would you get a jar, please? You can collect them and put them outside."

"Friends? In the cabinet?" Trey bounded to the cabinet and yanked open the drawer. He grabbed the packages of chemicals in the drawer and threw them—and the ants—into the room with a shout. I leapt away.

A few girls squealed as ants landed on them, their desks and their books. One student screamed; some climbed onto the chairs. Others backed toward the walls or the doorway.

Mr. Winters jogged in, breathless.

"What is it?!"

I sucked in another deep breath before I answered. "The room is infested with red ants." My voice shook. I reached up and brushed my hair off my face, imagining ants crawling up my neck and across my scalp.

A few students pushed out the door. More screams erupted and more students rushed past.

"Out in the hall, students. Remain calm." Principal Winters boomed from beside me. He calmly motioned to the fleeing students. "I'll handle this, Jamie. Take a break."

I sat in the teachers' lounge, my hands wrapped around a coffee mug half full of steaming brew. I had never dreamed Trey would pull a stunt like this. Could I ever regain control of that class? I wasn't sure I wanted to try.

How could I have forgotten that potassium chloride was stored in my cabinet? What would the sheriff say if he thought to look there? The chemical's presence would seem unusual except to a scientist: sodium was an essential nutrient for the human body, and the compound served several purposes in experimentation.

I poured another cup of coffee and let the steam swirl up into my face.

"Jamie! What's all the commotion down at your end of the hallway?" another teacher asked as she stepped into the lounge.

I sipped my coffee. "Demon student," I finally said. "Trey Woodard. He planted red ants all around the classroom this morning."

She squinted at me. "Trey Woodard? Are you sure?"

"No one else in that class, or in this school for that matter, would have done such a thing."

The other teacher shook her head. "If he planted ants, he didn't do it this morning or even yesterday after school. He has had study hall before and after school since the semester started. Trey does not goof off in study hall anymore. The kid really does want to get into pre-med at UNM."

I rinsed out my coffee cup. "So you say. Trey must have had someone else plant the ants. He was behind this."

I walked as sedately as I could through the hallways and back to the classroom. Outside my room, students lounged against the walls or sat on the floor. Trey Woodard was not there.

"I wouldn't go back in the room yet, Mrs. Aldrich," one of the girls said. "It's full of pesticide fog."

I sucked in a quick breath and pulled the door open. Nate Simmons and Walt Adams, fellow science teachers, held brooms and dustpans. Working in pairs, they swept up piles of dead ants while the custodians sprayed pesticide along the baseboards. The windows had been opened; the ceiling fans circulated fresh air laced with bug spray.

Winters looked up. "We are about to get them all. Feeling better?"

"Where's Trey?"I asked.

"Don't blame this on Trey. I personally know he was in before-school study hall. Don't you keep your classroom locked? How could he, or any student, have gotten in?"

"You are telling me a staff member did this?" I glanced at the other two teachers.

Winters shrugged. "We'll look into it, but meanwhile, don't assume Trey Woodard had anything to do with it. You have fifteen minutes left to pull your class back together. I'll send the students in."

Grumbling, the students filed in, glancing around the room and under the seats before they slid into the desks.

"Let's use our remaining time to review your homework assignments. We'll have our quiz tomorrow as scheduled."

The students groaned and opened their books. I took my usual spot beside the desk at the front of the room and read the review sheet aloud. I did not touch the desk or open another drawer or cabinet.

Behind my every thought was the memory of ants swarming over the potassium chloride box in the supply cabinet drawer.

CHAPTER 34

When the students left my room for lunch break, my skin still crawled with the imagined sensation of ants. I could not stop myself from peering around the room, watching for red ants scampering between hiding places under desks or cabinets. I fidgeted; nausea tightened my stomach. For the last part of the morning, only half of my mind focused on the classroom and the familiar lessons; the other half seethed with images of red ant mounds.

I tried to focus on Sam. He was crossing the Texas Panhandle on I-40; maybe he had already made it to Amarillo. He would soon be at my house. *Thank God.*

I pulled my purse from the bottom drawer, checked it for ants, then headed for the door. Kate's memorial service was set for 1 o'clock. A student teacher had agreed to cover the hour of class immediately following lunch period.

Principal Winters met me just as I stepped into the hall.

"Jamie, stop assuming every negative thing that happens is Trey Woodard's fault," he said. "That's not the case."

I shrugged, knowing I was not going to win the argument about Trey. Winters was solidly on his side.

"I heard about your stepdaughter. A missing child has to be stressful. Why don't you take this afternoon and tomorrow off? I'll cover your classes."

My mouth dropped open. Winters never offered to take anyone's classes or gave an afternoon off.

He smirked at my expression. "I taught chemistry and biology for years. I think I'm qualified."

Winters and I had never discussed his teaching background or his Masters studies, which had led to an advanced degree in school administration and his current position. For the first time since he had begun work here as the principal, I was curious. *Where had he gotten his degree? When?* I glanced at my watch. There was no time right now.

"A student teacher is covering the next hour while I go to my friend Kate's memorial service," I explained. "But, if you're willing to cover for me here later today and tomorrow, I'm grateful. I *am* in the middle of a family crisis with my stepdaughter."

"Give me your lesson plans and I'll take it from there."

My lesson plans for the next two weeks had been torn from my planner. And tomorrow's quiz was still on my home computer.

"Could I email the information to you tonight? I don't want to be late for the memorial service."

Winters nodded. "Sure. Take the long weekend to do whatever you need to do."

I returned to my desk and scribbled class details for the remaining afternoon sessions on a yellow pad while Al Winters hovered nearby.

Fifteen minutes later, I pulled into the half-filled lot of the funeral home. In the candlelit foyer, I picked up the small memorial pamphlet and walked down the aisle to sit in the front of the chapel. More than three dozen people waited in the pews for the service to begin. I recognized people from the yoga class, as well as neighbors and friends from work.

Would Joshua McDaniel attend the service? I scanned the chapel, but didn't see him.

I slid into the pew to sit beside Kate's editor, Mark Hamm.

"Hi," he said, his mouth turning up in a smile imitation. Emotional pain dulled his eyes.

"Hi." I glanced around the chapel; Kate's parents had not yet been seated.

"I miss her," Hamm whispered.

"Me, too. I still can't believe it happened."

"I keep thinking—," he stopped himself mid-sentence.

I peered at him. "What?"

"The piece she was working on. I never should have allowed her to dig into something so serious."

"You think whoever killed her had something to do with the trafficking ring?"

"Don't you?"

I chewed at my lip as I realized that in my heart I was still afraid her death had something to do with Ben's research request, or me. Potassium chloride was a strong link between the three of us.

Was her editor right?

It felt like a dream as I watched Kate's parents and her sister step to the front row of the chapel. The scent of lilies and mixes floral bouquets hung in the air.

Her sister, Claire, walked to the podium and gave the eulogy for her older sister. A friend from the gym sang an old Carole King song, "You Got a Friend," which had been Kate's official anthem.

Tears cascaded nonstop down my face. Elsewhere in the room, people sniffed. I closed my eyes.

At home after the service, I unlocked the front door and stood in the hallway, listening. The hair on the back of my neck stood up. Except for the low hum of the refrigerator, the house was silent.

I could not get past the unreality I had felt at the memorial service. Even now, inside my home, my dress smelled of lilies. Another smell lingered in the air, masked by the aromatic candle scents. I couldn't identify it. My head buzzed.

A walk would do me good and help clear my thoughts. I

climbed the stairs and changed my clothes, slipping on cropped yoga pants, a t-shirt and walking shoes. I also strapped on the ankle bracelet I had begun to wear this past summer. The stretchy cord held a small pouch where I had stuffed a dollar and a tiny battery operated laser light I sometimes used at night.

The image of the tree in Becca's sketchbook flashed into my head as I clomped back down the stairs. I stopped in the living room where I had left the sketchbook propped beside Ben's photograph of the old tree; its limbs bent low to the ground like the arthritic limbs of a giant.

Comparing the two images, I was more convinced than ever that the photograph and the sketch were of the same ancient tree at Fort Union, only steps away from the old Civil War earthworks fort. Ben and I had spent so many weekends exploring those ruins. For hours, he would walk the star-shaped mound of earth, daydreaming about the past. How many picnic lunches had we spread beneath this giant, out-of-place tree? More than I could count. I was certain that some of those picnics had included Rebecca. But she would have been so young. This was not a sketch drawn from memory.

If what Maria had said was true, Rebecca had only moved into the dorm two days before she went missing. Why would she have taken the time and effort to go to Fort Union during those first few hours?

Once again I wondered, what had Rebecca been doing out at Fort Union? *What was I missing?*

I had promised to email Friday's quiz to the principal. What he didn't know was that I hadn't yet written the test. The week had passed in a blur. Composing a quiz for biology classes had been the last thing on my mind. Somewhere on my computer, I had saved the file of last year's test questions. I could reword the questions, add a few new ones and send the quiz on to Winters.

In the office, as I reached into the file cabinet for the test folder, I clicked into my mailbox to check my unopened emails. First in the list was an email from Sparky. The subject line read, 'The Perk at 4. Blue shirt.' The message part of the email was blank.

Simple enough. Even at 4 p.m., the Perk's regular customers would be enjoying a latté and biscotti, as close to English teatime as residents of the Southwest ever got. I checked my watch. 2:30 now. I had plenty of time to create the quiz, take a quick walk and then make the 4 o'clock appointment. I also had time to contact Sheriff Clay, to let him know my plans. He could post undercover officers at the Perk.

I hit the reply button and typed, 'I'll be there.' I sent the message. Sparky immediately signed off.

Someone rang the front door bell. I hurried down the hall and peered through the peephole.

"Mildred. What's up?" I asked as I pulled the door open.

"What's wrong?" Mildred fired the question back at me.

"Nothing. Had the chance to take the afternoon off. I'm working on tomorrow's quiz. Something bothering you?"

"There was a van here this morning. Thought it might have been a repair company, but there was no company logo or phone number decal on the side panels. Didn't see anyone get out. Seemed strange." Mildred blinked and looked past me toward the kitchen. Her folded arms kept her denim jacket tightly closed.

"When was this?"

"Nine. Parked here a good hour. Did you call a repairman?"

I remembered the odd feeling I'd had when I had returned home. I had passed it off, thinking I was disoriented after the memorial service. "Maybe we ought to have a look around," I suggested.

"Yes. Let's do that," she agreed.

Together we trudged around the house. The plants in the flowerbeds along the house looked late August dry and spindly except for the succulents or native New Mexican species. The soil or grass had not been disturbed.

"Are they still landscaping next door?" I asked. "Maybe the yard crew parked their van on my drive since it's closer to this side of their yard." I peered through the bushes, which formed a boundary between my yard and the yard next door.

"Somebody's done some trimming," Mildred said. Clipped branches lay helter-skelter across the lawn. "Looks like their pay didn't include cleaning up. Must have been that white van I saw earlier. Yard man, no doubt. The Carters are away until Sunday." Mildred kicked at a branch, sending it flying underneath a bush. "For what it's worth, I got out the binoculars and gave that van a good look. Wrote down the license tag number. It's on my steno pad at the house."

I stepped around a huge holly bush and into the neighbor's yard. A white van was now parked on the stretch of driveway that curved behind their house. "Look, there's your van. Someone is working at the Carter's house. There's nothing to worry about, Mildred. But thanks for telling me. You never know."

Mildred frowned at the van. She shrugged. "Certainly. You sure nothing seems out of order inside your place?" We came around the corner of the house and stepped onto the front porch.

"Lights work, phones work, electricity's on. Everything's fine, Mildred." I stepped inside the house. "Thanks, again." I waved goodbye and closed the door.

In the hall, I stopped and listened. Something nagged at me. I peered through the peephole and saw Mildred still standing on the porch. I opened the door. "Mildred?"

"This." She pulled a thick packet of papers from under her jacket and waved them in my face. "I found these. I'd forgotten about them until last night, after I left you the box." Her mouth quivered and a frown fell across her face. She rubbed at her eyes.

I took the printed pages.

"Ben left these with me weeks before he died. I suppose he didn't want speculation to continue after he was gone," Mildred said.

"Speculation? About what?" I took the pages Mildred held out and motioned her back into the house.

"Two years ago, when I told Ben about Jodie, he told me he'd followed all those cases. He seemed to understand how upset I was, knew that losing Jodie had changed my life. Now I see it might have been more. Maybe he knew what had happened to her."

She plodded into the living room and dropped onto the sofa.

I began to read the typed pages. Incredulous, I read fast, then had to pause and reread. I read aloud.

Paul has no conscience. He had none when he kidnapped Maria. I'm sure it was Paul who kidnapped and killed Rita Gainsborough. I shouldn't have provided his alibi. But there was so much at stake. Since then, the stakes have gotten even higher. God, if Jamie knew . . .

I shook my head. "Rita Gainsborough? Who's that, Mildred?" I pressed. "What happened?"

Mildred fingered her chin. "A girl was kidnapped and killed at the University in Albuquerque when Paul and he were studying there. Ben told me he was a person of interest but the police never found enough evidence to charge him. Without real evidence, the police eventually dropped the case. Someone found out about it at the first university where he was employed. They refused to grant tenure. So Ben moved on."

"If charges were never filed, why would he have thought he should keep it a secret from me?"

"Ben also provided an alibi for Paul, who was also another person of interest. The alibi was not legit. Later, I think Paul blackmailed Ben. Everson never worked more than fifty miles from Ben. He stayed close to serve as a constant reminder during Ben's first marriage."

"What was it with these guys?" I asked.

"It was all about Paul. Him and Paul."

"But he hated Paul. He told me as much."

Mildred stood up. "I don't know. A family thing? Maybe they were related."

"Ben's parents are dead. No sibling, aunts or uncles. What did Ben tell you about Paul Everson?"

"He didn't tell me. Not that he didn't have several opportunities. Instead, he left these papers with me." She fidgeted and then looked off over my right shoulder. "I think about all the nights he and I sat out on the porch having a beer. Nip of cold coming off the mountain. He'd get to talking nights like that. Stare up at the moon and talk. I think he'd forget I was there. I was glad to have some company, to have somebody telling me something important. I let him talk. But he never told me this. Just left these papers in my care."

It was hard for me to imagine Mildred being quiet and listening for more than a minute or two. And, it was hard to believe she hadn't looked at these papers in the two years since Ben had left them with her.

"So, did Ben think it was Paul who told his first employer that he had been a person of interest?"

Mildred nodded. "It's all here." She motioned at the pages. Ben said Paul admitted it."

I thumbed through the pages. Another typed note confirmed what Mildred had just told me.

"Ben could have had the evidence reviewed. DNA results are clearing convicted criminals every day," I said. This new information puzzled me. What exactly was the relationship between Ben and Paul?

"Look at the pictures."

Beneath the few hand written pages were old class photographs from Ben's grade school years.

"Look for Ben and Paul, Everson and Aldrich."

Seconds later, I found the answer she knew I would find. I sank onto the sofa. There, in their 6th grade photo, Ben and Paul stood side by side, both listed with the last name of Aldrich. The resemblance between them was clear. Brothers. "Why didn't he tell me?"

Mildred shook her head. "After all that happened between them, he must not have wanted anyone to know. I think Paul was his fraternal twin. The two boys grew up together until their parents died. Ben was adopted by his uncle, Paul by an aunt with the married name of Everson. Their adoptive parents are all dead, too. Because of what had happened when they were young, then the adoption, and all that came later, Ben considered Rebecca the only blood relative he had."

"But she's also Paul's only blood relative."

Mildred nodded and glanced up at the sketch and photo of the tree. "Fort Union?"

I nodded.

"Paul and Ben both served on the Fort Union board. They spent hours researching historical documents and the site. Unique earthworks." Mildred blinked. "Remember the magazine article that cited the kidnapping account of the woman who got away? The women were kept underground."

My throat went dry. "What if it was out there, in the tunnels of the earthworks?" My heart began to hammer. "Maybe Rebecca and Maria are prisoners out there right now."

My cell phone chirped in my pocket. I pulled it out and glanced at the display, an alert from a local news channel.

Body found at Highlands University.

"Mildred, something's happened out at Highlands."

A minute later, I punched the off button on my phone with an extra hard jab. "I can't get anyone at the University to take my call, Mildred. Maybe there's something on TV." I turned on the local cable channel. An uneventful weather map hung on the screen, but headlines scrolled across the bottom.

A body found in a maintenance area of Highlands University has been identified as Joshua McDaniel, a professor. Investigators on the scene indicate McDaniel is a homicide victim. More information to come.

"Joshua McDaniel," Mildred repeated. "Wasn't he Ben's replacement in the history department?"

A shockwave rolled through my body. In my mind, Joshua had been the most likely candidate to have been Honeybone. Now he was dead. I grabbed my cell phone again and punched in Clay's number.

"Sheriff Clay here," he said, sounding irritated.

"I heard Joshua McDaniel has been murdered."

"Damn reporters," he mumbled under his breath, barely loud enough I could hear.

"What happened?"

"Mrs. Aldrich, I am not at liberty to say. His family has been contacted, but we are not releasing details to the public as of yet. We'll do a news conference later, when we know more. Suffice it to say it was foul play and he was found in the garage area where campus maintenance vehicles are stored." He coughed. "It's nothing for you to concern yourself about."

"He was a suspect in Kate Gerard's murder, wasn't he?"

I could imagine the sheriff's mouth in an annoyed frown at my question.

"We didn't find anything linking Joshua McDaniel to Kate Gerard other than meeting Kate for dinner that night in Santa Fe. He claimed she was alive when they parted and we have no evidence to indicate otherwise."

"Do you have other suspects? Maybe Joshua had figured out the truth. The killer got word of it and murdered Joshua. Someone like Paul Everson, for one. Have you looked at his history before he came to Highlands?"

"Of course. Paul Everson's application to Highlands states that his parents are deceased. He listed no siblings or close relatives. His references and his record from the last three places he was employed are sterling."

"And before that?"

The sheriff's sigh exploded into the phone. "Before that, who knows? Would there be any reason you can think of to go back any farther? We're talking 15 years here."

"There's got to be something," I said. "What about during his graduate work?"

"Mrs. Aldrich, if you know something about Everson's past, you had better tell me. I do not have the time or the manpower to check out wild suppositions. We are following all reasonable leads, I assure you."

I slumped into a living room chair.

"Okay, I'll tell you something that you probably need to know. Joshua McDaniel was murdered. The M.E.s initial conclusion is that his heart stopped. An autopsy will tell us why. It could be potassium chloride again."

I disconnected and set my phone on the table. *Who had killed Joshua? And why?*

I watched as Mildred stepped away on the front sidewalk, her shoulders slumped and her usual marching gate slowed to a walk. I still had questions about Ben, still wanted to review the things she had told me. I grasped the doorknob.

Something sharp pricked the skin at my throat.

A hand slammed down over my mouth.

The odor of sweat folded over me. I recognized it as the same scent that had hung faintly in the air when I got home earlier.

"Turn and go back toward the kitchen. Slow."

The low harsh voice, close to my ear, moved with me as I turned and forced my legs to walk.

"Keep moving."

My brain raced through self-defense tips. *Go for the eyes. Go for the crotch. Use the elbows.* Were those wise moves when there was a knife at your throat?

Behind us, the front door opened. "Jamie? I forgot—"

My assailant jerked me around to face Mildred at the front door. A second man stepped up beside us.

"Don't come any closer," he shouted at Mildred. "He'll kill her—or I'll kill you."

The arm tightened around my neck.

Mildred lunged toward us.

The knife whistled as it sped though the air. Mildred fell to the floor.

A chill shook my body. "Mildred?" She laid still, one hand outstretched toward me.

"Don't try anything," the voice growled in my ear. "Don't scream."

The knife pricked the first layer of skin on my throat. His arm cinched tighter around my waist.

My assailant turned and together we moved toward the kitchen. I stumbled. He jerked me upright. We staggered down the hallway.

"We're going out the backdoor and through the hedge," the second man said. "You yell or try to get away and his knife is going to slice and dice." I moved when the man moved, in a macabre dance toward the door.

The knee pushing into the back of my right leg propelled me through the kitchen. "Open the door and go through," the second man said.

I lost my footing as we maneuvered down the steps of the deck. He jerked me to my feet and steered me toward the hedge and the neighbor's back yard. The white van was still parked behind their house. I was sure it was the same van Mildred had seen in my driveway earlier today.

I should not get into the white van.

"Rebecca and Maria will be glad to see you." The second man chuckled.

"Rebecca?" I jerked and the knife jabbed. Blood trickled down my throat.

"I'll take you to them. If we don't get there . . . Well, I doubt they'll survive the night."

The knee bumped me again. We lurched through the bushes.

"Are you Sparky?" My voice quivered. Even as I asked, I felt sure that neither of these men was Sparky.

Was Mildred dead?

"Don't talk. Move."

Under my breath, I cursed the full-grown conifers protecting my backyard from the north wind and providing privacy from neighbors on all sides. The trees blocked vision but not sound.

"Where are we—"

The knife sliced. I gasped.

"Don't talk!" the voice growled.

"Remind me why we are taking her?" The man behind me snarled. He poked my leg with his knee again. "She's too old to bring any money."

"Be quiet, stupid," the second man said from behind us.

Evergreen branches lay scattered across my neighbor's lawn. The back doors of the van, parked nearby, stood ajar.

"Keep moving. Don't give me an excuse to cut you again."

Panic exploded in my mind. *I should not get into this van. I had to get away.*

We reached the open van doors. The second man stepped in front of us and threw open the doors. The arm around my waist released. "Climb in," he grumbled.

Two huge ravens flapped their wings noisily from their perch atop my neighbor's towering cottonwood tree.

Run! They screeched. *Now.*

I jerked to the right.

A hand slapped over my nose and mouth. Reflexively, I sucked in a quick breath.

My head filled with chloroform fumes and the world blackened.

CHAPTER 35

Friday, August 25

I awoke with a start, one arm pinned beneath my body. My hand ached. I stretched my fingers slowly. The sensation of pins and needles poking my flesh traveled through my limb as my nerves returned to life.

My eyes felt scratchy and dry. I opened them, blinked and blinked again.

Blackness stretched in all directions.

Panic closed my throat; I struggled to find air to breathe. I blinked, swallowed and blinked.

Calm down. I turned, searching the darkness for any tiny speck of light. *Nothing.*

I tried to slow my breathing by counting. One . . . two . . . three . . . breathe.

"Hello?" I called. Silence echoed back. My heart thudded in my ears.

The ground felt stone hard beneath me. I touched the floor. I was laying on a thin foam pad barely a half-inch thick and a scratchy blanket.

The damp, cold air bit into my skin. I shivered, and wrapped myself in the meager blanket.

I tried to remember. I saw the wide-open rear doors of the white van in my neighbor's back yard. I remembered wanting to run. If I had tried, I had not made it. They had drugged me.

Hadn't my abductor said he was taking me to Rebecca and Maria?

"Rebecca? Maria?" The darkness absorbed their names.

I reached out, feeling for walls, furniture, anything. I leaned as far as I could to the right and then to the left, letting my fingers skim the ground. My fingertips touched only the hard uneven earth floor. Gritty dirt packed into my fingernails.

Panic climbed up my throat, and the lingering scent of chloroform sickened me.

I rose to my knees, willing the panic to go back to my stomach and stay there. It didn't. I vomited into the blackness. When there was nothing left to vomit, I pulled my knees to my chest and rolled myself into a ball.

Sometime later, I crawled off the pad and onto the dirt floor. A few feet further on, my head butted a wall. I ran my hands over the rough surface, scratched at it with my nails, then pressed my nose against it and smelled stone.

I turned around and crawled back to the pad and across it, straight ahead. When I found another wall within a few feet, I scuttled back to the pad and turned left, crawling forward until I found the third wall. I scrambled back to the pad again.

Only one wall remained. Would I find a door? *What good would it do to find the door if I was locked in, surrounded by unbearable, impenetrable blackness?*

My breath caught. I wanted to scream.

Fight the panic.

I squeezed my eyes shut, realizing I could not fight the darkness. It just was.

In the silence of the earth room, my heart pounded.

Find a way to get out.

I rubbed my cold hands along my thighs, feeling the warm knit material of my yoga pants. My mind sparked. I wiggled my toes. I still had on my walking shoes and the ankle 'safety' bracelet. Its small pouch was still tucked down into one shoe. Inside was the laser light.

My cold fingers struggled with the snap, opened the pouch, then closed around the little light Matt had given me as a stocking stuffer last Christmas. My fingers trembled. I pinched the round disk.

The tiny light blazed in the darkness, illuminating a hazy six-inch circle. I pointed the beam and let it crisscross the room. The light was barely strong enough to reach the four walls from my little pad in the center of the cell. I stood up and stepped toward the one wall I had not yet touched.

Pointing the light midway up the wall, I moved the beam across it slowly, keeping my finger tightly pressed against the button. There had to be a way in and a way out. But it wasn't here.

I moved the beam from the top to the bottom of the second wall, walking closer; then, I stepped along the wall, scanning the surface using the light. No door.

At the next corner I released the button and stood in the darkness, listening.

No sound. No light.

The darkness enveloped me. Panic constricted my throat. I squeezed the laser light on to banish the blackness.

How long would the tiny battery last?

I thought about the fruit cellar, remembering my brief imprisonment at the homestead in Osage County last spring. I had thought I had banished my fear of small spaces and the dark, but now that fear roared in my belly every bit as strong as before.

I turned off the light. I breathed. I calmed myself.

My first sweep of the next wall section with the light showed a wooden frame and a square paneled opening halfway up the wall. I leaped the few steps across the little cell and shoved at the door. It didn't budge.

Something scratched behind the panel. I scrambled back to the pad, pulled the blanket over me and curled up on my side as a slice of light cut across the small room and fell onto my face. I played 'possum until, with a scrape, the door closed and the light disappeared.

My heart stuttered. I forced myself to breathe deeply, steadily. An earthy damp smell filled my head. I was not ready to confront my abductor. First, I needed a plan. False lights sparked on the backs of my eyelids.

I blinked repeatedly, struggling with dry eyes and sticking contact lenses. The false lights pulsed. I pressed on the laser light and let the little circle run over the floor of my prison to another wall. I took a step closer. The light illuminated a black square. An airshaft?

The opening was above eye level and little more than six inches across. I turned my ear to the opening and listened. *Was that a sound?* Something. Or someone. I could almost make out words. A voice? Someone sobbing?

A hard shiver raced down my back. Even if I could enlarge the shaft, the thought of pushing myself into and through that little tunnel turned me to jelly.

It was my worst nightmare. A small, dark place. A place to get stuck. A place to find things, like human bones. I shuddered.

I backed across the little room and onto the thin pad.

The voice did not belong to Maria or Rebecca. My mind was playing tricks. There was no one else down here. Only me and whoever had brought me here.

I didn't know what day it was or what time of day. Was it still Thursday?

My mind leaped to Sam. He had been getting close to Las Vegas when the two men abducted me. Where was he now? *Was he searching for me?*

Had he found Mildred? *Was Mildred dead?* A mental snapshot of her crumpled body in front of the front door crowded into my thoughts and took over.

I wrapped my arms around my knees and swayed. Little fireflies flitted on the back of my retina. The hazy outline of the air duct, the last thing I had seen with the laser light, wavered behind the fireflies.

I shivered and pulled the scratchy blanket closer.

Faintly, in the distance, came the sound of a woman weeping.

"Maria?" I asked the darkness. "Becca?"

Even if it was one of them, I could not reach them through that tiny passage. My dry throat ached and my swollen tongue clogged my throat. The sickening scent of chloroform lingered in my nostrils and my stomach roiled again.

My head and eyes throbbed.

The person who had brought me here would come back and bring water and food. *Wouldn't they?*

Sometime later, when the door swung open again, I did not play 'possum. I sat, arms clasped around my legs, the blanket over my shoulders. I had tucked the laser light back into the pouch on my ankle bracelet. I squinted at the light from the open doorway and the shadowed figure who peeked in.

"You're awake," a soft voice whispered. "Hungry? Thirsty?"

I rested my head on my crossed arms.

"Not nearly thirsty or hungry enough, I guess," the whispery voice snarled.

The door creaked shut and the light was gone, leaving me once again in total blackness.

My body shook. That was it then. No compassion, no kindness from my abductor. The cracks in my dry lips stung and my raw throat throbbed. How could they have left me without water?

As easily as they had locked me into the blackness. Not good.

You are on your own. Do something, Jamie.

I tossed off the blanket and reached for my laser light. The little beam guided me around the perimeter of the dirt room. Earth scent filled my head. Where was I?

I trudged around the cell once and then again. With the light on, my head cleared. The panic diminished.

Think.

My mind clicked.

A few days ago I'd read through the articles and papers from Ben's office. One article had discussed the earthwork tunnels used in forts of the Civil War. Mostly used to store munitions or for shelter during sieges, the tunnels were unique to those times. No one had ever mentioned tunnels at Fort Union.

Maybe Ben had never mentioned underground tunnels in association with the earthwork fort because he—and the board —did not want the public to know they existed. After nearly one hundred and fifty years it seemed unlikely the tunnels were safe or even partially usable. That is, unless someone had been repairing and using them.

Paul?

I stopped in front of the small airshaft and listened. The stillness was absolute. I shuffled along the wall to the doorway. Slowly, I ran my hand around the doorframe, feeling for gaps in the stone or the sandy grout which sealed the wall together. How long would it take to dig an opening large enough to crawl through? Certainly longer than the time it would take me to die of thirst if my captor did not come back.

I clicked off the light and crawled back to the pad. No need to waste the light while I came up with a plan.

Rebecca and Maria had to be here in this same earth prison. Why else would they have brought me here?

I stood and made a slow circle, swinging the tiny spot of light around the room again, this time at the base of the walls. In the corner farthest from the door, the light illuminated another dark square.

This opening was bigger and framed in wood like the other. I shone the light inside. Wood beams reinforced the ceiling and walls. This tunnel looked almost big enough for me to squeeze through.

Where would it lead?

I listened. Silence.

Cool air vibrated a loose strand of hair on my forehead.

I could either go through the narrow passage or sit here and leave my fate up to the person who had abducted me. He had not shown me any kindness. Did he intend to rape and murder me?

One of my abductors had said, 'She's too old to bring any money.'

A terrifying thought filled my head. Was this a holding space for the human trafficking ring Kate had been investigating? Were there other cells down here like this one containing not just Becca and Maria but other women to be sold?

With a gulp, I slowed my breathing, hoping to still the knocking of my heart against my ribs. I squatted on the hard earth in front of the passageway.

When my children were young, I had played games in the dark with them. They would turn out the lamps and creep around the room, trying to find me. Our games of blackout hide and seek never failed to cause the hair to stand up on the back of my neck. Why should this feel any different?

I slid my body, arms first, into the tunnel. As my shoulders touched the rough walls, I swallowed a lump of fear.

Using my toes, I pushed myself farther in, at the same time pulling myself with my forearms. *Push. Pull.*

I moved a few inches and then a few more. Other memories of darkness crowded into my mind. Childhood tunnel memories. Black eternity. My lifelong claustrophobia festered in my brain, alive, well and strong.

Panic exploded. I shoved backwards with my toes and, at the same time, pushed backward with my forearms. I had to go back to the cell, back to the known darkness. I could not do this. The tunnel was too small, too tight.

A muscle cramp stabbed my foot and skewered up the bones in my leg. I gritted my teeth. My whole body tensed. A spasm ripped across my shoulder muscles, arching across my back.

Oh my God. I was going to die here, right here, in this black tunnel beneath the fort.

Control it. Some tiny bit of sensibility in my mind whispered to me.

Control it. I slowed my breathing.

Relax. I thought of yoga. I thought of Kate. She had died at the hands of a killer. Without me to find that killer, her death was meaningless. I had to survive. I did not know where I was crawling to, or how many more yards down this tunnel I had to go. It was possible the tunnel might close up right in front of me. It was also possible the tunnel would collapse. Who knew how old this structure was or how sturdy? A dusting of earth snowed down on my face from the tunnel ceiling.

The little earth room I had left now seemed a safe haven. I tried again to move backwards. My other foot cramped. Once again, panic exploded in my brain. My chest heaved in silent sobs.

What about Rebecca? The young woman was alone and scared. I had to find her for Ben if I could, or die trying. *"Unforgettable . . . that's what you are . . ."* The tune played in my mind.

I didn't want to die. I had to keep trying for Ben. And, a few miles away, Sam was waiting for me. I wanted to see him again. I did not want to die here where no one might ever find me.

I wanted to see Alison get married.

I wanted to see Matt's children.

I wanted to see the sky and smell the desert rain in the wind.

Inch by inch I pulled myself forward. The gritty tunnel floor shredded the skin on my forearms.

Push, push. I clenched my teeth. The sandy floor dug deeper into the wounds on my arms and the heels of my hands.

My toes and my elbows shoved me forward through the narrow space. My shoulders scraped the tunnel walls.

The muscles in my arms, back and legs ached.

The nerve endings in my scoured arms screamed.

If mice or rats lived in the tunnel, they had scampered on ahead of me. Who knew what I might be scooting over? Pill bugs, worms, roaches, beetles? Excrement from vermin?

So far, no spider webs. I shuddered. Spiders were the least of my worries.

Was the tunnel getting narrower? My shoulders hardly fit. They ached, bruised by contact with the tunnel walls.

I drove myself on.

No, I told myself, *I won't get stuck.*

No, the tunnel isn't closing in.

I could not go back. I had to go forward, inch by inch, by inch.

What if my captor had blocked the passage ahead, and had snuck into the cell to block it behind me as well?

What if he had anticipated I would crawl through the passage and intended for me to entomb myself here alone in the dark?

Panic exploded again. I stopped. Counted, breathed.

I was in the dark with Alison and Matt, crawling around the living room.

My lungs labored for air. My breath grew ragged. My heart pounded.

The nerves in the heels of my hands and forearms shrieked. My back muscles clenched. My leg muscles cramped.

Oh, God. I can't do this!

I sobbed, gasped as I forced myself forward with forearms raw and throbbing, muscles trembling. I pushed with aching toes. My mind raced. Fear clogged my throat.

I can't do it. I'm going to die!

The four sides of the tunnel pressed in, too close, too tight. I inched forward, shoulders scraping.

I pushed with my toes. I pulled with my forearms. My body didn't budge. I laid my head on the earthen floor of the tunnel.

I'm stuck.

I'm going to die here.

I love you, Sam.

I squeezed my eyes tightly closed.

Something inside my body did not want to give up. My brain worked. *I was not in a tunnel, not under the ground, not going to die...* The thoughts hammered.

Something pricked at my consciousness. I lifted my head.

There it was again. A voice?

Once more, I struggled to pull myself forward with my arms and push myself with my toes.

I moved a centimeter.

I listened.

A voice chanted.

"Madre de Dios. . ." The voice pleaded and then quieted.

I scraped another centimeter forward through the rough earth tunnel.

Another centimeter. *Another.*

The voice echoed. When it stopped, I stopped. I listened.

The voice chanted.

I squirmed my way down the tunnel to gain a few more inches of bleeding, raw pain.

The voice stopped.

"Who is there?" A shaking voice whispered in the darkness.

CHAPTER 36

"Maria?"

"Eeek!" A female voice yelped. "I go crazy!" She moaned.

I scrambled another few inches through the tunnel, ignoring the screaming muscles in my arms and back and toes, trembling from exhaustion. I sucked in damp, stale air laced with musk and sweat. Abruptly, the pressure of the confining tunnel against my arms and upper back ended. I pulled myself into a seated position.

I gulped air and peered into the darkness. "Maria, it's me."

The woman's moan ended with a gasp.

I flicked on the little laser light. The tunnel had opened into a cell like the one I had just left. Maria huddled on a pad, her arms wrapped around herself, her hair a wild mass of black curls circling her head.

She stared at me, eyes huge. "Jamie? It is you?" Maria sat frozen.

"Yes, it's me."

Maria threw herself at me, wrapping her arms tightly around my shoulders. "Oh, Jamie, oh." She patted my head, my back and my arms, and then hugged me tight. "How you find me? How you get here? Madre de Dios, gracias." She stroked my hair and then held me at arm's length. "How you get in? We get out that way?" She pointed toward the dark corner where I had crawled in, her eyebrows puckered in a question.

"There's another cell at the end of that tunnel and another locked door."

"You crawled through there to find me? How brave. But how do we get out?"

"I don't know. How did you get here? Who brought you?" My whole body throbbed. I took in the thicker pad on the floor, the pillow and the pile of blankets. Maria had been treated slightly better than I had.

She ducked her head and covered her face with her hands. "I thought he was taking me to Rebecca. He said he was. But I have not seen her. I fear she is dead," Maria wailed.

"Shhh. Did Paul bring you here?"

Maria dropped her hands and looked at me. "Paul told me Becca was here and he would take me to her. I took the chance. I have been here in the dark ever since. What can we do?"

"Paul left you here alone in the dark?"

Maria shook her head frantically. "No, no." Something thudded outside the locked door. Maria flinched. "He will come back soon. What do we do?"

"Did he touch you, hurt you?"

Maria shrugged. "Not really. He sits. He brings food, light, a clean pot. He asks the same question again and again. I give my same answer. He goes. I think he will keep me in here forever until I give the answer he wants."

"What question? What answer does he want?"

"That he is Rebecca's father. That I will marry him." Maria's eyes closed and her chin dropped.

Rebecca's father?

I shone the flashlight around the little cell. The beam fell on a tray of dishes beside the pad. I swung the light toward the far corner where it revealed a lidded clay pot.

A scraping noise sounded from the other side of the door and light shone through a thin crack below it.

I turned off the flashlight and jumped to the far dark corner as the door creaked inward.

"Maria? Are you in here?" Paul Everson stepped down into the room holding a camp lantern. I reached down and grabbed the handles of the crockery chamber pot. Using what little strength I had left in my quivering arms, I hefted the pot toward Paul. It flew through the air, an unlikely missile. The lid clunked to the ground but the pot glanced off the side of his head.

He dropped the battery-powered lantern. "What the..."

I lunged to grab the crock again, lifted it and then smashed it down on his head. He crumpled.

"Take the lamp," I shouted to Maria. "Go!"

Maria grabbed the lantern and climbed through the doorway. She looked back at Paul Everson, who lay still on the cell's dirt floor. "But . . ."

I shoved her through the doorway of the cell, swung the door shut and pushed the huge bolt lock closed.

"Jamie, I tell you--," Maria began.

"We have to find Rebecca." I ignored the throbbing in my back, my feet and my hands.

Was Rebecca dead? Surely if Paul Everson thought Rebecca was his daughter, he would not have killed her. He would not have sold her into the sex trafficking world, either.

The lantern light revealed a curving tunnel stretching off in both directions.

We scurried down the tunnel to the left. At the first wooden door, I shoved the bolted lock open. A blanket lay on the pallet in the center of the empty cell. "I think this is where I was."

I turned away from my prison and continued down the narrow passageway. Maria held the light aloft. At the next cell, the door stood open. We peered inside. Although the cell was empty, it looked as if someone had been there recently. A blanket lay crumpled on the pad and a food tray with a few crumbs still on it rested on the floor near the door.

Once again, we turned down the hallway. Another doorway, another empty cell. Then abruptly the corridor ended in a pile of rubble.

"Back the other way." My heart raced. Pain pounded throughout my body.

Was Rebecca alive? Was she here?

We ran past the three open doors. A few yards farther down the hallway from Maria's cell, another door stood slightly ajar. I shoved it open. The room was empty except for the sleeping pad, a rumpled blanket and a tray for food.

Maria and I hurried on. In the light of the lantern, her face looked gray with despair. At the end of the passageway, Maria's light cast shadows on a stairway leading up. The steps carved into the earth had been capped with warped wooden planks. A final door in the wall a few feet before we reached the stairway was bolted shut.

Together, Maria and I shoved the bolt to one side and threw the door wide. A camp lantern sat on a wooden table, casting light throughout the cell. A mound of blankets covered a small cot in the corner. Two rocking chairs sat side by side in the center of the room. Rebecca, wrapped in a multi-colored afghan, huddled in one of them.

"Becca!" Maria shrieked. She tumbled over the threshold and into the room crying with joy.

Rebecca's eyes closed. She clutched at her mother.

"It's all right, baby. It is all right. Jamie saved us, my Becca." Maria patted her daughter and stroked her hair.

Rebecca smiled weakly. Her eyes, dark brown like Ben's, shown bright with tears.

I rushed down into the room and hugged her. "We need to hurry. Paul had at least one helper. We must be careful."

"Paul?" Maria questioned. "I need to tell you, Jamie—"

Rebecca frowned.

I grabbed Maria and Rebecca and nudged them toward the door. "Shhh. Come on. They'll be time later to talk."

I searched the room for something to use as a weapon. The cot, the chairs, a chamber pot, the lantern. Nothing else. I picked up the lantern and stepped out into the narrow passage where Maria and Rebecca waited.

The stairway up was the only way out.

"Follow me, close," I whispered.

I started up the earthen steps. Seconds later, our climb ended in another corridor. This one had a ceiling of rough-hewn beams and cell doors with barred windows. Dust and the rancid scent of sweat hung in the musty air. Another stairway led up eight feet to a wooden trapdoor.

I climbed the stairs and shoved at the trapdoor. The wooden slab creaked and then swung up.

I crawled over the last step into a sparsely furnished room and stopped. Behind me, Maria and Becca scrambled up the ladder and into the room. We were in the Officer's Quarters, one of the restored buildings of the fort.

"This way," I whispered, grabbing Rebecca's hand. The three of us crept through the small restored house. At the front door, I peeked out onto the wide gravel promenade and got my bearings. Bright starlight and a dim quarter moon lit the way. The three of us limped past the ruined block of buildings toward the dark square of the visitor's center.

"We're going to be okay," I whispered over my shoulder to Maria and Rebecca. Rebecca hung onto her mother, her face pale, her eyes huge and dark. Maria stumbled on the gravel walkway.

"I try telling you, Jamie," Maria scolded as she hurried to keep up. "Paul brought me here to find Becca. He did not lock me up. Someone else took me after we got here. I not see Paul again until now, after you came to my cell."

I scanned the shadows of the ruined fort and then looked back at Becca as the three of us scurried on. What was Maria saying? My mind spun. *Paul did not lock her up?*

Rebecca tripped and then righted herself. I grabbed her arm to steady her.

"You mean Paul handed you over to someone else when you got here?" I asked.

Maria shook her head. "No. No. Paul and I walk in here when it was black night. Someone grabbed me, pulled me down, covered my head. I hear fight. That's all I remember. I end up in that little room. Alone. No Paul."

"If it wasn't Paul who put you there, who was it?"

Maria began to sob. "I'm sorry. It's all my fault."

A half block away, faint lights shown through the rear windows of the visitor center.

Just a few more steps to the phone in Park Superintendent Owen Mabry's office. Then we would be safe.

"Who locked you in the cell?" I asked as we reached the visitor center's door. The padlock hung open on the thick security chain locking the handle of the door. I pulled the handle and the door opened. Inside, dim display lights reflected off the waxed wood floor and cast an eerie glow throughout the large room.

I hurried across the space to Mabry's office. The door opened a crack when I pushed against it, but then refused to move further. I peered through the crack and saw Owen Mabry, his head lying in a pool of blood.

"Jamie! Maria! Rebecca! Welcome!" a voice boomed from the other side of the exhibit room.

I knew that voice.

"I didn't expect you all here together but it's just as well." Principal Al Winters stood in the center of the exhibit hall. He smoothed his hair across his bald spot.

"Al?" My eyes had to be playing tricks. Another man swaggered from the shadowy library and into the exhibit room.

"And this is my cousin, Craig Sanford, but then, you two have already met."

I looked from one man to the other. *Al Winters. Craig Sanford. Cousins?* I remembered the photo from the yearbook, the one where Craig sat with Paul behind Ben and Maria in the stadium bleachers. It could have been a much younger Al Winters sitting on the other side of Craig.

Sanford snickered. "Hey, Jamie. You don't look so good. You look like you have been rolling in the dirt, scraping through a tunnel or something. Not a good look for you." He walked closer, leering at me.

I had heard this voice before, in my home, in my kitchen. He had pressed up behind me, his knee pushing me out of the house and into the white van.

Winters rubbed the top of his head again and rocked on his toes. "Gosh, I hate this. You worked so hard to get out of that cell. You know I can't let you go, Jamie. I have my reputation to consider, and as much as I like you, really like you..." he shook his head. "Not gonna happen. Now Maria, she knows how to keep a promise. She has kept her mouth shut for years. I can trust her. And her daughter... Well, she won't say anything against me. She knows I love her and after all, I am her father." He glanced at Maria, sneered at his cousin, and then took a step toward me.

Sanford moved to Rebecca and patted her bottom. Maria shrieked and charged at him.

I gathered what energy I still had and focused it on the muscles in my legs. I leaped toward Al Winters. He side-stepped, teetered and slipped. On his way down, he grabbed the uniformed Union soldier mannequin and clutched the saber hanging from the mannequin's belt. I kicked his hand and the sword clattered to the floor as the mannequin fell. I kicked again, this time aiming for Winters' crotch. He doubled over and fell with a gasp.

I whirled. Maria and Rebecca had Sanford pinned to the floor. Maria, swearing in Spanish, battered his head with one of her shoes; Rebecca sat on the man's lower legs.

As Winters writhed on the floor, I ran to the desk phone and punched in 9-1-1. "Need the sheriff at Ft. Union Visitor Center. There has been an assault. Send an ambulance."

I hung up the phone and turned back to the room.

Huffing, Winters heaved himself up to his knees. He glanced into the dark exhibit room and sighed.

Someone marched through the shadows and into the room.

I blinked to clear my head.

Mildred was dead, wasn't she?

The woman stared at me through her thick lenses and smiled. "Can't tell you how much I didn't want this to happen, Jamie. If you had left things alone . . . That would have made it so much easier," Mildred said.

"What?" I stuttered.

Winters lifted himself to his feet.

"I'll handle this from here on out, son. You've made a mess of things today." She glared at him first and then grinned at me.

"Let...me...up." Sanford shoved Rebecca off his legs and swatted Maria away. "Sluts. Like all the rest." He leered at Rebecca and reached to caress her cheek with his finger. Maria slapped him. He backhanded her to the floor.

Mildred glared at Sanford. "Stop, Craig. Can you control yourself for one minute? You are no exemplar specimen of manhood yourself, nephew. Mr. Honeybone." She rolled her eyes.

"So, what are we going to do with them?" Sanford asked, jerking his head to indicate the three of us.

"The same thing we did with all the others," Mildred said. "Sell them. Our connection won't mind three more."

Her eyes roved over Maria, then Rebecca and me.

"Two of them are a little used. And the third ... We'll get a good price for her. When is the transport due?"

Sanford looked at his watch. "Twenty minutes."

"You can't sell my daughter, mother," Winters whined. "She's your granddaughter, after all."

"*If* she is your daughter. I have my doubts." Mildred stepped toward a front window and peered outside. "Looks clear so far. No white knights in sight. And none expected." She smiled at me. "Gives me a moment of time to clear up some things, Jamie." She laughed. "I know I don't *have* to explain. However, I would feel better ending it this way."

"Ben loved you. Trusted you," I said. The muscles in my

legs shook beneath me. *How could Mildred have been a part of this?*

"Oh, appearances aren't always what they seem. Ben had thrown himself into research. Wanted to help find out what happened to my 'daughter.' Investigated twenty years of 'disappearances' in the region. He was too good at the research. Got your friend Kate involved. Then he discovered I did not have a daughter. I had a son, Albert." Her eyes shifted to Winters. She spat onto the floor. "A stupid son."

Al stiffened.

"What did you do, Mildred?" I asked. I was horrified by the enormity of her crimes.

"I did what any good friend would have done. Al brought me some potassium chloride from your biology lab. I slipped it to Ben. Enough of the endless suffering."

I lunged for the saber on the floor, grabbed it and rolled back to my feet. The nerves in my abraded arms shrieked and the sword quivered.

"Don't move again, Al," I pulled the sheath off the sword and aimed the point at Al's midsection. "Don't come any closer Mildred. I'm not afraid to use this."

"But that would mean you assume that I care." Mildred rushed toward me. I lifted the sword. I was not expecting the hilt of the sword to jam into my stomach as Mildred ran full on into the blade. Eyes open, she slipped off the blade and to the floor. I gasped for breath.

"Mother?" Shock evident in his wide eyes, Al bent over Mildred. His hands pressed into the gaping, bleeding wound. "Don't die, Mother."

Mildred's blank eyes stared up at the ceiling.

Cries of pain roared behind me. Maria cursed. The outside door flew open and Paul Everson rushed into the room. "Maria? Darling?" He rushed across the room and threw a hard punch at Sanford's jaw. Sanford crashed to the floor.

I kept my eyes on Winters. With Paul's help, I had no doubt Maria and Rebecca could take care of Sanford.

Sirens sounded outside. Winters groaned.

The door crashed open again and this time a swarm of police officers rushed in.

Sam.

He dashed across the room, his handsome face blanched white.

My body shook as he took the bloody sword and circled his other arm around me in a half-hug.

Sam planted a kiss on my cheek and brushed my hair from my eyes. Both of us watched Al Winters. The man crouched beside his mother, still trying to staunch the flow of blood from her gaping stomach wound.

Another uniformed man stomped across the room, glanced at me, and then at the old woman who had been my neighbor.

His look moved to Maria, Rebecca and Paul who towered over an unconscious Craig Sanford. "Here's Sanford, he's a wanted felon, and you . . .?" He squinted at the man crouched beside Mildred. "Al Winters? The high school principal?"

Outside, sirens shrilled as more law enforcement officials arrived.

I peered down at Al Winters. His eyes shifted from his mother's still body up to me.

"When I came here, two and a half years ago, Ben didn't recognize me. And Paul wasn't about to tell him who I was." He closed his eyes and stiffened. When his eyes opened again, they glistened with tears. "I'm far from being a nobody. It took Trey Woodard to finally get you to notice I was an effective principal, a real human being." Al Winters glared.

I scooted closer to Sam; he tightened his grip around my waist.

"You and your mother killed Ben." My voice broke.

"You're like that slut Kate," Al Winters continued. "She wouldn't let Craig get into the same hot springs. So, he fixed her a drink. Added something extra. We already knew how well potassium chloride worked." He grinned.

I shuddered; the room tilted. My stomach twisted. "Craig killed Kate and you helped him do it." I stared into snakelike eyes, unremorseful and uncaring. "And the girls at the University. You kidnapped them and sold them?"

"That was Craig's deal. He was into the girls, the computer foreplay, the maneuvering. He has always liked the University girls. And they liked his nerdy computer persona. He grabbed them, sold them to the traffickers and pocketed a nice bit of cash. But while they were under our care out here, he never hurt them, I made sure of that."

Sanford groaned. Maria slammed her foot into his stomach. Two deputies jerked Sanford to his feet and handcuffed his wrists behind him.

Deputy Sheriff Steve Ross led Al Winters and Craig Sanford out of the visitor's center to the waiting police cars. The medical examiners assistants loaded Mildred Bodke's body bag onto a gurney.

Paul Everson drained the glass of water he had just filled in the museum's kitchen sink.

"I knew Winters was shady," Paul said. "Knew it ever since high school. Neither Ben nor I put it all together. We were too busy blaming each other, thinking the other one was responsible for what had happened to Rita, the woman who was Al Winters' first kidnap victim."

He lowered his head and closed his eyes. When he spoke again, he kept his eyes closed.

"Rita had been dating me at the time, even though I had a big crush on Maria. Ben thought I freaked when Maria chose him over me. And I thought he'd been behind the kidnapping, that it had been a payback to me for being the one who made love to Maria first." He paused and wiped one hand over his face and chin. "There wasn't much trust between us. Too many things had happened for us to be friends. We were competitors, almost enemies."

"I know that you recommended Craig Sanford for the job at Highlands. Why?"

"Yes, I vouched for Sanford. He was a hometown boy. I didn't know he and his cousin Al were in it together. Had been ever since Rita."

Sam laid his arm across my shoulders; I stepped closer. "Al Winters helped Mildred kill Ben; and Sanford murdered Kate," I said. "Joshua must have figured out Craig Sanford was Honeybone. Rob's investigation was headed in the same direction but they ran him down before he could turn in his report."

Paul's look met mine. I saw traces of sorrow and regret but something else, too.

"I still don't understand what happened between you, Ben and Maria."

"Foolishness is all it was. Immature foolishness." He straightened and stared into space. "Ben and I were so intent on besting each other we didn't see there was someone else around who was truly dangerous. If I had not seen Al out here last week, sneaking back to the parking lot from the old earthworks, I never would have put it all together. Then I never would have brought Maria here. And you wouldn't have been kidnapped." His body sagged.

"But Rebecca might not have been found," Sam said. He grabbed my hand and squeezed my fingers.

Warmth surged through me. I stared at Paul, searching for any resemblance to Ben. I found it in the line of his jaw, the shape of his ears and his cheekbones. One question remained.

"What about Rebecca? Why does Al think she's his daughter?"

"Ask Maria. Al was obsessed with her and Maria used him more than once when things were rocky with Ben, as they often were." Paul shrugged. "After Rebecca was born, she ended the relationship with Al for good. Rebecca is Ben's daughter."

"He raised her, he loved her," I said. "It never would have mattered to Ben."

Maria stepped over to stand beside Paul. Tenderly, she touched his forehead, where a purple bruise swelled. "Are you okay, my Sparky?" she asked. Paul's eyes softened as he looked at her.

Sam drove the truck up the driveway and popped the parking brake as the vehicle slowed. I winced as I scooted across the bench seat to the door. It would be a while before the pain of that agonizing crawl through the tunnel eased.

My front door flew open. Matt, Alison and Sam's basset hound, Queenie, rushed down the steps. I closed my eyes and savored their embraces.

Somewhere, I knew that Ben was feeling the love, too. His family finally knew the truth.

Human Trafficking in the United States

Human Trafficking (a.k.a. slavery) is and has been an institution throughout the world for most of human history.

Information on the current state of the problem can be found on several websites, including those for the National Center for Victims of Crime (www.victimsofcrime.org) and the U.S. Department of State's Bureau of Justice Statistics (www.bjs.gov.) Other sites containing information include the International Justice Mission (www.ijm.org/), and the UNICEF Report on the State of the World's Children (www.unicef.org/sowc/.) Operation Underground Railroad (https://www.ourrescue.org) is one program which provides assistance for children who have been enslaved.

Human traffickers kidnap victims for use in several types of businesses. At the time of *Ant Dens: A Suspense Novel* publication, the breakdown is:

- Prostitution and Sex Services: 46%
- Domestic Service: 27%
- Agriculture: 10%
- Sweat shops: 5%
- Restaurant and hotel services: 5%
- Other: 8%.

Within the Prostitution and Sex Services category, 94% are

female. 83% of those who are sex-trafficked in the U.S. are U.S. citizens. Racially, the statistics show the following:

- 40.4% are black
- 25.6% are white
- 23.9 % are Hispanic.

Within the Labor categories (54% of trafficking), here's the breakdown: 66% are female, 34% are male. Racially, the statistics show the following:

- 55.7% are Hispanic
- 14.8% are Asian
- 9.8% are black
- 1.6% are white
- 18% are other.

Other nations besides the United States whose citizens are often grabbed by traffickers are from the following areas: Malaysia, South America, Asia, China, India, Eastern Europe and Russia.

About the Setting

Although I am a native Oklahoman, I love our neighboring state of New Mexico. Just like in Oklahoma, there is much to explore. The Ant Dens story gave me an opportunity to introduce readers to two places they may have never heard of: Las Vegas, New Mexico and nearby Fort Union National Monument.

Las Vegas, New Mexico—Las Vegas was established in 1835 and was laid out in the traditional Spanish Colonial style with a central plaza surrounded by buildings which could serve as fortifications in case of attack. Las Vegas soon prospered as a stop on the Santa Fe Trail. In 1846, Stephen W. Kearney delivered an address at the Plaza of Las Vegas claiming New Mexico for the United States.

The Atchison, Topeka and Santa Fe railroad reached the town in 1880 and a station and related development was established one mile east of the Plaza. Las Vegas boomed during this railroad era and became one of the largest cities in the American Southwest. Turn-of-the-century Las Vegas featured an electric street railway, an Opera House, a Carnegie library, a major Harvey House, (The Hotel Castañeda) and a university (now New Mexico Highlands University.)

The Las Vegas Carnegie Library, built in 1904, is the only surviving Carnegie Library in New Mexico. Its Neo-Classical Revival architecture resembles Thomas Jefferson's Monticello.

The Museum & Rough Rider Memorial on Grand Avenue was dedicated in 1940, the first such museum established by the decision of Theodore Roosevelt's Rough Rider's regiment (the first Volunteer Cavalry Regiment of the Spanish-American War.) The group named Las Vegas their official reunion home and held their first reunion in Las Vegas in the Plaza Hotel, June 1899.

Las Vegas has over 900 historic structures listed on the National Register of Historic Places. Many notable homes and buildings were built in the 1890s during the town's heyday. The town features six separate historic districts including: the Bridge Street Historic District, Old Town Residential District, Railroad Avenue Historic District, Lincoln Park Historic District, Library Park Historic District and Douglas-Sixth Street Historic District.

Here a sampling of films partially or entirely shot in the town of Las Vegas (who knew?):

- The 1994 film Wyatt Earp, with Kevin Costner

- Several scenes in the 1998 film *John Carpenter's Vampires* were filmed on the plaza

- *The Hi-Lo Country* (1998) and *All the Pretty Horses* (2000)

- The 2001 documentary *Freedom Downtime*

- The 2007 film *Wild Hogs* starring John Travolta

- The 2007 Coen brothers' *No Country for Old Men*

- The 2008 film *Beer for My Horses* starring Toby Keith and Rodney Carrington

- The 2009 thriller *Not Forgotten*

- The 2010 film *Due Date* starring Robert Downey Jr. and Zach Galifinakis

- Scenes for the 2011 film *Paul* starring Simon Pegg and Nick Frost with Kristen Wiig, Jason Bateman, Bill Hader, Seth Rogan, Joe Lo Truglio and Sigourney Weaver

- The 2012 A&E TV Series *Longmire* starring Robert Taylor and Katee Sackhoff (subsequent seasons have filmed in and around the town)

Visit the Las Vegas, New Mexico's official website to learn more about this historic city and this beautiful region of New Mexico. www.lvfiba.org.

Fort Union National Monument -- Fort Union was built in 1851 on the famous Santa Fe Trail. The trail, composed of trade networks established by North American Indian tribes long before the Spanish arrived, became a major line for commerce and settlers moving across the plains. The original wooden fort was built as a military post to secure commerce on the Trail and to establish a federal government presence in this part of the Louisiana Territory designated in 1846 as the New Mexico Territory.

Ten years later, with the start of the Civil War, the Territory faced a new threat: the Confederacy saw value in the immense resources of the Southwest. The wooden post was abandoned after construction was finished on an earth fort built in the shape of a star. The fort included a critical arsenal. Military leaders anticipated that an important battle in the Civil War would take place near Fort Union. The actual battle happened miles to the west at the Battle of Glorieta Pass.

After the war, a military fort was no longer needed,so construction began on the third fort to be built at the Fort Union site. Made of adobe and constructed by skilled Native New

Mexicans, this fort was the largest military installation west of the Mississippi River. Troops from this fort patrolled the Santa Fe Trail and provided escorts for mail stages and wagon trails. These troops also fought in the Indian Wars. The Fort Union depot and arsenal provided fire arms and supplies to an entire network of forts throughout the west and was critical in providing the western territories with supplies and household goods. In 1859, when railroad lines became the major supply lines feeding the West, Fort Union was bypassed. The supply operations were phased out, and the depot closed down in 1883. In 1891, the troops left as well, leaving behind only a caretaker. In 1894, the War Department relinquished claim on the land to the original owners.

Now, Fort Union National Monument includes a visitor's center with historical displays and a 1.6 mile trail where visitors can visit the ruins of the adobe fort. Ruins of the second star-shaped Civil War earth fort are visible. The site of the original wooden fort is located across a grassy meadow between the visitor's center and the Sangre de Cristos mountains.

From the Author

Writing has provided an outlet for my busy imagination ever since I learned to write in the second grade. Although I have always worked professionally in jobs requiring extensive writing ability, it is writing fiction that makes my muse dance.

While working as a historic park planner and naturalist for the Oklahoma Tourism and Recreation Department, the pairing of history and mystery solidified in my writing. Then, as a special feature writer for the Ponca City News in the late 1980s, my love of little known places and ordinary people expanded.

Everyone has a story, every place has a life of its own. The writer's job is to ferret out that story and that life and make it real for the reader.

—*Mary Coley*